THE
BODY
POLITIC

ALSO BY BRIAN PLATZER

Bed-Stuy Is Burning

A Novel

THE
BODY
POLITIC

BRIAN
PLATZER

ATRIA BOOKS

New York London Toronto Sydney New Delhi

ATRIA
BOOKS

An Imprint of Simon & Schuster, Inc.
1230 Avenue of the Americas
New York, NY 10020

First Atria Books hardcover edition March 2020

ATRIA BOOKS and colophon are trademarks of Simon & Schuster, Inc.

For information about special discounts for bulk purchases, please contact Simon & Schuster Special Sales at 1-866-506-1949 or business@simonandschuster.com.

The Simon & Schuster Speakers Bureau can bring authors to your live event. For more information or to book an event, contact the Simon & Schuster Speakers Bureau at 1-866-248-3049 or visit our website at www.simonspeakers.com.

Interior design by Silverglass

Manufactured in the United States of America

1 3 5 7 9 10 8 6 4 2

Library of Congress Cataloging-in-Publication Data has been applied for.

ISBN 978-1-5011-8077-4
ISBN 978-1-5011-8079-8 (ebook)

For Mom, Dad, and Jamie

Will you have this man to be your husband,
to live together in holy marriage? Will you love
him, comfort him, honor and keep him in
sickness and in health, and forsaking all others,
be faithful to him as long as you both shall live?

—TRADITIONAL

Contents

THE
BODY
POLITIC

Fall

1

Water tumbles down the black marble wall and slaps flat against the floor in time with the music. When the music speeds up, so do the pulses of water, falling, slapping, and disappearing as the next pulse falls and slaps. Tess watches it. Sips her vodka. She tries to block out everything but the water. Is it possible she sees dirt in it? Could the water not be filtered? Why, she sighs, would it be? But still, the room is dark and she must be ten feet away from the wall. Those would have to be large chunks of dirt in that water for her to see them. The music speeds up. The dirty water falls faster. It hesitates only briefly now at the wall's top lip before it falls. Tess is drunk. High. Thirty-seven years old. She feels strong. She dances in self-contained fluid movements along with the filthy falling water and the crowd around her. The music, pot, vodka, dirty water, and wall nearly fill her mind to capacity. Or nearly empty it. Nearly. She holds her glass by her thigh. She sways to the music. Nobody is looking at her, so she dares herself to drop the glass, and she does! She watches it fall, clenches for the shatter and shards, but it bounces, rolls, and settles onto the marble floor. She's disappointed. The music slows, but the others keep dancing around her. She tries to forget the glass. There's no falling water, then the music surges, and the water falls again.

Tess leans against the bar, waiting for another drink. She thinks she recognizes a man in the bar mirror and freezes, but it's no one.

A stranger. It would be fun to run into someone who could tell her what the show was like—what she was missing. They could dance together! It's not like she's doing anything wrong. There are powers beyond her control that have made her drop out of her dream role weeks before opening night. She's got no secrets. She's only had three vodka tonics. And the giant bag of weed. But forget her life onstage. Forget everything but the music.

The club is bright with white lights scanning the dancers, bars, water walls, candles, and bronze cages hanging from the sky. Dancers inside the cages wear animal masks. Their muscles are oiled to their bikini lines. One is a tiger. Another is a moose. A moose? Mooses aren't sexy. Mooses? Moose. Tess forces her way to the middle of the large dance area beneath a caged man dancing in his underwear and a tiger mask. Tess roars up at him, and, farther away, across the deafening music and crowd of a thousand, the moose impossibly roars back.

It's late but Tess wants to keep going. She hasn't done it yet, truly forgotten, had the moment she'd set out for. Once, when Tess was a girl, without her mother there to watch her, she started on one side of a big open field, stared at the sun, and ran as fast as she could with her eyes wide open. Eyes, legs, and lungs raced to see which would fail first. The field went on far longer than she could have run. Nobody else was around. The sun was bright, and her eyes were burning, but so were her lungs and her legs. She was outside herself, recognizing, at seven or eight years old, the pain in the various parts of her body, and curious, as though a bystander, about which part would stop working before the others. She twisted an ankle, stumbled, screamed, but kept running. Tears blurred her vision, and she gasped for air. But she kept running. She wouldn't stop. She'd have to physically break before she stopped.

She woke up hours later in bed with washcloths on her wrists, her aunt pacing by the door. And to this day she doesn't know what happened. Which part of herself failed her? Which part let her down?

Tess rushes the remainder of her drink into her mouth. The ice clicks cold against her teeth. She's failing at forgetting. At manufacturing another out-of-body experience.

A tightrope walker is crossing between cages. Tess is dancing in the middle of everyone. The music is building and thickening. Tess opens her eyes to better feel the boys and girls jump along with her, up and down and up, banging against her arms but gently. Tess wants to yell, so she yells. She wants to fly up to the cages and grab the tightrope and swing up into the lights. She wants to live in the moment, in the light. To forget the past and the future—and live only in the teasing, itching present. And for a moment, maybe five, ten seconds, there she is: thirty-seven years old, scratching, blooming, and on fire.

2

"It's daytime! Daytime, Mommy Daddy! Daytime!"

It's four hours later.

Tess is still drunk. Her mouth tastes like cigarettes she doesn't remember smoking.

David has been in bed since his *dance well, love* text at 9:30 the night before. But he's the one covering his ears with his pillows.

"Good morning, sweetie," Tess whispers to Ethan.

"Max is still *sleeping*! *Silly Max!*" Ethan says. "Time to get up, the sun is awake, Mr. Golden Sun, please shine down on Max, silly Max, get up Mommy Daddy Mommy Mommy Mommy!"

Okay, Tess thinks, and then says, "Okay, okay, let's let Daddy have some space . . ."

"But Mommmmmyyyyyy, it's daaaaayyyyy tiiiiiiiimmmmmme," Ethan says. He then carefully positions his four-year-old fists and begins pounding Tess's back, punching down on her at each syllable: "Get up, get up, get up, I have to go peeeeeeee!"

Tess focuses on what is good. That David is not complaining. That Max is still in bed. That she hasn't vomited, and it doesn't seem as though she will. It's dark, she can't see, but she can't bring herself to turn on a light. Her stomach is in her throat and nose, and her head is hollow but for what feels like a pair of scorpions kicking the shit out of each other.

She gropes her way to the bathroom, smells urine, clamps down her jaw.

"Mommy, you don't feel so good?" Ethan says.

"I'm still tired. I went to a party last night," Tess says.

"Did you have a cupcake?" Ethan says.

"I did," Tess says. "I had three cupcakes, and now my tummy feels sick."

Ethan's eyes widen in amazement. He's unsure whether Tess is joking. His face sours into jealousy, followed by opportunism.

"Did you bring one home for me?" he asks slyly, as though it's no big deal, as though he's not at that moment sucking on his fingers.

"Take your hand out of your mouth," Tess says. "I'm sorry. I'm just joking. There were no cupcakes. I was just working with some friends. It wasn't a party."

"That's not nice," Ethan says. "Max"—Ethan turns to his brother, who has appeared beside him—"Mommy is not nice. She said she ate cupcakes but didn't say the truth."

"Eha no cupcake?" Max says, wanting only his brother's approval. He wants the cupcake not for himself but for Ethan. Two years old, and he can taste the injustice of his brother having been tricked.

"Silly Max!" Ethan says, smiling and hugging his younger brother and then pushing him to the floor.

Max cries. He cries and cries.

Ethan looks to his mother to gauge whether she's going to yell at him, and when he is satisfied she won't, he says, "Max is a baby."

Max cries louder, lying on the tile of the bathroom floor, occasionally stifling his tears to check if Ethan notices how sad he is.

Tess grits her teeth against the urine smell. Someone has peed. She sniffs in Max's direction.

"Let's get dressed," Tess says.

"No!" Max screams, on the floor, legs and arms splayed. "Eha!" he begs for his brother.

"I can't listen to this," David says.

Even after fifteen years together, Tess is still caught off guard by how big he is. He blocks the natural light from the bedroom window. Everything is dark. His shadowed face grimaces behind his fingers. His lips contort, and she suffers her inability to help him. Her love for him is exasperating. She'd fallen in love with his buoyancy and good cheer, and now she loves him for the hope he'll get back there again. She silently begs him to hide his pain from the kids so they won't suffer as she does, seeing him like this. She'd run to him and pull his face to her neck right then if it wouldn't cause him more pain, if she weren't so tired and nauseated, and if the kids weren't around.

Instead, she says, "I got home late last night. I'm trying not to vomit."

"I'm sorry," David says. "I just can't. My vision is already gone. Max was in bed for a minute, and I scolded him."

A week ago, Tazio made a joke that since the accident it's like Tess is raising three boys, and now she can't stop seeing David like that: a big broken boy.

"Who peed?" Tess says through clenched teeth. The smell of it is overwhelming her stomach. She needs to eat.

"I can't," David whines. "I'm sorry, but I can't."

"It's okay. I've got it," Tess says.

"I'm sorry." He slouches to the ground, his back against the hallway wall. Max, no longer crying, finds his way to his father's lap.

Eight months ago, David fell off the ladder up to a long slide attraction at an upstate New York apple-picking orchard. He fell because he was showing off for her. She knows it, and she thinks he does, too. They haven't talked about it in any detail. The fall or what led up to it. And it's too late to control any of what led up to it anyway. What she can control is getting the kids dressed. And making it through the morning without throwing up. Five years ago, she would have taken a shot of vodka now to level her off, but there are words for people who do that, especially people with kids. She knows she can't complain that the room is spinning. But she wants to. She wants David to know that yes, her symptoms will only last the morning, and yes, she brought them on herself, but for this moment, she's as bad off as he is.

She brings the box of Cheerios into the bathroom and shares them with the boys.

"We can eat in the bathroom," she says, "because it's a special day."

"You always say that," Ethan says.

"There are a lot of special days lately," Tess says.

Max reaches out from David's lap. Tess hands him some Cheerios, and Max stuffs the entire fistful into his mouth.

"Let me change your pull-ups," Tess says.

"No!" Max says, loud enough to rouse the scorpions.

"Okay, finish those bites first," Tess says.

"Big bite!" Max says.

Max was in David's arms when he fell. It was a long fall. Watching the two of them in the air—David holding Max, Max reaching for Ethan still on the ladder, Tess realizing Ethan could fall, too, and then waiting, waiting for David and Max to hit ground—she shakes off the memory. She won't allow the images into her head again. Here Max is. He's okay. Nearly a year later, he's still sensitive, cautious. But the cut on his head has healed. David shielded him on the way down, positioning his body—and head—between Max and the cold pebbly dirt.

She'd had the affair, which led them to take time apart, which led David to smile and jump and climb after they reconciled in ways he'd never felt pressured to before. He was trying to show Ethan and Max that Daddy was back and everything was okay, *better than okay*, as David would say. That everything was great.

But she still can't fully blame herself for any of it. The affair was nothing so important. The fact of it was important, but the thing itself hadn't been. She and Jonah barely spoke. After late rehearsals, when she got over the strange joy that *the* Jonah Carr was focusing all that attention and magnetism on her, they drank themselves giddy and stumbled into bed. This life right now seems like too much punishment for something so fleeting. She acknowledges that she took a few moments for herself, but moments are nothing in comparison to a life. Her life is with David. She hurt him, and she wishes that hurt back so much— every day she wishes away that pleasure and passion and mostly that hurt—but the retribution of mornings like this one feels totally out of proportion with her crime.

Also, and maybe more important, Tess has a hard time making sense of her role as perpetrator after a lifetime of victimhood. The last eight months aren't even close to enough to make up for the previous thirty years.

The Cheerios are helping ground Tess's stomach. She's eating and eating. And so are both boys, in various states of undress. Bathroom breakfast. Let someone judge her. Let David dare to. He's back in bed. She stuffs as many Cheerios into her mouth as possible and both boys laugh.

"Really big bite!" Ethan says.

She remembers the moment—her mother's mouth, an arm on the counter for support—she owns the moment and dismisses it. She has spent her entire life seeing, remembering, imagining, and dismissing those five minutes so many times that she can no longer separate her memory of it from her fantasy of it, from one psychologist's attempt to rewrite the memory with something less vicious, less—in the psychologist's own words—*inescapable*.

Tess has lived her whole life with people feeling sorry for her. And though she has also spent her life insisting that they not pity her—insisting that this original wound made her into a woman who was stronger than everyone else and thus more prepared to take on whatever came her way—that didn't mean she wasn't also a victim. She embraced her victimhood. That she was a victim, she told herself and others, made her strong. And the fact that she created an awful situation that led to her husband's brain disorder didn't make her any less of a victim. In fact, it made her more of one. Most people face, at most, one—she thinks as she watches Ethan help Max into Thomas the Train pull-ups—one tragedy in their lives. This qualified as Tragedy Number Two. And she is doing her best to get not only herself, like the first time, but also now her kids and husband through it in one piece.

"I'm sorry," David calls from the bedroom. "I love you. I tried. I just can't."

"It's okay," Tess says. "I've got it."

"Thanks, love," David says under the covers. "You have fun last night?"

Ethan and Max are at the coffee table now, sharing a Teenage Mutant Ninja Turtles sippy cup full of a bubbly orange mix of orange juice and seltzer. "I have my turn first," Ethan says, "and then you have your turn. You're the little brother."

"Totally," Tess says. "But would have had more fun if you'd been there."

"We've got some time between now and then," David says.

"I know," Tess says.

David gets upset when she mentions anything that might

happen when he feels better. It emphasizes that he's still so far away. That he can't be out of bed past 9 p.m., that he can't dance, be around loud music, talk much, see flashing lights, who knows what else. It's exhausting to need to be so careful around her husband. She's exhausted. She turned down one of the most exciting opportunities of her career—the role she'd have been the understudy for was onstage the entire show and sang the majority of the songs—to be beside him, exhausted. She knows he is suffering. But who the fuck isn't?

"I love you," Tess says. "I'm going to drop the boys off and then try to take a nap before heading out in the afternoon. Can I pick up anything?"

"No," David says. "I'll be here waiting with open arms!"

Tess, smiling, cringes. She drinks a cold can of espresso from the refrigerator and helps the boys with their shoes.

3

Tazio is in the kitchen when Tess returns home from dropping off the kids. The house smells of salmon and rice. Tess's shoulders relax. She can nap while Tazio reads to David, or while the two of them watch TV. That's what they're doing now. Watching MSNBC, with their feet up on the coffee table.

"Sage butter?" Tazio says, leaning over David to pour. "No? There's some on there already, but only a bit because I wasn't sure if butter was on the list."

Tazio's voice is precise. He enunciates the two "t"s in butter. He sounds British, but it's just an affectation. His father—whom Tess never got to meet—was born in Italy, and his mother is Mexican from a few generations back, but Tazio grew up on Long Island like David. A kid from the suburbs who should have spoken mall American like everybody else, but ask him to say the days of the week, and "Wednesday" comes out in three crisp syllables. Every Wednesday in February, Tess used to ask everyone around to quiet down so Tazio could announce the date. "Today is Wed-ness-day, Feb-rew-ary the third," he'd amiably reply, and their college class would cheer. It should be pretentious, and maybe it is, but there's something about Tazio's demeanor that people are attracted to.

Watching Tazio pour a small gravy boat of sage butter over David's greens, she notices for the thousandth time that everything about Tazio—except for maybe his lips—is sharp. Precise. His movements, his pronunciation. He is all nose and elbows. Even his attitude is sharp. Tess never knows if he's serious. He's wry. Severe, even. But how could she think that, watching him serve her husband? He has become a kind man. Tazio was an unreliable friend to Tess in college, promising to show up for lunch and then disappearing for a week, or, while shopping with Tess in Pearl Paint, sneaking unpaid-for brushes into her bag. And then he started surprising her. First, by delaying graduation for a year to work in North Carolina on the campaign for that narcissist sloppy-Ken-doll John Edwards. And then, since the accident, caring for her husband.

Tazio is tall and thin, like a crystallized version of David. David is bigger, sillier, more careless, and less in control; or maybe that's just a kind way of saying David has acne and unruly hair and should lose a couple of pounds, while everything about Tazio is perfectly in place. Tazio, every day, wears gray tailored pants and a white dress shirt with white Adidases and his Italian grandfather's watch. When Tazio introduced Tess to David that night at Abel and Cain, David appeared to her like a version of Tazio at which God had taken a couple of lazy swipes of an eraser and then abandoned, leaving a smudged, bloated copy.

Now, next to Tazio on the couch, David waves off the extra butter and eats from a bowl in his lap of what looks like brown rice, salmon, and stewed greens. It's ten thirty in the morning.

"Smells good," Tess says.

Tazio rises to help her fold the double stroller.

"Bok choy, more in the fridge, just a little garlic and the butter, no soy sauce—MSG—just the butter, so it's not as good as it could be," Tazio says. "A container of rice, too. And arctic char. I made too much for just me and Angelica."

"Maybe for dinner," Tess says. "I mean, thanks. You made for you and Angelica what happens to be perfect for David's regimen?"

Tazio smiles.

"Thank you," Tess says. "I don't know what we would do without you."

"Don't be silly," Tazio says. "I'm between jobs. I have the time."

Tess hugs Tazio tightly. He returns to the television. Tess wants a shower and a nap, and with David out of bed and entertained, she has a real chance at both.

"You guys relax," she says, but fearing she sounded sarcastic, as it's the middle of a weekday, she adds, "I mean it. Relax. And fuck Trump."

"Fuck Trump," David says, raising his water to Tazio, who distractedly clinks his glass with David's.

Tess pours herself water from the Brita on the counter and chugs. She's no longer drunk, just dehydrated. She's about to tell David that Max was a mess at drop-off. That he clung to her and cried. But she looks at David eating, watching politics and listening to Tazio, and she can tell that something's not right. She isn't sure if it's one or both of them. They're watching Jeffrey Lord parrot Trump best he can. "They're not all rapists," Lord says. "How many times do I need to say this? They're not all rapists, okay? But that doesn't mean we want them here. In our country. These are not the best of the bunch that are coming over here, believe me."

"I can't take this shit anymore," Tazio says.

"It's totally bananas," Tess says. "Can't they get anyone better to represent him? Pence? Even Christie?"

"I can't take it," Tazio says.

David's not going to break the silence that follows, so Tess continues. "I mean, just on a strategy level: Who thinks putting Jeffrey Lord or Rudy Giuliani on CNN is going to benefit anyone? These're the country's least appealing people."

For a moment it looks like Tazio is going to start yelling or even crying, but he steadies himself. Though it feels like months since Hillary lost, it's only been three weeks. Other than the night of the election, Tazio has for the most part shown few signs of despair. Now he stares at Trump's big healthy face, just as he'd stared at nearly everything when she met him almost twenty years earlier at Cooper Union, where they both studied to be painters. His stare is so conspicuously discerning. Tess could never tell if this was because Tazio was brilliant or because he cared so much about seeming so. Maybe the two weren't mutually exclusive. Tess has always tried so hard at everything, but Tazio was more talented than she was, both technically and in terms of gamesmanship, which people cared about in a way she never could. Gamesmanship: a gendered word for a gendered world of men making other men feel smart. Tazio always had explanations for his work that surprised people. He had big dramatic ideas and punch lines. He considered himself Mexican, still spoke to his mom in Spanish, but was named Tazio Di Vincenzo and talked like a member of a bygone aristocracy. He inspired curiosity: more than curiosity, attention. And his work *was* smart, much smarter than everyone else's.

Apparently, Tazio had the same reputation in the tiny world of the Hillary communications office that he'd had in the tinier world of art school. The thinking man's artist turned into the artistic thinker. The intuitive whiz who knows how to reframe the question. Or knew how, at least, until Hillary lost. He won't talk about it, but it's clear he's not only pissed off that Hillary lost, but also that no one listened to him as the ship sank.

Tess remembers one painting he did at school, a realist landscape portrait of George W. Bush hiding in the woods or something, and when you turned it upside down, it was a perfect painting of that lady in a coma, Terri Schiavo, eating a big fancy dinner. It was freaky and a parlor trick, but funny and sad, too. And though to be honest Tess thought the whole concept was dumb, because who turned paintings upside down, and even if someone did, it didn't really make much sense on a conceptual level—like why is Terri Schiavo the inverse of George W. Bush?—their professor went on and on about how Tazio's painting exemplified the artist manifesting a political view. How after Bush stole Gore's presidency, an artist literally could not be apolitical. Every portrait was a portrait of its time.

Now Tess smiles at what she would have thought back then if she could have seen this portrait in front of her: her husband eating arctic char prepared by Tazio Di Vincenzo as Tazio sits loathing President-elect Donald Trump.

"Jeffrey fucking Lord," Tazio says in his odd patrician patter. "He was a Reagan guy?"

Tess doesn't know, and David doesn't seem to be listening.

"Turn this off," Tazio says before realizing he's sitting on the remote. He hits the power button and exhales.

Without Tazio, where would David have gone for those couple of months after she told him about Jonah? To his parents' on Long Island, which would have been worse. He would have been crushed by his mother's empathy. Angelica deserves credit for putting up with David living on their couch. That said, a sad chatty David on the couch must have been better than a sick silent David in Tess's bed. Preaccident David, even sad, was pretty lovable.

And Tess loves him still and will love him for the rest of her life. She reminds herself not to lose this fact, the most important of her life. He *will* get healthy again. She *will* have her life back again with him. They will have their life back together. She'll hunker down until they can start living again for real.

Tess drinks another glass of water. She feels sleep coming on.

She'll take a nap and feel better. She'll feel good. It felt good to be herself last night and then take care of the kids this morning. Even if she feels like shit, it feels good. Even if she feels like shit still. There's something fantastic about being thirty-seven years old. Young enough to get drunk and dance alone in a club, old enough to have kids she'd die for. It is the life she dreamed of, and when David gets healthy again, she'll have it all. Ethan is thriving, and Max will be okay. David will get another job. She'll be able to work again. Money will stop being a concern. They'll be adults and parents. They'll be fine. They'll be better than fine. They'll be great.

4

The next morning, Tess wakes up feeling better, takes Ethan and Max to school and day care, returns home, and David is gone. This is not so unusual. He sometimes has appointments with his body-worker, Monica, and though those tend to be in the afternoon, alone time for Tess is too valuable to question. She showers, naps, and eats the Halloween candy that Ethan probably won't notice missing and is bad for him anyway.

But when Tess returns home that afternoon from an audition, David is still not there, which makes it seven hours, by far the longest he's been out since the accident. He isn't responding to texts or the two messages she has left on his cell.

That night, when the kids ask where Daddy is, she tells them he's at Tazio's house, and they panic that he's gone again for a long time.

"No," she says, "it's just one night," but Ethan doesn't trust her, and Max follows Ethan's lead.

"No," Ethan screams when she approaches him on the floor. "Don't look at me!"

She leaves him to cool off, returns ten minutes later, and it's the same. Max silently stares at Ethan and is rigid when Tess approaches him.

Another ten minutes later, Ethan and Max are under the covers together in Ethan's bed, Ethan rubbing Max's back.

Tess's heart melts. She relaxes into something like real joy. She bends to kiss their foreheads.

"Don't look at me!" Ethan screams.

"No look Eha!" Max says.

They are silent until the next morning. Tess, without much sleep, is exhausted. Tazio hasn't answered his phone, David's voice mail box is full of Tess's messages and who knows what else. The boys ask where Daddy is, and Tess tells them he's with Tazio on one of Tazio's vacations, but he'll be home soon.

Dropping Ethan at school, Tess lingers with his teachers. She takes Max to get an orange juice before dropping him at day care. She goes to the bank to take out two hundred of her remaining two thousand dollars, picks up milk, yogurt, and eggs. And finally she returns home, hopeful that enough time has passed. He's still missing.

He could have fallen in the street and been hit by a car. He could have gotten dizzy walking down the stairs to the subway. She calls the three Brooklyn hospitals she can think of. She texts his parents. She would give anything not to have cheated on him. She can't raise these kids without him. They have so many plans. To live abroad when the kids are in college. To save up and buy a small place by a lake where the boys can swim and bring their own children someday. Even at his angriest, he's never been the type just to leave. The kids or her. Tazio has pulled this shit for as long as she's known him, but not David. She calls Tazio again. She doesn't have Angelica's number and realizes how strange that is. She emails Angelica, who is probably too busy at barre class or getting her hair blown out or seeing patients to respond.

Tess takes a shower. Thinks to check David's medications— the Serzone and Lexapro—in the medicine cabinet, and the little bottles are missing. She knows this is a good thing, but she doesn't feel it as such. It means he planned to be gone for more than an afternoon. Still, she likes seeing the cabinet empty of meds. She imagines a time when she won't have to watch him swallow them, his back and neck tight. She hates watching him try to relax as he ingests medications that don't seem to be doing any good. She wants him to take more of them, or different ones. She wants the doctors to figure out what's wrong more than she's ever wanted anything. For his pain to go away, and for her to be able to live again. But the medication takes months sometimes to kick in, so the doctors don't want to change anything prematurely or take him off something that could cure him. That would be an unforgivable miscalculation, and David and Tess have the rest of their lives to consider. Sure, every day might feel unlivable, but in the time frame of years, the prudent course must always be taken. Tess understands, but she hates those little pills. They're so tiny compared to his big body, and they're an unreliable magic. No one knows why he's dizzy or, really, why these pills might help. Maybe one day they'll make him start to feel better. Or maybe they won't. There's nothing she or David can do to make them work faster, yet they have become the most important thing in her life.

Tess checks under the sink and by the bed just to make sure they're really gone and not just hidden. She takes a shot of vodka from the freezer. Falls asleep. When she wakes up in the afternoon, he's still not there. She cancels an audition for a series of car commercials and opens David's laptop to look at his calendar, which shows an appointment with Monica for the next day but nothing yesterday or today. She picks up the kids, puts them to bed, tries to sleep, gets them ready the next morning, attempts to joke them out of their sulking, drops them off, still with no word from anyone.

She returns to the calendar to confirm what time his meeting with Monica is supposed to be. He won't miss that. Unless he's hurt, or something truly bad has happened. It's at 3 p.m. She'll go to his appointment. It's as good a lead as any.

She closes the calendar and notices, for the first time, scattered among other files on David's computer desktop, an icon titled DR. B. Dr. Burgurski is the psychologist David had been seeing before the accident and then stopped seeing after talking for the hour became too difficult. He'd told Tess they'd been emailing and that Dr. Burgurski was sending him questions to facilitate David's keeping a "prompted journal" they sent back and forth, but Tess hadn't followed up to ask how it had been going. The way David had told Tess about it made her think he'd dismissed the idea as juvenile.

Tess double-clicks the icon. The document grows as she scrolls.

5

DR. B

What were you like growing up?

Healthy. My parents were healthy, too. Healthy enough. I mean, my father had kidney stones and my mother lay on the couch in the morning paralyzed with fear of going to work. I sometimes threw up from anxiety when the babysitter came. But we were healthy in the ways that mattered. And we stayed healthy for a long time. Within reason, at least. As I got older, my body didn't work in all sorts of normal ways. I needed glasses starting in first grade. In eighth, I stopped being able to digest dairy. I had bad acne in high school and I started losing my hair at twenty. But I ate whatever I wanted and never got gross, I don't think. I binge-drank without consequence all through college and business school. Life was relatively easy.

Or it should have been. I think a lot about the conversations Tazio and I had in college. I was up at Columbia, and he was at Cooper Union. We met Friday nights to drink until I threw up or Gerard kicked everyone out. Gerard ran Abel and Cain, a cocktail bar. But it was more than that. According to *Esquire*, Abel and Cain was responsible for starting New York's cocktail renaissance. We drank there every Friday night for free because Gerard was friendly with one of Tazio's professors who recognized Tazio as both a talented craftsman and a serious drinker, and tapped him to build Gerard's new booths in exchange for free booze.

Abel and Cain was an eighteen-year-old's paradise. The wood was oiled, the leather soft, the ceiling tin, the straws made by Tazio in stainless steel, and the ice chipped off a giant block behind the bar. For a few months, Gerard decided to give away warmed cashews and almonds along with the drinks; then it was fresh strawberries and mascarpone. Once I overheard a woman order a Cherry Coke and Gerard say, "I wish I could, but cherries are no longer in season." The asshole must have been sitting on that line for years in hopes that someone would order a Cherry Coke in winter.

Tazio and I spent Friday nights in our corner booth pretending we belonged. Tazio drank straight whisky, and I drank whatever complicated thing Angelica wanted to pour. We were both in love with Angelica. We guessed she was a year or two older; was half black, half Asian; and was Gerard's ex. Tazio and I built a whole dumb world around Gerard based on hints he'd drop of his previous life as a coke fiend, a classics scholar, a basketball phenom. According to what Angelica told Tazio later, Gerard was just a prep school kid who took money from his father to open a small bar. He liked to dress up in suspenders and slicked back hair, and tell stories. He was a genius at making drinks, and he built a life around it. I've still never tasted anything as good as his mint daiquiri.

Fuck, I miss drinking. And eating gluten, and dairy, nuts, citrus, avocado, MSG, dried fruit, lentils . . . drinking all that Pepsi and coffee as well as the liquor . . . eating chocolate. But I'm getting off the point. And I don't really miss eating lentils all that much. But Pepsi, beer, and wine. Pizza, pasta, bagels, a normal fucking bowl of soup. Cereal. What I'd do for a bowl of Smart Start and a chocolate chip muffin. But Monica, whom I'm following now when it comes to all this stuff, won't allow it. She says one muffin is the same as one hundred. That my cells will have to regenerate all over again.

The point is that the drunker I got at Abel and Cain, the more I stared at Angelica's neck and collarbone—the area where her shoulders met her neck and dress—while Tazio and I talked about what I was reading or how stressed I was about the essays I needed to write. I bring all this up because though Tazio was already by far my closest friend and I looked forward to these Friday nights for the whole week, mostly I remember us fighting. You ask what I used to be like, and the answer is I think that I was really nice. I was fun to be around. I was happy by disposition. But sometimes when I drank—especially with Tazio—I was still me, but with the kindness stripped away.

I was probably subconsciously angry, as you'd put it, that Tazio had a string of artist girlfriends while I was still a virgin. Less deeply submerged was that I was taking all these literature and philosophy classes at Columbia but could never seem to explain the ideas to Tazio in a way that he wasn't able to debunk or think of a way to argue around. I often found myself, whether I agreed with myself or not, defending exaggerated positions with increasing anger, and drinking with increasing speed.

I didn't know then that Tazio would develop a national reputation for pith or cleverness or whatever it is from some of the most powerful people in the world. Then, I just knew that Tazio was much smarter than I was. I could tell him about, say, how, according to the theory of utilitarianism, what mattered most was to maximize happiness for the most people, and without thinking much about it, he'd say, "But what about the poorest of the poor whose life is fucked just because everyone else is a little happier? Even if the total happiness quotient or whatever is higher, there shouldn't be a society that totally sacrifices the most miserable and suffering." The main problem with the theory—the problem it took three entire sessions of Contemporary Civilization for our class to reach—just fucking occurred to him.

Tazio knocked back whiskies as I ordered South Side Swizzles, Sidecars, and mint daiquiris, and I couldn't just be proud that someone this naturally smart was my best friend. Instead I argued that when people are conditioned to suffer, they cease feeling pain in the way we think about suffering. The truly downtrodden don't live lives of constant horror, I explained. They get used to their condition as much as anyone else does. "When you live in Africa and have seven grown kids and you've lost five in childbirth already," I said, "then there's *no way* seeing a family member get sick is as painful for you as it is for a mother in New York who's only had one kid. It just isn't."

"Really?" Tazio said, sipping, thinking. This was when he could still drink and find things funny in a detached, ironic way.

"Think *logically*," I said. "Having expectations that your kid might die *must* make it easier when it actually happens. Think about how much it fucked you up when your dad died. Now imagine how much better it would have been if you still had nine more dads." I talked with this hideous bravado in order to prove our friendship to myself, to Tazio, to the universe. I could say anything to him, and he wouldn't balk at it. I literally couldn't offend him. "Having so many kids *must* make it easier. You're not thinking about what it's like there."

"Where?" Tazio said.

"In poverty-stricken countries," I said.

I'd written a report about health crises in India for a class I took to fulfill my Major Cultures requirement.

"I don't know," Tazio said, downing his fourth, fifth, twelfth whisky that evening. "I'd hate to be used to a condition where I had the expectation that one of my kids might die . . ."

I think about this particular conversation a lot, because I wish that at that moment he'd kept going and taken me seriously enough to tell me to shut the fuck up, because was I really saying that people who suffer just get used to it? Was I really saying that sick people, people in mourning, people who have lost loved ones, and by extension enslaved people and who knew who else, get so accustomed to their pain that they experience their lives less harshly than I did back then knowing I'd need to wake up hungover with a twelve-page paper to write?

I want to strangle that little kid in that bar talking about things he didn't know anything about. I don't blame him for being coddled. I don't blame him for his lack of broken bones or for thinking that his essays or homesickness or virginity was hard. But I do blame him for his lack of a basic empathy, and I wish now that Tazio had told me back then to get over myself. That I didn't know what I was talking about. That I didn't know sickness, death, or, for that matter, suffering of any kind.

If I'd been made more aware of that back then, I feel that somehow God or karma or my own consciousness would be less cruel to me now.

Now. Tazio and Angelica will be married next summer. And even though I've got this fucking brain disorder no one can figure out, what I'm really distracting myself from is that Tess is going to leave me again, this time for good.

AUGUST 2, 2016
As simply as possible and without focusing too much on Tess, describe what happened and what it's like now.
Five months ago, I fell off a ladder trying to carry Max up to the top of a slide at an apple-picking place in upstate New York,

and ever since, I've woken up every morning feeling a debilitating combination of drunk and hungover, and I feel that way all day until I go to sleep. My vision is blurry, my thoughts are scrambled, and I'm overwhelmed by my surroundings. If I talk or interact with people or feel any stress or anxiety, it gets worse.

I was climbing up to give Max a chance to go down the slide. Tess and I had recently reconciled, and we'd agreed to take the kids on more outings, adventures. Ethan had already gone down the slide twice, and Max wanted to go. The ladder was tall and steep, so he couldn't climb it by himself. I was holding Max in one arm and gripping the rungs with my other hand. But Ethan wanted to beat us up to the top. Ethan was laughing. Max was laughing. I could tell Max wanted to get up top first, and since he rarely won anything, I sped up. But I only had one arm to climb with, and Max isn't little anymore. Ethan was faster than we were. There wasn't room for him to pass us, and I thought it would be dangerous if he tried to get around us, so I leaned to the side a bit to let Ethan by, and just at that moment, Max kicked out at the ladder. I lost my grip. Ethan watched us as we fell, and, holding Max, I remember thinking I could take care of Max. I could make sure I hit ground before he did, but Ethan, Ethan had to hold on. And, thank god, he did.

A week after the accident, when my symptoms weren't resolving as promised, I called the doctor who had dealt with me most often at the hospital. He agreed that the problem went beyond my eyes and sent me to a neurologist who put me through a CT scan, an MRI, blood work, an eye exam, and vertigo tests. Everything came out fine. He had no idea why I was experiencing these symptoms. Something probably got knocked off-kilter in the fall, the neurologist told me. "Knocked off-kilter" was how the fucking brain expert put it. "Maybe concussion related?" It would probably heal by itself, but he prescribed a combination of antidepressants, which he said often helped in ambiguous circumstances.

Tess had to drop out of her upcoming role as the understudy for the lead and member of an ensemble in what in this case is supposed to be the next hit Broadway musical written by an aging pop star—and she'd been hoping it would grant her more exposure because the actor she was understudying for had both a massive role in the show and TV obligations that conflicted with two weeks of performances. Therefore Tess would have opportunities to fill in and be seen as a lead herself. Before she got pregnant with Ethan, she'd had some big understudy roles— *Billy Elliot*, and even *Phantom*—but this was going to be the first where she was all but guaranteed to have a real opportunity to star. Instead, she just takes care of the kids and me, auditions for commercials she so far hasn't been right for, takes care of us again. Evening work is impossible with me unable to be alone with the kids.

But even with our new routine, I can't completely hide from the boys, and I can't not talk around them. When I tried to interact with them silently, at first they laughed and played along, but then, when they realized it wasn't a game, they cried until I talked again.

What is it like now?

There's no language for it that hasn't become a cliché. It's like living in a nightmare. It's hell. It's unbearable. I bear it, of course, but it's impossible to bear. It's not really pain. Or not only. If I had a broken foot, or even if I was constantly, every day, breaking my foot, at least I could teach myself to ignore it. I could distract myself. But it's my brain. I can't focus. It's the lens through which I experience everything. I fall sometimes. My brain thinks the ground is moving, so I bend a knee to regain balance, but I'd already been balanced so I fall. I've fallen at home once, standing in a subway car once, and three or four times in supermarkets and other stores. Something about the clutter of the aisles makes me worse. It's never happened when I was with the boys, thank god, and I haven't been hurt beyond a scraped hand. In that way I've been lucky.

But those are rare events. The day-to-day of brain fog is the torture. It's impossible to ignore that I can't focus or think clearly. I can't *think* clearly. I can't *do* anything. Writing this is about all I can handle. If that. Talking makes it worse, showering makes it worse, napping makes it worse, eating makes it worse. I don't know why. No one does. But what is it—the feeling? It's hard to describe. It's a constant pressure, a frenetic vibration, a feeling of being overwhelmed by my surroundings. But it's also an imbalance. A loss of vision. A complete loss of control. It's as though someone is constantly taking my brain and yanking it down and to the side. It's like that moment when you know you've drunk too much and you're going to need to vomit, and you're not sure if you can make it to the bathroom. It's that feeling all day, every day. When I'm watching *Daniel Tiger* with Max. When I wake up from nightmares of falling— falling with Max in my arms, Ethan falling after us—in the middle of the night. When I try to think of some way to make Tess happy. It's pressure, pain, panic, and a crushing lack of clarity. I'd rather be in a wheelchair. I'd rather be blind or deaf. I'd obviously rather be mute. And I don't know how long this is going to last. If I knew that I was going to need to suffer like this for a month or for five years, say, I could do it. I could grit my teeth and suffer through those years knowing I'd be able to emerge out the other end grateful and so excited to live every new day. Even if life was delayed two or five or ten years, I would know that I could eventually get my job back, be promoted to vice president, make a solid mid-six-figure salary— enough to send the kids to summer camp, let Tess stop doing commercials, even buy a place upstate, in Kingston or Woodstock or somewhere, where we could play catch in the summer and ski in the winter. Everything I worked so hard for my entire life. But this might last forever.

If only I'd held on tighter. Or not taken Max up at all. Or been more stern with Ethan. Or if Tess had called Ethan back down. If I hadn't been so cavalier. So intent on everybody having fun. I could have held on tighter. I didn't know.

Mornings are the worst. My brain needs extra time to right itself. I used to love rolling around in bed with Ethan and Max before making them scrambled eggs and toast with bubbly orange, but now I sleep in fear of the moment they'll wake me.

This morning, it was Ethan.

"It's daytime, Daddy!" he yelled at a few minutes after six. "Maxman, wake up, wake up!"

Ethan sprinted from his room into ours, with Max following still groggy, carrying his green stuffed snake.

Max was sucking on the snake. Ethan dove up into my bed. My vision was still only slightly blurred. Not fully occluded. Tess was in the shower. Ethan grabbed the snake, said, "Baby toy! You're a baby Max is a baby Max."

I scolded, "Ethan! Why would you do that?" which was enough to fully blind me. The walls felt like they were tipping toward me. I wanted to tell him to be nice to his brother, but I couldn't find the words.

I lay back down and took deep breaths, both boys swarming over my body.

"Please," I managed. "Please."

"Daddy?" Max said, head to my knees, feet at my shoulders. "Daddy no feel so good?"

Ethan, upright and beside the bed, hit Max on the arm.

"Eha hit me . . . ," Max started crying.

Tess ran in from the bathroom, still wet from the shower. She hugged Max. I tried to relax. I tried to take deep breaths and count slowly like the neurologist had told me to, but I was hyperventilating. I couldn't see out of either eye. I had to hold the bed or else I felt I'd fall through.

"Come, let's go peepee," Tess said, physically pulling Ethan off me.

"With Daddy!" Ethan said.

I was crying.

"Daddy is sick?" Ethan said.

"No!" Max yelled.

"Ethan!" Tess yelled.

"No!" Ethan said.

"Let's all go pee," I said, mustering the courage to slide out of bed. I wiped my eyes. Some vision had returned, but the tension and discombobulation were still there. Needles and pressure in the front of my head, and my jaw clamped down. I tried to breathe deeply. I tried to relax.

The light in the bathroom was too bright. I couldn't find the toilet insert Max sat on to pee. I could see shapes but not colors.

"Max first," Ethan said.

"Where are you?" I cried out for Tess.

"Right here. Okay," Tess said. "Max first."

"I'll go get everyone bubbly orange," I said, steadying myself on the wall on the way to the kitchen.

"I'll do it," Tess said. "You rest."

"This is my life," I said cruelly to Tess, expending energy I didn't have for reasons I didn't understand. "Let me."

"Sorry," Tess said.

I didn't move. Together, we watched the kids scream.

"I'm not angry at you," I said.

"I know," Tess said.

"Max went peepee on the floor," Ethan said. "I clean it up!"

"No," Tess and I both said, but I said it too loudly. I had to sit down on the floor. Ethan started crying and hugged me. I wiped tears from under my eyes.

"Daddy is sick again, Mommy! Mommy Daddy is sick."

"Leave the paper towels," Tess said. "I'll clean this up. Fuck!"

"Tess," I said.

"Mommy?" Ethan said.

"Sorry, baby," Tess said.

"Give me paper towels," Ethan said. "I clean it."

She gave them to him. I was still on the floor holding my head. I wanted to laugh or be proud, but I couldn't see or think.

"I cleaned it all up!" Ethan said, dozens of paper towels in one hand mopping at Max's bare feet, the diminishing roll in the other hand, Max crying, Tess retrieving her own bath towel to mop up both boys. It was only Monday morning, and we'd been awake for less than fifteen minutes.

But nighttime can be as hard. Like last night, I tried to put Ethan to bed on my own.

"Daddy?"

"Yes, Ethan?"

"Can I ask you something?" he said.

"Of course," I whispered.

Whispering felt better, for reasons doctors couldn't explain. They couldn't explain any of it.

"This is your house again?"

"This is my house."

"Okay, Daddy. You're not going to sleep other places anymore?" he said.

"Like the hospital?" I said.

"No, like before that," he said. He meant, of course, the weeks after Tess had told me about Jonah and I stayed with Tazio.

"This is my house, baby, and I'll always come back," I said.

"I'm not baby, I'm a big boy."

"Okay, Ethan."

"Daddy?"

"Yes, Ethan?"

"My penis is hard," he said.

"Penises do that sometimes," I said.

"Can you make it soft?"

"I'm sorry, I can't."

"*Please* can you make it soft?" he said.

"People can't make other people's penises soft," I said.

"I said please!" he yelled, suddenly furious. "Not nice!" I started to breathe scared, shallow breaths. If he went from presleep tired to fighting me, I wouldn't be able to control him. I was living my life scared of him, scared he'd act like the four-year-old he was, and I'd try to manage him and be bedridden for hours because of it.

"It will just go away," I said.

"Please make it soft!" he said.

Tess came running.

"If I could I would," I said. "I'm so sorry."

"Make! It! Soft!"

It's the kind of thing Tess and I would have laughed about later. Instead, just listening to him yell was too much for me. I had to lie down on our bed as she told him that penises were like sponges that get filled up with all the water and blood and pee and saliva swishing around in the body, and we needed to wait for the water to slosh back on its own. I'd only meant to rest, but I fell asleep at seven thirty and awoke again in the morning to their screams.

AUGUST 3, 2016

Who do you really rely on through all this?

Tess. Tazio. And the hope that the meds will start working. Mostly Tess.

I was trying to make an impression on her and the kids, which is why I fell. She knows it. I know it. But there it is. She slept with Jonah Carr, the only Broadway star I could name. She admitted it. My guess is it happened a half dozen times? Maybe ten? Her kissing his mouth, his chest . . .

Six months before the accident, she sat in front of me on a dinner table chair, having pushed away the coffee table we usually ate on. I was on the couch, which we bought with my signing bonus out of B-school. She was sitting in front of me just as she usually sat when breaking important news to Ethan. She wore sweatpants and a T-shirt. She was beautiful as always, her skin pink and her eyes a Caribbean fucking Sea blue. She looked like Anne Hathaway, but less cartoony. Once, on the subway, some teenage girls giggled their way to Tess and asked, "You're her, right?"

"Thanks for saying hi," Tess said. "But I like to keep things quiet when I'm out." At least, I think they thought she was Anne Hathaway. Tess wasn't as sure.

But six months before the accident, she spoke in her competent, kind voice: her voice-over voice. She did some radio commercials, and this was the voice she used. *Two-point-oh-liter four-cylinder excluded MSRP from eighteen-four two-sixty.* Her voice was the first thing that scared me, even before she'd told me that there were problems. I asked why, what kind, when, and she started to cry. In five minutes she told me that her life, as wonderful as it was, must have been unfulfilling in some way she didn't understand, in ten about Jonah and that she'd ended it, in fifteen that she wanted to fight for the family if I did. Fight for the family. I was filled with a rage I hadn't known I was capable of. My mind got hazy and I starting yelling at her. *Fuck! Fuck you! Do people know? Is this whole life pretend? Jesus fucking Christ, you lying fucking asshole. Fuck you, walking around all this time knowing that all this is fake. That our life isn't real. Jesus fuck. Fuck!* I wanted to throw the slate coaster she'd brought back from Brazil. To see the cabinet door crack and buckle. I looked at that coaster, but I didn't do anything. I couldn't act. I just screamed. She cried. The kids woke up, and I drank at a bar I'd never been to until I was too drunk to stay awake.

I stopped being able to put in the hours at work. And this was before the accident. Long hours at PepsiCo were not conducive to jealousy and an eagerness to rush home every night, even when home was Tazio's couch and a laptop to check Tess's social media. I was only a year into the job, still repaying my business school loans. I'd been with Tess for more than a decade. We'd moved in together after college, then business school and her months in regional productions, and then marriage, kids. And suddenly, because of Jonah Carr, I didn't want her anymore. Or I wanted her, but I didn't want to want her.

It's funny that the reason I started seeing you is because I wanted to be able to support Tess. I wanted to be there for her in ways I maybe wasn't psychologically prepared for. I was checking all the boxes. You complimented me for that, said it was mature and sensible, said what she went through was so uniquely horrible that no partner could be prepared without putting in real work. I think I forgave her partially because I wanted our family to be together for the boys, and partially because I loved her so much I'd have forgiven pretty much anything to get her back. I'll add to those two partiallys that I also believed that what she went through as a girl was enough to make her relationship with me so complicated that I was willing to dismiss the affair as having less to do with us than with her own fucked-up shit. But now I don't know if maybe that last one is a distinction without difference.

It's unbelievable that she was in the room when it happened. I thought she was joking the first time she told me. She said it in such a casual way. We were drunk. She said, "You're not going to believe me, but my father was in jail for eighteen years."

"I believe you," I said, staring at her face and thinking about sex. We'd started having sex just a week before and we were still in that time in the relationship where all other activities seemed things to do before and after but never the thing itself. I wanted to kiss her mouth, her neck, I wanted to make her gasp and clench. Her clothes seemed beside the point. We were sitting at a restaurant, and for the first time in my life, clothes seemed like these strange drapes of fabric that separate people from touching and looking. I was young and overcome by her. She was only the second girl I'd slept with, and I'd never been in love before. I had always thought of myself as very ugly. I wanted her as much as I was amazed she wanted me.

She said, "He was in jail for killing my mother, and I saw him do it. It was with a knife."

I wasn't sure what was going on. I didn't want to fall for some kind of joke, but I also didn't want the person I found myself in love with to be someone who'd put me on the spot like this by joking about her father murdering her mother, just to see how I'd react.

But she kept talking:

"Mom and I that year celebrated my fifth-and-a-half birthday with a big vegan stew," she said, and again, I didn't know if she was joking. We were at an Italian place in the West Village we still go to sometimes. I didn't laugh, but I guess I indicated thinking it was funny to make vegan stew for a child's half-birthday, so she explained: "I'd decided that year it was my favorite, but I think it's just because it took the most preparation and I liked going to the organic store and then rolling the dough for dumplings, cutting the veggies, arranging them by color."

Tess was telling me the story as if she were a kid again. It was weird. I was looking at her and wanting her. So her talking and remembering like this was jarring in and of itself, irrespective of where I knew the story was leading.

She went on. "My father was wearing his suit, sitting on the couch, watching the news. I knew I couldn't just tell him about the veggie stew, so I asked him if he wanted me to pour him a Coke. He didn't say anything, so I brought him a can from the fridge. Mom was already sleeping or else I wouldn't have dared. The can was cold. I felt brave. My father kissed me on the cheek, hugged me tight, said good night, and I turned back to my room, just at that moment realizing I hadn't even mentioned the stew!"

Tess was looking at me, but she wasn't telling me the story as much as she was accessing it like a file in her brain's memory folder. It was freaky to watch and made me love her more. It made me want to hear all her stories—to access all of her. It was as if I saw a mechanism where I could peer into so much more of her than skin and breath. The moment she was leading up to was the most significant of her life, and though I hated whatever I was about to learn, I was also thrilled it had occurred because she was now able to share it with me. She trusted me, and we were crossing this threshold together.

"When," Tess said, "I turned back toward him, he said, 'Jesus! What now?'

"I went back in the direction of my room so he wouldn't see if I started to cry, and I felt it—the cold and then the dead weight—before I knew what it was. I was on the ground crying from the pain. I saw the can next to me spewing soda in a spray through a small hole that must have formed when it hit me. He'd thrown it hard. If it hadn't hurt so much, maybe I would have found it funny. Like, who throws a full can of Coke? But I probably would have needed to be much older to think like that, and it had really hurt my head, and I didn't know if he'd done it as a kind of cruel joke or not, and if not, then what, you know? Mom appeared, cringing, and then she kept her eyes nearly closed. She tucked me into bed and told me to be quiet. She said it wasn't a good idea to give my father anything he didn't ask for, especially at night. My father changed channels on the TV from news to some kind of music."

I looked up at Tess.

She said, "Why did she stay married to him? Of course that's the question. My aunt's answer was that Mom loved him, and when he was violent he wasn't himself. He wasn't the version of him that she loved. It was a sickness, Mom told her, and it wasn't fair to blame a good man for the sick part of him. When my father was younger, my aunt said, he was the smartest man they'd ever met. My aunt never liked him, but nobody could doubt how smart he was. Being around him was like living inside a book. It's hard to leave a man like that. Hard to blame him when he starts to rot. Hard to leave a sick man in that situation when you love him and have a child together."

Hard to leave a sick man, she told me back then.

Tess was wearing jeans and a T-shirt. Now, when she gets ready for an audition or even sometimes when she takes the subway into Manhattan to perform, she wears black pants and Banana Republic–style blouses that make her look professional but slightly stuck up. These clothes accentuate something— maybe her turned-up nose or the contrast between her dark hair and pink cheeks—that makes her look as though she had been popular in high school and still has the possibility of cruelty somewhere in her. She was popular in high school. Miserable and popular, but, until recently, I hadn't thought she was still capable of causing pain to anyone but herself. At that restaurant with me a dozen years ago, she was so much the perfect version of herself that it kills me to remember it.

"A few months after the Coke incident," she said, "my mother put a lock on my bedroom door, and only she had the key. She told me I had to go to the bathroom before I went to bed. That very night, my father broke the lock by pushing and pulling hard, and he came in and methodically punished me. It wasn't usually wild, his physical abuse. He took me off my bed and said, 'You know better than this, Tessie, you know better, yes you do,' and he held my ear with one hand and smacked me across the face with the other. I was scared that on my face someone would be able to see blood or a bruise the next day, but I felt my eye and nose, and they were okay. I ran to Mom in their bedroom.

"When he came back home, it was for breakfast on a weekday morning. It's the only morning I remember him at breakfast. He ate a bowl of cereal and wore a dark blue suit. He was excited to teach me how to do a cartwheel. I was wearing my school uniform. He taught my mother and me how to do cartwheels. I kept looking at my mother, but she wouldn't look at me back. That day at school was normal, and then Mom picked me up and we went straight home, and she said it was important that I not see my father that evening. I asked why and she said because we didn't want him to be angry again and that his head was bothering him and things were bad at work and he wasn't feeling well in general since he broke the door, she was sure I understood.

" 'Your father loves you,' she said, 'but he has a mental—that means brain—problem, and when he drinks he hits people, and the same brain problem makes him want to drink.'

"I didn't know what to say because I knew all this. It was obvious.

" 'He is working on it,' Mom said, 'and he loves us, and I love you and him, and we are a family. So even if it hurts sometimes it's worth it because nothing is as important as family. Remember that. No matter how bad it gets. Nothing is more important than family.'

"I said I understood, and I did. What she said made sense. I don't remember what happened that afternoon, but then I heard Mom screaming before dinner, like she'd burned herself on the stove really badly. I thought we were alone in the house, so I ran to the kitchen to maybe get Mom some ice, but Mom was with my father, who was holding a knife.

"I shouted, Mom shouted, 'Go away, go into your room,' and my father shouted, 'This can't go on, it can't go on like this, live in the real world, you fucking bitch,' and she slapped him and then he came down with the knife into her shoulder. My father was wearing a brown button-down shirt, which was too casual for him, and his face was scared. Mom's face was also scared. She was so pretty, even when she was scared. I started throwing up, which I think my mother saw. I continued to puke, my mother looked at the knife in her shoulder as if she was seeing it for the first time, and my father pulled the knife out of her shoulder and lifted it again and brought it back down into my mother. My mother stopped yelling. My father was crying now and hugging my mother, saying, 'Julia, Julia, I love you, I love you, Julia, Julia, my love,' and then to me, 'Tessie, Tessie, Julia, I love you, I love you, I love.' "

Tess was crying mechanically, but it didn't overwhelm her. She wanted to finish the story.

"I told him I loved him, too. I wasn't even crying anymore. That's when the blood came. I don't remember anything that happened for more than a month after that."

Some days I think I'm lucky to be with someone who's suffered. Seen what she's seen and survived true depression. Other days I think I need someone less damaged, someone who can devote herself more fully to helping me. Of course it is worse to see what Tess saw than to live through what I'm living through, but this is happening to me now, and I guess I'm not in a very empathetic place these days.

She watches me when I take my morning meds. Lexapro and Serzone. Antidepressants are supposed to help suppress the buzzing, the instability, whatever it is. Explanations are always presented to me with dumb metaphors. Antidepressants supposedly "swathe" my brain in a "layer of protective" something or other. Maybe they've helped a bit. They're supposed to take two months to start working and then people see increasing improvement over the next six months to a year, but my doctor has bumped up the dosage twice over the last four months, so now I'm on these heavy meds that make it hard to piss and add a floating feeling to the dizziness. But it's a heavy floating. It's hard to explain.

Tess watches me take the medication as though I might, seconds later, announce that I'm all better. And though I want the exact same thing as she does, I get angry with her for her inability to hide what she wants. When of course she wants me to feel better. I do the same thing: brace myself before I take those pills, with hope that today will be the day. But I have the decency to hide that hope. I feel like every day I'm sick I'm disappointing her, the kids, my parents, everybody. I don't want to let her down, and I don't want to admit how badly I want this to be over. But obviously I do. Who wouldn't? So I feel bad for her, and she feels bad for me. And I resent her for feeling bad for me. All to what end? My life is still completely fucked. I can't talk to people. I can't work. I can't interact with my kids. Or her. She'd said she wasn't fully satisfied before all this. Imagine what she feels now. I can't be with her on any meaningful level. Her past may be psychologically scarring, but I can't live my goddamn life.

I find myself competing like a lunatic with the person I love most over who has experienced the most of what kind of pain. I need her to take care of me, and I'm scared to ask. *Now that I'm weak*, I want to ask: *Now that you'll have to take care of the kids alone while also taking care of me, now that I can't do anything for you, can't have fun, can barely move, now that I look like this, can't really have sex, don't want to have sex, can't parent or work for who knows how long, have left you to do everything, to sacrifice a career that you were just starting to feel good about, now that I hurt our baby and made our other boy watch—are you still here, promise me you still want to be here?*

AUGUST 4, 2016
So it's only Tess and Tazio?

I'm surprised by the number of friends who haven't reached out. High school and college friends I know have heard about the accident but who still, three months later, haven't texted or emailed. Then there's the majority who contacted me for news and, at the end of the call, said to let them know how they can help. I told them it would be great if they could bring over a roasted chicken with vegetables or maybe take the kids on a weekend to the zoo or a museum. And then, nothing. I don't know why. Before I was sick, they'd have brought over dinner, no problem.

But for some reason I'm angrier with the people who do check in. Being in the position to tell them that I'm not getting any better makes me flinch whenever they ask. And people check in so infrequently that when someone does, I want that person to know the full extent of it.

They text, *How're you doing?*

I write back, *Struggling.*

They write, *Tess doing well?*

I answer, *It's really hard trying to get in her auditions while taking care of two kids and me.*

Kids healthy? they write, looking for any possible way to get out of the conversation on a positive note.

But I don't let them. *It's hard for them having me as sick as I am and Tess frustrated.*

I want to scream at them: *How dare you ask how I'm feeling? Can you really not know?*

As the days went on, I felt lonelier and lonelier, cut off from those who didn't ask and furious at needing to explain myself to those who did. Tazio and Tess made up my entire emotional world.

But I couldn't have full conversations with Tazio or Tess without exacerbating the symptoms, so mostly I tried not to complain. I told them I wanted to hear about their lives. But delivering monologues exhausted them, so now we watch a lot of TV. After those two conventions, the only way Hillary loses is if she fucks up the debates. Tazio comes over before and after work on the campaign, but he doesn't talk about what's going on inside the Brooklyn compound. He acts like he wants to watch CNN but he turns it off before too long.

I'd always been the happy-go-lucky one. The big silly guy who told jokes and didn't care if his hair was messy. I was kind, my parents were kind, girls liked me if they'd just been mistreated by an asshole and were looking for someone they could trust. I made them laugh. I wasn't moody or irregular. Even at work, when people bitched about the hours, bosses, and weekends at the computer, I tried to joke about wives, kids, salads, *The Bachelorette*, Joe Biden, Drake, Eli Manning, and iced tea. Sure, we were working corporate communications at a massive consumer packaged goods company, but our job was trying to get more people to drink sweetened iced tea. It could be funny! Anything could. But sitting at home with blurry vision, trying to watch TV as Trump told Anderson Cooper that the racists were the ones "who prioritized advancing blacks ahead of whites not on merit but on quotas even after a black man has been president" made me start thinking about murder. Not in an active, Google-"bomb-making" kind of way as much as a psychological one. Like how kamikaze pilots were trained to think during World War II. If I could make the world a better place by sacrificing my petty, suffering life for a worthy cause, then so be it. I don't know. Maybe that would just lead to President Ted Cruz.

I see my boys in the morning and evening. During the day, I sleep and watch the news.

But Tess is accustomed to striving. To working hard to accomplish goals and not letting her past define her. As she became a teenager, she suffered with what she describes as depression, but she willed herself out of bed and then out of the house and finally to good grades and friendships. She was never the most naturally talented artist, but she was admitted to the most selective art school in the country. She has charisma onstage and has been singing since grade school, but she doesn't have the best voice on Broadway—she trained and made a career for herself.

But now, at home, all she has to strive for is my health. She hates that there's nothing she can do. Regardless of who's at fault, she hates that she's stuck not working toward an achievable goal. So she emailed, called, Facebooked, and Googled, and made me a series of appointments with practitioners who have helped other people with ambiguous disorders like mine.

"You have to do something," Tess said one weekend. "This can't last."

"I'm taking the medications. I'm waiting for them to fully kick in, or then to try the next one. I am trying."

"The first appointment is tomorrow," she said.

Two Mondays ago I saw Rachel, an herbalist.

She opened the door before I rang the bell to her Bed-Stuy brownstone. "You look twenty-five, but you're shriveled up," she said. "You've got the life sucked out of you, you poor thing. You poor thing, you. Come in, come in."

She was Australian, I thought, based on her accent. I didn't know whether I liked her warmth or was repelled by her pity.

I'd promised Tess I would go in with an open mind. What better than someone who could cure me with herbs? Her house smelled of chicken soup.

"Take a large sip of this tea," she said. "And tell me everything you put into your body."

She was probably forty-five years old, but her sagging clothes and pity made her seem much older.

I told her about the acne cream, Propecia, and the antidepressants.

"Why are you on Propecia?" she said.

"Hair loss," I said.

"But why?" she said, smiling as if in recognition of a great sorrow.

"Vanity?" I said. I told myself to remain steady. If she could cure me with herbs, I could endure her judgment. But these thoughts catalyzed some kind of neurological chemical that flooded my brain. I struggled to regain my breath. I blinked until I could see again.

"Your hair looks full," she said.

"Propecia works," I said, trying to smile.

"It's poisoning your liver," she said. "And the acne cream. How long have you been on it?"

"Ten years," I said.

"Ten years! You know it's an antibiotic, right? So it is killing all the good bacteria. There's hope for you yet. No wonder you're dizzy. All these medicines in your system."

"Well, I was fine until I—"

"Tell me about your diet," she said.

"I eat well. I eat low-sugar cereal with soy milk every morning, lean proteins and vegetables, I've stopped drinking alcohol or caffeine since the accident, just seltzer, really, with orange juice sometimes."

"Cereal is just sugar, and soy milk has estrogens in it, so you probably feel a high as you're eating the cereals, but then you crash, and it imbalances your system. And there is nothing worse than seltzer. Nothing. The reason you want it is because we're programmed to yearn for it—water used to be filled with bacteria, so beer and other fermented beverages were safe, but seltzer creates gasses and disrupts your intestine, so no more seltzer, and, like the cereal, OJ is just sugar. Also, you want fat in your meals. Do you eat fat?"

"I cook with olive oil?" I said.

"You should be eating a piece of butter like it's delicious cheese on your bread every morning. Instead of cereal, you should have egg and toast with avocado and three sardines. And of course take a bit of chicken soup."

"For breakfast?"

"Yes. You need to rebuild that good gut bacteria. You need to take chicken soup three times a day, whether for a meal or with the meal, but I always carry two thermoses of it around with me, and I make sure my children do, too. The reason your brain hasn't healed correctly is your stomach is out of sorts, and there is a direct line between your stomach and your head. I'll give you the prebiotic-probiotic pills for you to take, and you'll start drinking pickle juices and kefir and sauerkraut and ghee and beef stews, and you'll take chicken soup at least three times a day. We'll get you off the Propecia and acne meds and antidepressants, and passionflower! I'll make you a tincture of passionflower! Here, try this. I mixed it in anticipation of your arrival. Do you feel better? Do you still feel dizzy? Are you sure? Well, sometimes it takes a while to work.

"So the passionflower at night and the skullcap during the day and no more Propecia or acne meds or antidepressants, and raw milk. Gallons of raw milk. It's illegal in New York, but the most fascinating woman sells it in the back of a diner not too far from here. I gave it to my newborns. It's liquid gold. I stand by it, and eggs with sardines for breakfast with chicken soup, and you can buy fermented fish oils from me, too, and the prebiotic-probiotics. There's hope for you yet! I'll see you same time next week? Cheer up. Don't look so down. This is good. Smile. Once you start eating better and taking herbs and removing the poisons from your body, you'll be back in shape in no time."

She charged me $200 for the session and another $350 for the pills and tinctures. I bought a bottle of water at a bodega and took a prebiotic-probiotic and a fish oil capsule and some skullcap in the subway station, and I cried all the way home.

Something was seriously wrong with my brain, and I had just spent $550 on the promises of raw milk. My job wouldn't keep me on a leave of health for more than another year. My brain was spinning and my eyes were dull. I could barely see colors when I dragged myself up the stairs at my station and didn't get out of bed until the next afternoon when it was time to see the chiropractor.

"I can already observe you are misaligned," Lauren said. She was the same age as the herbalist, but smaller and formally dressed in a long pearl necklace over a black blouse. She crouched like a monkey on my back in order to smooth my bones into place.

"Is that good?" I said after I inhaled the air she'd pressed out of my chest.

"Well, it's bad for your brain."

"I mean is it good because it could be the source of my dizziness?"

I was on the table, facedown on the doctor's paper, feeling optimistic.

"There is a direct line between your spine and your brain, and your spinal cord runs right through your spine into your brain, so if it is pinched anywhere in there, of course your brain is malfunctioning. I'm working on the theory that in the accident, you misaligned or damaged something in your spine or neck, which damaged the spinal cord and isn't allowing full function to return to your brain."

"Yeah?"

"I could have gone into any kind of healing—medicine, acupuncture, pharmacology—but this is where I felt I could do the most good. We make two things in this country—disease and debt. And I don't know a thing about money, so I cure disease. Or I allow your body to cure itself. Let me show you what I mean. Say 'Life is beautiful' and hold your thumb and middle finger together."

"Life is beautiful." She tried to pull my fingers apart but couldn't.

"Say 'Life is terrible' and hold your thumb and middle finger together."

"Life is terrible," I said, and she easily pried them apart.

I was crushed. I'd been starting to trust her. What she was saying about a nerve being pinched from the fall made sense, felt like actual medicine. Why did she need to give me this shitty demonstration of quack science?

" 'Above the plain of right and wrong there is a field,' " she said. " 'Meet me there.' Have you heard that one before? I believe that we're all just bags of molecules. Think about that. Listen to this one. One of my patients was on an airplane. She bought a bag of chocolate chip cookies and sat down in her seat. After takeoff, she started eating the cookies."

She asked me to turn over, and then, with sweeping motions, like my chest was a tablecloth she was flattening, she pushed my ribs, pulled at my shoulders, and kneaded my stomach.

"Well, the old lady sitting next to her reached over and took a cookie out of the bag and ate it. Then my patient ate a cookie, and the old lady ate one, until there were no cookies left. At the end of the flight, the old lady got off the plane without saying thank you or anything, and my patient thought, *What a nasty old bitch*, you know, eating her cookies like that without saying thank you.

"Well, my patient stood up, opened the overhead compartment for her carry-on, and she saw her bag of cookies there. She'd been eating the old woman's cookies that whole time. What she thought was a nasty old bitch not saying thank you and my patient biting her tongue was actually the reverse. She was the bitch! You see what I mean?"

She gently pushed my ribs, pulled at my neck, and kneaded my stomach muscles.

"Now, you might feel better as soon as you sit up, or you might feel shaky for a day or two while your brain gets accustomed to full function again. But we're on our way."

I felt exactly the same.

"See what I mean?" she said.

"No," I said, desperate to feel. I couldn't see her well. I couldn't think of the words to tell her how badly I'd wanted her to be right.

"This takes time," she said. "Some of my patients don't feel truly healthy for a month or two." I could sense her fear, and I wanted to tell her it was okay. No one could help me. She didn't need to feel bad about it.

Instead, I said, "But how do I know whether all the time and money—this is expensive—is going in the right direction?" I spoke in a frail voice I didn't recognize as my own.

"You have to do something, right?" she said. "I'll see you next week. I know it. I'm going to cure you."

The next day, I entered a cramped apartment on the Upper East Side, and Monica smiled, greeted me, "David!" She was younger than the others, a native New Yorker was my guess. Jeans and a simple cotton T-shirt. The room floated and bounced; my vision was already blurry from a bad morning with the boys.

"I can tell you're off-kilter, come sit down," she said. She spoke like a New Yorker. As though she didn't give a shit whether I sat down or not.

I told her about my blurry vision, the dizziness and disorientation. The memory elicited, as it always did, the moment of impact, my head hitting the ground, and then Max's head hitting mine. I shuddered. Monica put a hand on my shoulder. She asked me if anything made it better or worse, and I told her that talking and stress made it worse and nothing made it better.

"Come up on here," she said. She had a massage table laid out in the center of the living room full of plants and crystal animals.

She spent twenty minutes asking me to focus on different parts of my body as she worked them, and then she told me to breathe deeply. To fill up my chest and then let it collapse like a balloon.

She asked me who in my family when I was growing up was most miserable, and I told her about my mother having trouble getting up to go to work in the morning.

She asked about my appetite (poor), sex drive (nonexistent), and sleep habits (all I wanted to do was sleep since I started the antidepressants), and she asked how my professional and personal lives were going. I told her about how I can't work and how Tess cheated and we'd just reconciled before the accident. Monica told me she wanted to be fully honest with me and that she'd already heard about the breakup and reconciliation from Angelica, who was her dentist.

"Angelica is telling her patients about my personal life?" I said.

"Only after she asked me if I thought I could help. But back to you. You're happy to be back home?"

"I'm so happy I have them back," I said.

I started to tear up.

"Except . . . ," she said.

"Every day is a hell! I can't work or play with my kids or be around my wife or anyone, really, in any kind of normal way. I'm preventing my wife from working, and I can't work, and . . ."

Talking like this made it worse.

"Can you visualize, I mean, imagine, the life you want?"

"Yes," I said.

"No, I mean can you feel it in your body?" she said. "Enjoying a new job, playing with your kids?"

"No," I said.

I lay on the table taking deep breaths. Monica's hands found creases between my bones and muscles, created space, and moved on. She did something like what the chiropractor had done the day before, but this was very painful. I'd barely felt the chiropractor.

"I know this hurts. It's supposed to. I'm waking your body up, so it can heal itself. That's what—keep breathing—that's what you have to do. That's what you have to feel. You have to feel everything you want coming true."

She started pulling harder at muscles and tendons. In my legs. She asked if I felt pressure in certain points. I felt close to blacking out from the pain.

"That's okay," she said. "It hurts. Cry. Our bodies cry when we're in pain."

She released her grip on my calf and positioned her hands on the other calf. Before her fingers found their way under the muscle, I clenched up, and she told me to breathe.

Then, "Repeat after me," she said. "I now have permission to enjoy what I've created."

"I have permission to enjoy what I've created," I said.

She squeezed, shooting pain from my leg up through my back, snapping my neck up and then down on the table.

"Fuck!" I yelled. "Fuck. Sorry."

"It hurts, right?" she said. "But it also feels kind of right? Like I'm loosening something that's solidified or atrophied in the wrong way?"

I sniffled back tears.

"You don't need to think there's any validity in what I'm asking you to do. Feel free to roll your eyes if you want. Just get used to saying it."

She pulled at muscles in my leg more softly now.

"Relax into it. Let your leg go entirely. And don't forget to breathe."

I relaxed.

"Good," she said.

Repeat, "I'm learning that change is safe."

"I'm learning that change is safe," I said.

"Your body has been dizzy for months now. It wants to stay dizzy."

I breathed.

"I'm learning that change is safe," she said.

"I'm learning that change is safe," I said.

"I'm learning that it is innocent to have what I want."

"I'm learning that it is innocent to have what I want," I said.

"Your abdominal muscle on the side, here, is tight. Do you feel the tightness here?" she said.

"Yes," I said. "But please—"

She squeezed, and it felt like a razor blade pulled at my stomach. She let go. I gasped for air.

"Your body received a shock, and it has not allowed itself to recover from it. It's still in shock. Through bodywork and mental processes, we have to force it to recover. It won't recover by itself."

I breathed and felt her hands on my chest. She pushed down, hard, with both hands, dug fingers under both sides of my ribs.

I shrieked, and she held me down.

"I'm learning to trust the unfamiliar," she said.

"I'm learning to trust the unfamiliar," I whimpered.

"I'm learning that change is safe."

"I'm learning that change is safe," I said.

"I'm learning that it is innocent to have what I want."

"I'm learning that it is innocent to have what I want," I said.

"You don't need to be your mother. You don't need to carry her sadness into your home. Her tension. You are free to let the blood flow in your body where it needs to, to release the muscles that are cutting off your nerves and vessels."

"Should I see a psychologist? Is that what you're saying? I was seeing someone be—"

"Breathe," she said. "Imagine, feel in your body playing with your children and feeling good. Feel having dinner with your wife and the room staying still and your eyes working. Feel it all. Don't imagine it in your head, feel it in your body. And sit up."

I sat, and the room swung as though at the end of a long rope.

"Jesus," I said.

"This is good," she said. "Your brain needs to reacclimatize itself."

"I've never felt worse," I said. "I'm about to vomit."

"Then vomit," she said. "I'll get a bag. I taught your body how to find its correct equilibrium and get the vital fluids flowing again. Not only blood but waters and interstitial and lymphatic fluids."

I looked at her. She was five years younger than I was, and I'd let her torture me.

"I feel much, much worse," I said.

"That's your body trying to regain its composure," she said.

"I feel woozy," I said. "Have you been to any kind of medical school or anything?"

"Yay!" She jumped up and down, having ignored my question. She was clapping and jumping without any of the irony from an hour before.

"What?" I said. "I'm dizzier."

"That's wonderful," she said. "I have an opening same time next week. You can pay me then. Cash, please. It's two hundred dollars per session."

"Sure," I said. Together, Tess and I had less than ten grand.

The rope that the room was on snapped, and the floor jumped. My knees buckled. She caught me by the arm. She was like a little kid. "Yay!" she said. "We're going to get you healthy! Go home and celebrate with Tess."

The next day, Thomas the acupuncturist was on the fourth floor of a former factory in an industrial strip in Williamsburg. Pipes were exposed throughout the unpainted stairwell, but the office door opened up onto trimmed plants in clay vases on antique side tables, Victorian couches, and midcentury modern chairs.

"David! Sucks, man, what you're dealing with. I read through your forms and know I can help. The people who come in here, they suffer from everything. Terrible, rancid skin, constipation, erupting boils. There was one guy who threw up all this disgusting blood and bile every time he went from a reclining to sitting position; I had to keep a garbage can next to the table for him. Women on birth control who want to get off it, but when they do their period is so heavy and painful they're in bed for a week, can't go to work, you know. And my basic approach is the same. Make sure the gut is healthy, the energy is steady, make sure you're eating well, sleeping well, allow the body to start healing itself, and I help it out with supplements, with acupuncture, and with anything else I can think of along the way. Make sense?"

He was fifty, probably, but looked and talked thirty. Wore shined shoes, tight jeans, a dress shirt with two or three buttons unbuttoned, and a shock of graying brown hair, messy and somewhere between the style of a Californian surfer and European intellectual.

He had me lie down, and he placed a series of vials on my stomach.

"I buy all these old dusty, decaying medical books—books your neurologist would say are total crap—and they make me feel right because the stuff I'm doing has been around for hundreds of years, you know? I've been to dental school, but I'm not convinced the medical way makes any more sense. The people who come in here, their blood tests are clean. They're told they're in perfect health. But they're dizzy or in miserable pain or they can't get out of bed. They're told they must just be depressed. And sure, they're depressed because their life is shit now. Some of them literally have to shit all the time. Can't be away from a toilet for more than ten minutes. And doctors and pills can't help them. Everyone tells them to have a better attitude. To buck up. But it's like, fuck you, man, you try having a better attitude when you've got to shit all the time. My way of doing things works."

I laughed. He was right. I was depressed. No one understood me. They did tell me, or at least imply, that a better attitude would make me healthier. Monica the day before told me as much.

The acupuncturist was lightly touching the muscle on my inner arm as he placed each vial on my chest, testing, I gathered, to see if various vials made my muscle twitch.

"I treat a lot of musicians here and they tell me that I'm tuning them, you know, like they tune their broken-down, aging instruments. I think there's something to that. Like I see where the energy is going in your body and where I can increase flow, and I try to help you regain your natural state.

"Because after an accident like you had, your body is permanently in this fight-or-flight state. It has settled into this cross-wired state where it has to ease itself back. All the medications you are taking are trying to dull the crossed-over state so you don't feel so crossed over anymore. What I'm going to try to do is to enable the body to uncross itself."

He put needles in my feet and inner arms. They barely hurt. He was a lovely guy. I lay on the table for a half hour.

"See you next week. Oh, and start taking these supplements. At breakfast, take one cardio, two zinc, two calcium, one ortho, and two hydro. At lunch, take two cardio, two zinc, two calcium, two ortho, and two hydro. At dinner, take two cardio, four calcium, four ortho, and seven hydro. And, before bed, take four hydro and four calcium." He charged me $320 at the door and scheduled me for the following week.

I had appointments scheduled again for Monday through Thursday.

I missed them all. I didn't call to cancel. I didn't respond when they called or emailed to confirm. I was sick and getting sicker. I ate big bowls of cereal and took all the tinctures and pills and potions with bottles of seltzer. Every day I took two Lexapro, two Serzone, one Propecia, some acne cream, some passionflower, some skullcap, four fish oils, two prebiotic-probiotics, five cardios, four zincs, twelve calciums, seven orthos, and fifteen hydros. I spent Sunday at the toilet vomiting, my boys taking turns bringing me seltzer to sip.

I cried more that week than I'd ever cried in my life. Tess told the kids I had the flu. Max got into bed with me and cried, too. He explained, in his way, that he'd had the flu shot (and gotten a yellow Band-Aid), so he'd be okay. I was ruining their lives. Tess told me I had to move out if I was going to keep crying like this. I could be sick at home, but not like this. I told her I was depressed, and she was being cruel. She apologized and cried, too, and told me how sick it was making her, my feeling like this.

On Monday of the following week—last Monday—twelve days after I met her, Monica showed up at our apartment when I was home alone during the day, lying in bed and staring at the ceiling. She said Angelica had told her where I lived. In a way, she saved my life. I don't know what would have happened if she hadn't come for me. She gave me a massage and took me

for a walk. I drank some water and ate some rice. We set rules
that I've been trying to follow ever since.

AUGUST 5, 2016

How did you and Tazio become so close?

We were always close. Starting in high school, we were close.
In college and for the few years after that, he continued to be
my best friend, but I think we kind of hated each other. Maybe
in your early twenties, everyone kind of hates everyone else?
He was so talented, so smart and capable. The question is, how
did the drunken antagonism disappear?

One explanation goes something like this:

Every morning, after his disastrous time with the Edwards
campaign in 2003, Tazio woke up at five thirty, went to the
bathroom, vomited, showered, listened to the morning news
on the radio as he shaved, dressed, and brushed his teeth, and
got to the liquor store just after it opened at seven to buy three
airplane bottles of Bacardi Gold, which was the cheapest,
worst-tasting hard liquor and therefore a daily ritual of mas-
ochistic asceticism. Tazio drank the three bottles outside the
store, got a black coffee from a bodega, and tried to work or
paint until noon, when he settled into the Puerto Rican dive
bar near his apartment and drank four or five double Dewar'ses
and then spent the afternoon trying to nap and paint. He didn't
eat until dinner, usually at five thirty or six: takeout, like Thai
or empanadas. After dinner, he went back down to the bar and
drank until bedtime. When he had a girlfriend, she usually met
him at home later on. He drank about twenty-five shots (over
a fifth) every day. He passed out at around eleven, woke up the
next morning, and did it all again.

There were better and worse years. He'd control the drinking enough to consult for a municipal race or New York tech start-up. He even worked as the chief strategy officer at a small company that was trying to bring arts education to public and charter schools, but he fell back into the same self-destructive routine. In 2007, he disappeared for over a month and I still don't know where he went. The following year, I think, he trashed a gallery and got into insane physical fights. Or maybe that was earlier. It feels like he hasn't painted in years. Tess and I hardly saw him for months until, when Ethan was born, he came over daily with homemade baby foods and handmade toys. And then his liver started to hurt. He tried to stop drinking but couldn't. His stomach filled up with fluid, and his skin—and what were supposed to be the whites of his eyes—turned yellow. He took the subway to a hospital. By this time, he'd lost most of his muscle, and where his skin wasn't yellow, it was red from acne and burst capillaries. It was strange to see him ugly. I thought I'd like it, but I didn't. I thought I'd like to see him sober because all the slurred words and dumb conversations had been boring. But this kind of sober I didn't like, either. Sick was worse than boring.

He was in the hospital for a week. Then I was there to look after him until he could start caring for himself. His mother lived more than an hour away and couldn't take time off work. I told my boss at Pepsi that a family member was ill, and she was surprisingly cool about it. Tess and I had just moved to our current apartment, but I stayed most of the time at Tazio's place, bringing in gallons of cranberry juice, helping him bathe and use the bathroom, and making sure he didn't drink. My seeing him like that took away a lot of the artifice and competition, I think. (Who could doubt that he had lost?) And silently listening to classical music and NPR for all those hours created something powerful between us.

Another explanation goes like this:

Tazio's liver turned into scar tissue. Why? Because he's an alcoholic. Why? Because he is ashamed. Why? Because his father abandoned him, and he thought his life would be devoted to painting but then decided that art wasn't big or useful or important enough for him so he abandoned art to devote his life to politics where he lost elections as well as the drive to paint.

I couldn't be antagonistic with that.

Freshman year on Long Island everybody listened to Green Day, and I wore the costume—unbuttoned flannels over white T-shirts with jeans—but I didn't get the whining and dumb lyrics. I still mostly listened to my father's music: Paul Simon and Bob Dylan. Tazio was going through an all-black phase. Black leather jacket and black jeans and T-shirt with black motorcycle boots. It straddled the line between cool and ridiculous. His name and, if I'm going to be honest, ambiguous ethnicity made me think of him as cool. We had never hung out, but we knew each other from being in all the same accelerated math and science classes. He hung out with other kids who wore black, too. Goths, I guess we called them, but at our school they were just the kids who smoked cigarettes and didn't like Green Day. If I'd had any guts, I would have been one of them. And if I hadn't been so tall that the JV basketball team had to take me. These Goths didn't have piercings or call themselves witches or anything like that. At least, as far as I knew at the time. I kind of rooted for them. Maybe they did do witch stuff? I never spoke to a single one of them. From my vantage point, they just wore black clothes and seemed to be really comfortable around one another.

Then, one day, my mom was picking me up after basketball practice, and I heard Tazio listening to Dylan in his mother's car. He said it was "Isis"—this was decades before the Islamic State, of course—and I told him I liked that song, too, and had the same CD. *Bob Dylan's Greatest Hits Vol. II.* It was a two-CD set, my favorite, and Tazio looked me up in the school directory that night. He asked me about homework but quickly transitioned to Dylan. It turned out we both loved "A Hard Rain's A-Gonna Fall." We both listened to it at night when we were trying to fall asleep. Tazio told me the lyrics were just like poetry, and I told him my father said the same thing and I agreed. Tazio told me Billy Joel was the worst singer in the United States, and I told him that I loved living on Long Island, but Billy Joel was the worst singer in the world. Tazio said he did not love living on Long Island.

We spoke on the phone for hours that night and the next and next, and then, the following week, we counted down from three, two, one, and at zero we hit play on our boom boxes and listened to the entire "A Hard Rain's A-Gonna Fall" together over the phone. It was over ten minutes long. I heard Tazio's breathing during the verses we didn't know yet, and we sang the chorus together. For the first time in years, I wasn't self-conscious around someone my own age. I think it's because he had self-confidence, and when we were talking he included me in his little impenetrable bubble. We all knew that his dad had left a couple of years before, and I connected that fact with Tazio's intensity, or, if not intensity, then perhaps instinct to make every moment feel significant. When the song was over and we'd sung the last "And it's a hard, and it's a hard, it's a hard, it's a hard, and it's a hard rain's a-gonna fall," he said, "Right?" and I said, "The best," and he said, "Three, two, one," without indicating what he meant, and we pressed play again together. It was a good feeling to be so close with someone after only knowing him for a couple of weeks. To be at my house with the plastic basketball hoop up in my bedroom, and my homework spread out on the floor, and Tazio on the other end of the line feeling and thinking everything along with me.

6

The apartment door opens as though David has been waiting for Tess to read the last line of that entry. Or maybe she paused, paralyzed, after that final line. Her heart beat faster, and she couldn't have read on if she'd wanted to. She's been blankly staring at the screen for close to an hour.

Now David looks at Tess.

From the particular sound the keys made at the door, she knew it was him, but she didn't rush to close the computer. She wasn't the one who had to explain herself.

"You want to tell me where you've been?" she says.

"Monica is going to be able to fix me. I'll tell you. Put that away. You shouldn't be reading that," he says. "Come here."

Tess joins him in the living room.

"It's going to take a while," David says. "But she found a way to fix me."

David looks exhausted, flushed, red-faced, torn-fleshed; pimples have colonized his cheeks and forehead. Tess has trouble maintaining her anger in the face of David's suffering body. But that's not right. Anger is coursing through her. Anger is the most vital of her feelings, vying for primacy over her desire to soothe and comfort him.

"Sit down. Rest," Tess says, motioning to the couch cushion beside her.

She tries to compartmentalize. First, she feels relief that he's home. He's not dead, not run over. Ethan and Max aren't half orphans. She's not a widow. And she has him back again.

"Monica has been reaching out to her network," he says. "An audiologist says he's seen this before. People fall and damage the inner ear, which makes the brain lose its equilibrium. Initially, the condition is misdiagnosed as concussion, or maybe it's concussion related. Vestibular migraine was one possibility."

"And she says she can help you?"

But more than relief, Tess feels fury. David left her alone for days. Her and the boys. He hasn't acknowledged how painful it must have been, and that this type of pain—caused by the man she needs to be reliable acting erratic and then disappearing—is the exact type of pain she's lived her life fearing most. He wrote that he's scared she's going to leave him for good, and then he acts in a way that makes her want to?

But love is mixed in, as well. Her analyzable needs and understanding of her own tragedy and triggers have everything and nothing to do with her pheromonal, hardwired love for David, this hopeful, miserable man she's been living with for more than a decade. More than anyone else in her past or present, he is her family.

"The equipment is expensive," he says. "But Monica borrowed a set for me already, and even though I'm not supposed to feel any effects for a month or so, after the first time, I felt steadier. My vision was a little bit clearer. This was after two of my worst-symptoms days!"

And on top of Tess's relief, fury, and love, there are a million other less immediately comprehensible emotions and curiosities, like the need to know where he's been sleeping, what signals she has given him that she would leave him, what he knows about Tazio, if he's always hated how she dressed, and if Monica— regardless of her intentions—really can help him.

All these in addition to the creeping fear they'll be disappointed and that the whole thing is her—Tess's—fault. Because though she'd wanted so badly to create for her children the stable childhood she'd lacked, as soon as she had those children, she'd gone and fucked the whole thing up. Even after David abandoned her for three days, she can't look at him without feeling guilt and then fury at herself for putting herself in this position. Shame. Self-directed fury is shame.

So maybe David is right that Tess has some cruelty in her. But doesn't everyone? If not cruelty, then selfishness at least? Wanting to live a specific life in the moment you want to live it? At seventeen, she escaped her aunt's house and devoted her life to painting. At twenty-one, after half a decade of creating obscured images of her mother over and over, she was dismissed by one professor for "hiding beyond a superficial veneer of ambiguity" and another for painting "Mud! All I see is mud! You say it's a woman. What? Am I supposed to take your word for it? And what does this muddy woman mean?" So what did she do? Did she let these men's aesthetic whims define the rest of her time at school? No. She shifted out from under their influence and began appearing in friends' art films and then in real, narrative student films, until she found her way to off-off-Broadway, professional productions and showcases that, though they didn't pay, got her in front of her manager and, as important, an audience that let her forget her past and just be. Just do her work. The freedom was thrilling. When she landed the non-Equity tour of *Rent*, even the bus rides—with everyone sprawled out on the bus floor trying to sleep between cities—were thrilling. And when she was singing onstage, she felt flashes of high-adrenaline ecstasy that she never experienced in real life, whether in painting, sex, sports, friendship, or any other moment when she had to be herself and live within the confines of her own memories, needs, and fears.

Onstage, even in the ensemble, she was dependent on no one's selfishness; she waited for no one to let her down; she was able to be visible, vulnerable, and in the moment, in luxurious contrast to her real life spent playing the bit role of a woman devoted primarily to steeling herself against exposure. Maybe it wasn't cruelty that David saw in her. Maybe it was self-preservation.

So yes, she understands that when she had Ethan and Max, and she needed David, in a way she hadn't before, to continue behaving as wonderfully as he always had behaved, she revolted against being dependent on his behavior. And yes, scared or unfulfilled, she fucked up and slept with Jonah because everything in life can vanish at any moment, so one must seize pleasure wherever possible. And yes, she was inexcusably selfish, sacrificing everything for nothing, trying to scratch an itch she didn't understand.

But she has also been good. She took David's injury in stride because the benefit of fearing the worst was always being prepared for it. And when David disappeared for a few days, she felt fear but also that same resolve, that other side of the not-wanting-to-be-vulnerable-to-a-man's-trajectory coin, which was steadfastness and fortitude—for the kids, at least—in the face of disappointment. So she'd done bad, but there were far worse people out there, and she deserved to be treated with kindness, because everyone did. And because she'd married this man specifically for his kindness.

She processes what she's heard: "You were with Monica? At her home?"

"I barely saw her. I needed a place to rest."

She decides to believe him.

"You didn't want to see the boys?"

"Of course I did. But Tazio . . . ," David says, and plugs his eye sockets with his palms, rubbing his scalp with his giant fingers.

"What does your staying with Monica have to do with Tazio?"

"He left. He went down to DC. Without Angelica."

Tess feels a horrible rush of potential, a loosening of a still-buckled straitjacket. "Is the wedding still on?"

"I think," David says.

"He was just here and seemed fine."

"You just don't believe anything bad about Tazio," David says.

"What's that supposed to mean?" Tess says.

"Nothing. Forget it."

"Okay," Tess says. "How bad is he?"

"Tazio? He'll be fine."

"But then why didn't you call me?"

"I was with him. I was doing my best."

"That's why you didn't call for three days?"

"He said he wasn't going to drink, but he also said I could come if I wanted, so if he left that opening, I figured that meant he wanted me there."

After reading David's depiction of her long-ago account of her longer-ago childhood trauma, Tess realizes that she is unable to compartmentalize. David's incapacitation has coincided with—or, if such a thing is possible, caused—the intensification of her memories and associated pain. Human beings, she'd thought, were supposed to be able to handle one problem at a time. That was the way natural selection worked. You had to stop worrying whether the caveman loved you for long enough to outrun the woolly mammoth. But, for Tess, the more difficult David's condition made her life, the more she couldn't escape images of her parents.

"I was calling police departments," she says. "I was terrified. So were the boys."

David stares blankly. His body is so raw and in need of care that in spite of her anger she moves toward him and pulls his face down to her neck. David smells tired and a bit sick, sweaty; like himself but tinted with decay. The boys are young and will forget as soon as they see him again, even if it leaves them shakier and less confident in the solidity of their lives. And she is worried about Tazio, but the year or two after he got sober, he left for six months to travel through Asia. She'd worried then, too, but he was fine.

What Tess fears more is that David has changed. That he's not the same life-affirming, loving, gregarious man trapped inside a body that no longer functions, but that he is fundamentally different now. That with her infidelity and then his accident, he has become some other David who is not as concerned with his children. Whose first instinct is not to hold doors and help strangers. The David she married once shyly told her that when he walked past playgrounds and schoolyards, he hoped a ball flew over the fence so he could throw it back. He confessed it to her as if it was some dishonorable secret, but she'd known and loved that his greatest pleasure was making himself useful. Now, maybe he is different. Maybe this instinct has been broken by living every day through a fog of disorientation and pain. Maybe he's not the same man she could always count on. Maybe even if David does get his health back, everything is already ruined. He was with Tazio driving for hours, then alone all day—preparing to go to sleep, brushing his teeth, putting in his contacts, taking his meds, washing his face—and he'd chosen not to communicate with her. If he's not passively transforming into some new person, then he's actively establishing his independence.

"It's a start-up," David rambles. "There's tons of funding. All kinds of dried mango and coconut water just around to take. They were reminiscing and blaming people. Saying Robby Mook didn't want to pay some pollster, which was why the campaign had no idea what was going on in Wisconsin and Pennsylvania. And that leaders had too much faith in the American people. Didn't think they'd vote for a racist. They're going to find the real dirt on the administration. The connections with WikiLeaks. Polling machines.

"And oh—sorry! I'm burying the lede. He was down there with Satin of all people. He—she—is trans now and still goes by Satin. She's been lobbying. Mentioned something called FWD-dot-US."

"He hated that guy." Tazio had been so excited about Satin in the beginning of the Edwards days before everything soured.

"When I said that, Tazio just waved me off. I'm telling you, he was a fucking prick."

"You didn't say that," Tess says.

"Well, my adrenaline wore off, and I started feeling even worse. The lack of routine, no sleep, and all I could eat were eggs. None of the restaurants seemed to have vegetables. It was all fried food and sandwiches, and Tazio didn't notice or give a shit. I ate eggs for four meals in a row. Scrambled eggs and baked potatoes. I slept in the rental car. I was going to get a hotel for the next night, but instead I took the train back to the city. I told Satin to keep him sober, but I don't think she took it seriously. I said he's an alcoholic, he was hospitalized since she last saw him, and she said she'd do her best, but everyone there seemed kind of obsessed. I had to leave. I had to. So I went to Monica's to recuperate."

David has been talking for a long time. He gets this way sometimes when he's so dizzy, his vision so blurry, that he gives up and figures it can't get any worse. He needs a shower and twelve hours of sleep. But it'll be hard not to let the boys wake him, to let him tell them everything is okay and that he is home again for good. If he is, in fact, home again for good. She needs to ask it one more time.

"Why didn't you call me?" Tess says. "Text once to let me know you were okay, or what you were doing? I keep on asking you this same question. You had all that time by yourself. And then you were a subway ride away, and still . . ."

David looks down. He looks back at Tess. Their bodies have separated to opposite sides of the couch.

"I wanted to get away from everything," David says. "I wanted to try to just be myself away from people I upset."

"You could have told me that," Tess says. "You don't upset me."

"Are you in love with him?" David says.

"Who?" Tess says.

"Who do you think?" David says.

Of all the possible memories, this one comes in a flash, as a complete encapsulated moment she hasn't recalled for years. Tazio had been up painting for a night or two. Tess had taken pleasure in the performance—her two hands pulling his leg off the bed—of dragging him out of the dorm for a meal. The weather was painfully cold. She was underdressed. They went to the pizza and bagel place on the corner of St. Marks and Third. He ordered a large coffee, a plain slice, and a bagel with cream cheese, and was taking distracted pecks and sips. They both shivered.

Tazio wore a paint-spattered pea coat and had his hair cut tight against his scalp. His features were warm and large. Nearly pink. Especially his lips. Tess sipped tea and watched Tazio drink from the open fold in his paper cup's plastic top.

Tess didn't know if she wanted to be more than friends with him. She'd been looking for excuses to be around him. But there were always other girls. "You know Sienna?" Tazio said, pizza slice in hand. "From drafting? She won't leave me alone. Pretended to be waiting in my lobby for someone else . . ."

They were silent for a long time until Tazio said quietly, like he'd long ago figured something out and was saying it aloud now just to confirm it was true, "Sometimes when people see me, they see me in class or ordering a slice or whatever, and they have no idea. They don't know that they're in the same place as Tazio Di Vincenzo. They'll never know. I'm going to be famous. I might change the world. And nobody fucking knows it. It drives me insane! It's unbelievable!"

Tess giggled, caught herself, transformed her laugh at him into a laugh with him. He had something. That was for sure. Ambition, charisma, intelligence, talent. She liked—maybe loved—being around him. But he was absurd. Even at nineteen years old. Completely ridiculous. Impossible to rely on. Tazio then and now.

"Is that what this is about?" Tess asks David. She is ready to say what she'd long planned on saying if this question was asked of her, by David or Tazio.

"I see the way you talk about him," David says, disguising his sadness as anger. But when he actually gets angry he just turns sad. Sometimes she wishes he'd let himself be angry. Get it out. Act rashly. Throw a coaster, hit a pillow, or smash a hole in the wall. But she tears up seeing his tears. "The way the boys run to him with their arms in the air like they used to run to me."

"That's just not true! Tazio is their friend, but it's you they love. Tazio has been helpful," she says. "But I swear to god I'm not going to make the mistake I made again—with Jonah, I mean. I agree Tazio's been around too much. But now he's gone. Maybe it will be better to have him elsewhere for a bit." Here she delivers the line she's rehearsed for years: "We both love him as a friend, but we didn't marry him. You're my entire life. My family." She breathes. "That's why these last few days were so impossible. You're the love of my life. I read your journal."

"I walked in on you reading it."

"I'm not going to leave. I'm here forever, whether you like it or not."

They both pause, having heard something in the boys' bedroom. But it's nothing.

"I'm trying," David says. "I'm trying to get over it. But now look at me. I don't have a life. I'm worthless."

She backs into the kitchen.

"Well, I'm happy you've finally said it," she says. "Blamed me."

"Said what? I didn't mean . . . ," he says. "I know it was my fault I fell."

"You meant it," she says. She's crying because she can't bear to think about the details. To relive that day and David's fall with Max in his arms. She can't think about it. "I'm doing everything I can."

"I know. I didn't mean to say . . . ," he says. "This isn't your fault. I—"

"I do love you," she says. "I'm here for good. With you."

"No. I know. You shouldn't have read that. I love you, too. And I forgave you. I forgive you. I just wanted to see what it felt like to hurt you a little bit, too."

"Did you like it?" Tess says.

"Yes," David says. "No. No."

7

"Daddy's home!" Tess says.

"Daddy!" Max says.

"Where goed Daddy?" Ethan says.

"On a trip!" David calls from the bedroom, where he'd been trying to stay awake until he could hug and comfort the kids. "To make Tazio feel better!"

"Tazo and Angie?" Ethan says.

"Just Tazio!" David says.

"Tazo comed home, too?" Ethan said.

"Daddy home Mommy Daddy home Mommy!" Max says, looking for Tess to match his elation.

"Your shoes!" Tess says instinctively, but she doesn't care whether they take their shoes off.

The boys sprint—"Me first Maxy I seed Daddy first"—to the bedroom, where both jump onto the bed and then under the sheets with their father.

Tess's heart soars as David flings four tiny shoes out from under the covers and wrestle-hugs the boys.

"Daddy sandwich!" Ethan says.

Max is crying.

"You're hurting Max," Tess says, still from the doorway, still smiling.

"I got here first," Ethan says.

"Max is okay, I think," David says. "Are you, Maxman?"

But Max is holding on to David's arm and weeping.

Ethan is scared by the intensity of his younger brother's reaction. "It's okay, Maxy, Max Max," Ethan says through his own tears. "Daddy is home now. Daddy is back home. See?" Ethan gestures at David with both palms up.

Max cries and cries, clamping his whole tiny self around his father's arm.

Winter

8

Tazio was twelve years old the last time he saw his father. There was still a half hour left in *Batman Returns* when Mr. Di Vincenzo stood up from the couch and told Tazio to get in the truck. He lived in Ronkonkoma, ten minutes on the Long Island Expressway from Tazio's mother's house in Islip. Tazio was disappointed to be going back so soon. He'd been looking forward to spending time with his father, and all they'd done so far was sit at home and watch movies he'd already seen.

Tazio was small for twelve, and his father was short, too, but thick. Muscular, with a belly that seemed to increase his strength. They both wore heavy, oversize New York Islanders T-shirts, though neither could have named a player on the team other than Patrick Flatley, whom Mr. Di Vincenzo told everyone he liked because of the nickname "The Chairman of the Boards." Mr. Di Vincenzo's Chevy had been painted green for as long as Tazio could remember. Its cabin smelled of oily pipe wrenches, circular saws, plungers and toilet snakes, American Spirit rolling tobacco, and dried sweat. At Tazio's feet, a bright orange extension cord coiled over and around crushed cans of Rolling Rock and ginger ale. As they pulled out, Tazio hoped someone would see him riding in his father's truck. He wished someone would take a picture.

"Everything good?" Mr. Di Vincenzo said.

Tazio rarely spoke, not even to his mother and father. He knew other kids thought he was a weirdo. Later, when he grew up and became a thoughtful, brooding, handsome man, he would paint on canvases, have close friends, and confidently explain politics at parties to groups of strangers. But at twelve, he was quiet. His father had said that was okay, which made Tazio feel happy and also embarrassed.

They'd gotten onto the LIE but were heading in the wrong direction, driving deeper out on Long Island instead of to his mother's house. When Tazio realized this, his body filled with a tart, adrenaline-spiked heat that quickly faded and that afterward he would have done or said anything to recover.

"You good, *patatino*?" Mr. Di Vincenzo said. "Everything good?"

Tazio nodded, slightly warmed again by the pet name. *Little potato*. He watched the concrete partitions that divided the road from the trees and anchored the bases of the lamp poles. He loved his father so much he couldn't stand it.

"See those poles?" Mr. Di Vincenzo said, pointing with his forehead. "You think they're aluminum or steel? I'll give you two guesses."

Steel was too heavy and expensive. Aluminum was a surprise, though. Mr. Di Vincenzo was laughing, and Tazio realized with a twinge that it had been a joke. Two guesses.

"Look, I get you being angry with me, but I want things to be better between us. Okay? Hey, I'm a good guy, I promise. That's all I'm trying to be. If that's not good enough for your mother, then . . ."

Mr. Di Vincenzo shook his head at the windshield.

Better? Tazio hadn't known that things weren't good between his father and himself. Between his father and his mother, sure.

But to Tazio, his father was just his father. Papa. He called his father Mr. Di Vincenzo in front of customers. Some of the older ones would laugh and rub his head. Twelve was too old for a person to still be getting his head rubbed, but Tazio couldn't think of a way to bring this up.

He sat up higher in his seat and relaxed his hands, with which he had been squeezing and twisting the seat belt. They were pulling off at a rest stop.

"You'll see. It's for the best," Mr. Di Vincenzo said. "I never knew how to make that woman happy. This way she'll get you all to herself."

Tazio's hands tightened again around the seat belt. His father seemed to be finishing up a conversation Tazio couldn't remember starting.

"I love your mother. I always will. The problem is . . ." Mr. Di Vincenzo squinted at something in the rest stop parking lot. "The problem is that she's . . ."

The problem is that she's what? In the entire world, Tazio suddenly recognized, this was what he wanted most: to know what his mother actually was. She was hot-tempered, formal, Mexican in a way that often made him think, strangely, of lords and ladies. She spoke perfect, accentless English at her work and only ever Spanish at the house with Tazio. To his abiding shame, Tazio had always felt more comfortable around his father.

Mr. Di Vincenzo parked the truck. The rest stop was just a lookout point on a small cliff, the water below dark blue and choppy.

"Mama's what?"

"He talks!" Mr. Di Vincenzo said.

"The problem is that she's what?" Tazio said.

"I don't want to run down your mother," Mr. Di Vincenzo said. "I wouldn't do that."

Tazio felt like he could cry. He had been so close to a real answer. He clenched his jaw until his teeth squeaked. He wanted to tell his father to go fuck himself.

"You and me are the same," Mr. Di Vincenzo said. "We're good guys. We are. What else do they want? We're just good guys." He opened his mouth again, hesitated, and then said, "You know I'm going away. You're smart, yeah? I don't need to tell you." Without looking, Mr. Di Vincenzo reached over and rubbed Tazio's head. Tazio felt an unbearable urge to bite his hand. "I was thinking, though, sometimes you could just look out at the water. You know? If you ever think about me. Only if you want. I'll be looking back, okay? That's all I'm saying. I'll be thinking about you."

Mr. Di Vincenzo nodded out at the water, and it took Tazio a moment to understand he wasn't talking about the beach.

"What were you going to say about Mama?" Tazio said.

"Don't give her a hard time, okay?" Tazio's father said on the drive back to Tazio's mother's house. "You two gotta look out for each other now."

In the driveway, Mr. Di Vincenzo got out of the truck and came around to give Tazio a goodbye hug. Tazio just turned and went inside.

Even as a grown-up in Washington, DC, having left his fiancée and with his father long dead, Tazio thinks often about that afternoon. He thinks about it when people call him kind or loyal or good. Tazio is good. All his friends say so. David. Satin.

Even Tess. "You're such a good guy," Tess says, and Tazio laughs silently. A good guy. No such thing.

9

Tess drops Ethan off first. He sprints to the puzzle station with his friends. Max is okay—cautiously finger painting alone—when she leaves him. It's January, and the sky is cloudless and blue. Her only exercise since Max was born were a couple of months of private boxing lessons, which she can no longer afford. The thought of running on a treadmill or in circles or anywhere—just the inane act of running—makes her feel sluggish and sore. She senses it encroaching but fights it off. This isn't the time for depression.

She considers calling a friend from high school, but it's all too much to explain. Only David and Tazio understand, and she can't talk to either of them. Both are out of their minds. Drunk in one case on faulty neurological synaptic connectivity, and, in the other, on whisky. Tazio must be drinking again. To leave Angelica so soon after proposing. To not respond to Tess's calls. Ethan and Max are too young to talk to, obviously. She can't afford a therapist. Her aunt would judge or pray.

And Tess doesn't want advice. She wants information. About David, sure, but really about Tazio. Tess understands David, as far as anyone does. But Tazio? At the very least she needs to know why he's ignoring her. If David can't or won't say if Tazio's departure was somehow about her, Angelica might. So, as Tess enters her apartment, she messages Angelica and asks to meet. Says it's urgent. An hour later they sit together at a tiny glass-and-chrome table in a Williamsburg café.

"My partner—the worst—is on vacation *again*, so I've been squeezing in her urgent cases between my regular patients. I just this morning saw your email about David having gone missing," Angelica says, stretching her arms over her head. "Sorry. That's not true. I mean, my partner *is* taking another vacation, but I'm constantly on email. I just figured David was with Tazio, and I didn't want to get into it."

"I get it," Tess says.

"He okay now?" Angelica says.

"Tazio?" Tess says. Oh, she means David.

"David," Angelica says.

"What do you think?" Tess says.

"Did he come back, I mean?" Angelica says. "You found your man?" Tess hears contempt or sarcasm. Something cutting.

"Yeah," Tess says. "I found him."

Angelica stretches again, cranes her neck for a waiter. She's impatient. She only has forty-five minutes for lunch.

Tess has never been alone with Angelica for longer than the few minutes it took for Tazio to use the bathroom or take a call. They spent dinners together with Tazio and David, and they've been going to the same parties and weddings for years, but Angelica tends to sit quietly, judgmental or bored, in her designer dresses. Nothing about her suggests she's a dentist. If not a model, then a gallery owner or magazine editor.

"Have you heard from Tazio?" Tess asks.

"He knows I'm pissed. Uugghh," Angelica groans, flowering into a human being. A man looks at Angelica with pity or lust, and returns to his croissant sandwich.

"He hasn't called me back," Tess says. "Is the wedding still . . . going to happen?" She wants to get the question asked before the conversation turns confrontational. Angelica's face tries to recompose itself, but it can't finish the job. She stares off toward a group of young women who are entering the glass door cut out from the glass wall.

"I think," Angelica says.

"Sorry," Tess says. Sorry that the wedding might *not* happen, she meant, but it's possible it sounded as though she was sorry it would.

Angelica looks to her phone. Then up at Tess and seems to focus for the first time.

"You want to talk about Tazio," Angelica says.

"I want to know why he left," Tess says. "We miss him."

"Sweetheart," Angelica says. "Tazio didn't leave because of you."

"I didn't say—"

"He left because I finally told him the truth," Angelica says.

"What truth?"

"The truth about me and Gerard."

"From Abel and Cain?" Tess says.

It seems to matter to Angelica that Tess not think herself too important.

"My boss," Angelica says. "Both of our bosses. He had Tazio in twice a week to redrape the curtains and hammer out imperfections in the wall, and he all but told me how to dress. One day I was a grungy East Village NYU grad, and the next, a neo-geisha glam girl. Gerard transformed me into a half-reticent, half-willing, 1920s cocktail–knowledgeable goddess whose charm was as key, suddenly, to the bar's allure as his cocktails and house rules. No Name Dropping, No Star Fucking. Gentlemen Must Remove Their Hats. I'm laughing now, but everyone back then thought that stuff was so great. It *was* great . . ."

Though Tess is uneasy trying to figure out what any of this has to do with Tazio, sitting with Angelica makes her feel freer. Less of an adult. As usual, all Tess wants is a brief escape. She forgot what it was like to have friends. To vacation in other people's stories.

"You were in love with him," Tess says.

"Gerard was my entire world. He talked about Abel and Cain as this 'oasis of quality in the desert,' and he made me feel like an integral part of it. Clientele would sit—I'd see them waiting for him—and have two, three extra drinks on the off chance that Gerard would join them at their table. His being my boss was a part of it, but he cared so much about what he cared about, and he hardly cared about anything. At the time, it was just the bar, the drinks, his customers, and, I thought, maybe me. Like I was worthy of his attention when so few other things were. At first, I thought I was subverting Gerard's expectations when I made him buy me these little kimono dresses. I thought I was mocking the idea. But I was doing exactly what he wanted. And I liked it!"

It makes some sense that Tazio left Angelica as their wedding approached if she has always been in love with this other guy. If she's in love with him still.

"I liked it," Angelica continues. "I mean, I wasn't just out of college anymore. I didn't want to wear T-shirts and old jeans. I liked how I felt with straight posture. He seemed to have a greater sense of responsibility—of conscience—than anyone I'd ever met. He had rules, and not just for the bar. Rules about looking people in the eye, about gentlemen keeping any deal made on a hand-shake, about comping drinks to teachers, firemen, military, even grandparents. I think most people viewed it as excessive. I found it endearing, and I tried to follow his rules, too. Never be late. Never let people feel judged or uncomfortable. Gerard didn't value ma-terial possessions, and though he always dressed in wool pants, shined shoes, the white shirt, and suspenders, he hardly owned more than that one pair of pants. He'd switch up the suspenders to make the rest of the clothes seem different. With his bright blue eyes and dark hair slicked back on top and short on the sides in a way no one's worn since the 1930s. It was cool. He was cool! I don't know. I bought in." With her red leather jacket off, Angelica's white blouse looks custom made for her tall, thin torso. "I wanted to change, and Gerard showed me how."

The waiter delivers their cappuccinos in glass cups with glass handles, along with a bottle of tap water and two empty glasses. They both order the quiche of the day. Broccoli leek.

"I grew up a little Blasian tomboy," Angelica says. "And since my senior year of high school, I've been this fetish object, even to my boyfriends. Until Tiger Woods got famous, I was the only black Thai person anyone had ever seen, and as far as I know, Tiger Woods doesn't have a sister—Ladybug Woods, or whatever that lunatic golf-dad would have named her. No one knew what to make of me.

"So as much as maybe I hate to say it, it was nice at the bar, for the first time in my life, to have a clear role to play. Even if it meant leaning into the objectification. Gerard and I even practiced smiling. We'd huddle together in that little bathroom, take a bump, and practice our client smiles. I thought it was so funny. For the first time in my life, I felt powerful. In the dresses and heels and lingerie and smile, I'd found the costume for my superhero self. Sometimes Gerard called me 'Enchantress,' like that was my superhero name. It wasn't me, but it was."

Enchantress. It's so dorky and endearing. Tess would squirm with embarrassment if someone called her Enchantress. But Angelica felt it could be something other than silly or condescending. Her sense of grandeur and importance reminds Tess of someone. Of Tazio.

Tess is a good person.

She tries to get herself to back off.

To let Angelica and Tazio go through what they need to without her involvement.

Tess is married to David.

Let Tazio be or not be with Angelica.

Especially because, to Tess's horror (and delight), she really likes Angelica.

"And I liked how much Gerard liked it," Angelica says. "We'd slept together a few times, spaced out by more than six months each time, and each time I felt as though this was the time when everything would change. Each time I thought that this time he'd stop sleeping with other women and this would be the first step toward a relationship that would grant me all the meaning I'd been lacking. I wouldn't be single, you know—I'd be in love! I wouldn't just be waitressing—I'd be the queen of an internationally famous cocktail empire! But also, I wanted the companionship, stability, morning newspapers, eggs and mimosas. I felt that I didn't need to make a life for myself if I could slip into his. If his life could become mine."

"It was so dumb. So young, in retrospect. Each time we slept together, Gerard had this whole routine. He allowed himself more than his customary single drink at the end of the evening. Turned on the answering machine. Asked if I wanted 'a nightcap.' It's hard to imagine now, but the routine of it was equally off-putting and exciting. Like he'd seen the future and was just bringing it to fruition. As if I didn't have agency. I wasn't sure if I did. Each time, he slept over at my apartment. He showered in the early afternoon. He kissed me with a mint already in his mouth. He always carried around Altoids in a cigarette case. Each time, he told me I was his best friend, and that he was lucky to have shared such a 'wonderful night' with me. He was so awkward. So stilted and formal. The last time it happened that way, I promised myself that if it was going to happen again it would be under different terms or not at all. Though I didn't know if I was capable of keeping that promise. I would try my best. Have agency."

Angelica shakes her head.

"But it wasn't just Gerard. It was the entire world. I'd never cared about politics before we invaded Iraq. Even after 9/11. There'd been no real difference between the first Bush and Clinton and the second Bush. Clinton actually seemed like the biggest asshole of the three. But the idea of my country ordering troops to murder people, of actually sending American teenagers in to murder soldiers and civilians in other countries without a real reason, or, to be more precise, for pretend reasons . . . not being able to do anything about it made me insane. I felt empty and crazy. And this emptiness just made me want to be with Gerard even more. He was the only thing in my life that I thought could fill it."

"I never got to know Gerard," Tess says. "But I felt like that after 9/11, too. Like we had to do something about it, but everything Bush did was so obviously wrong." Tess can remember the frustration of the Bush days when every decision made was idiotic (Bush) or cruel (Cheney). But she never truly cared the way some people did. In fact, that other people cared so much comforted her. If Al Gore and Jon Stewart and Angelica were feeling enough fury, Tess herself could relax a bit and let them feel fury on her behalf. What was the point of adding her impotent anger on top of theirs? Especially considering the scope of her personal tragedy and how much emotional energy that required of her, she didn't have the capacity to care as deeply about politics. She was surrounded by people who, after 9/11, seemed so eager to play a role in the suffering and tragedy, but Tess already had her own. So she tried to focus on what mattered to her. Tazio, acting, David.

"I was so angry at everyone," Angelica says. "I stopped sleeping, and when I was awake I was buying all these new clothes, preening for Gerard and his clientele . . ."

"I know the feeling," Tess says. "Like you're living for someone else."

"Exactly! Like your inner life is tethered to factors you can't control! I disappeared inside my body," Angelica says. "I took drink orders. I even bowed sometimes. I get now that there was something aggressive about a brown girl bowing to a mostly rich white clientele, but my Thai cousins bowed all the time. I liked it. I was into the concept of 'respect' and what that meant and how to show it. Maybe there was some irony to it. I don't know. Gerard told me to stop bowing, that it was weird, but I kept on doing it. I was going through life as this 'mysterious woman' who was confident and happy but unapproachable. I thought it meant that I had a part of myself no one could take because no one could see it. But really, no one gave me enough thought to imagine it existed."

"I kind of know what you mean about how you looked," Tess says. "When Tazio first told me years ago that you two hooked up, I couldn't believe it. I mean, Tazio kind of has that superficial—sorry if that's offensive—but superficial appeal, too. But I was just amazed that *Angelica from Abel and Cain* would actually start dating anyone."

Tess provokes. Even when she doesn't intend to. She doesn't like herself when she's needling other people, forcing them to confront the truth as she sees it.

She takes a deep breath. Relaxes her shoulders.

"I guess my act worked on you," Angelica says, unfazed.

A cramped table of five young white women are sipping one another's coffees and laughing. All the glass cups look the same, but the women are stretching over one another for little tastes.

"Then, one night, you showed up with Tazio and David.

Maybe it had happened before, but I remember it as the first time those two had ever come in with someone else."

"Wait," Tess says now. "You're talking about that very first night? My first night with David?" The night when Tess chose between them.

Not only was that the night she chose David, but it was also the night she met him. Previously, she'd heard all about David from Tazio, but she'd gotten the feeling Tazio didn't want them to meet. Nicest guy in the world. Hardest-working guy I know. Most generous. Sweetest. Funniest. Dorkiest. Most earnest. Tazio had built David up to be an impossibly good man.

Even if Tazio were single again, would Tess let herself seriously consider it? After swearing to David she'd be with him forever. In sickness and in health. Not like that one broken promise matters in comparison to what it would do to her life and family. To her boys! It's impossible. Tess is happy to have that settled. It's impossible, and she doesn't want it to be possible. Tess can be Angelica's friend.

"I guess so. They were really young. David was goofy. He was so free with the voices and jokes, so easy, everything was funny to him. Tazio was self-indulgent, but it was clear he'd grow into himself. I liked his hands. And he looked more mixed back then. More Mexican, I guess. More like me. Not as dark as me. But browner than now."

"I don't remember that," Tess says. "You're saying his skin *looked* darker?"

Tazio likes to show off his Spanish, and sometimes he refers to himself as Latino, but he's never seemed anything other than white.

"I don't know," Angelica says. "It was probably that I only really saw him by candlelight. But yeah, he just seemed like being Mexican was a part of him more. Like he made weird self-deprecating jokes about showing me a real taco spot. No—that's not what I mean. I don't know. I just have these memories of him mentioning Mexican stuff all the time. Like, Thai-versus-Mexican came up a lot. Holidays, beaches, rice."

Come to think of it, it's the same with Angelica. Angelica looks different from most people. She is visibly black and Asian or some other equally gorgeous combination, but her father was a dentist and she's a dentist and her parents have a house in Connecticut in addition to a "compound outside Chiang Mai." It's possible that Tazio and Angelica hide their otherness when around her or that she's too blind to it, or, more likely, that their lives of, in Tazio's case, relative privilege, and, in Angelica's, real wealth override in some way their statuses as national or racial minorities. Though Angelica seems more Thai than black, and she also seems more Thai than Tazio seems Mexican.

"I also," Angelica says, "liked how much he and David liked each other."

"And I was the first person they'd brought there with the two of them?"

"You were different back then, too. More relaxed."

"I was younger."

"Don't get offended," Angelica says. "You just came off as chill in a way you don't anymore. You were laughing really hard at whatever David said. I brought your drinks and remember very much wanting to be sitting there with you instead of serving. It all felt so useless. My whole life did. I wanted to be laughing instead of working, instead of being so serious all the time. But in retrospect it must have been seeing you with the two of them that made me want to be with the two of them in a way I'd never realized."

"The two of them?" Tess says.

"Tazio. David wasn't my type."

Big friendly funny smart guys aren't her type?

But Tess, of course, gets it. David's appeal is lovability, not temptation. Angelica needs the allure. Tess has long credited herself with choosing David's kindness over Tazio's allure.

"What does this have to do with Gerard?" Tess says. The waiter serves them tiny slices of quiche on giant white plates. The forks and knives are bright silver or chrome, cast in right angles. There are no napkins.

"I thought you'd want to know the whole story. You seem so interested," Angelica says.

"Okay," Tess says, unsettled.

"So Tazio was supposed to be some art school prodigy," she says. "And now he had a full-time job on a political campaign. He was actually doing something. Talking to people who mattered—who could change the course of things. I mean, my father is my hero. He came over here from Chiang Mai and went to dental school for a second time and married a black woman for love. Can you imagine? But Tazio made me think on a larger scale. And suddenly he seemed so right for it—for that kind of scale."

"That's why we were all there that night!" Tess says, remembering. "It was a kind of going-away party, which was why he wanted his two friends together with him there."

"And you kept saying how proud you were of him . . ."

"David and I both were."

"You started getting close to David. You were really drunk, but still. It was clear how much you liked him."

"I did," Tess says. She remembers thinking from the beginning how happy a father David would be—how happy he'd make their kids. Not only did he have Tazio's approval, but that first evening together, she thought *this is the kind of guy who'd make my kids happy*. She'd never thought about kids before.

"I know Tazio was put off by seeing you guys together. I don't know if he was feeling jealousy over you, or over David, or both. The night was supposed to be about Tazio, and it became about you two. That's mostly in retrospect, though. In the moment, Tazio and I were rolling our eyes about you and David. I asked him if I could become a volunteer maybe, and he was excited, saying, 'Definitely! Definitely!' He was so eager and sweet."

A waiter asks if they want anything else. Angelica orders an espresso. Tess says she'll have the same.

"Didn't you say you had to go back to work?" Tess says.

"Nah. I told you I only had forty-five minutes in case this was weird. My after-lunch canceled this morning."

"You're such a freak!" Tess says, laughing. She's happier than she's been in weeks. Months, maybe. Since the accident or even before she told David about Jonah. Angelica will either leave Tazio for Gerard or marry Tazio and let Tess move on with her life.

"My time is valuable," Angelica says, and Tess can't tell if she's joking.

"So I was just wasted, talking to David, trying not to fall asleep?"

"You and David were getting really sloppy," Angelica says. "David slipped, or you let go, but David slid down the booth, and Tazio said he'd find you guys a cab and then come back if I wanted him to."

"The first night David and I hooked up was the first night you and Tazio did? How did we never know this?"

"Tazio asked if I wanted him to come back. Tazio was such a kid, but I liked him. But Gerard was there, too. Tazio put a hand on my leg, under the table, just a finger or two on my thigh. He asked me again if he should come back after getting you two a cab. Maybe it was because he was feeling left out of whatever you two had going on, but he said this was the last night I'd see him for a year. I remember hoping that Gerard was watching."

"And what happened?" Tess says.

"I told Tazio to go home," Angelica says. "To remember me when he was working in the White House."

"Why?" Tess asks more loudly than she intended.

Everyone in the café looks over. The women who have been sharing coffees glare at Tess, as though it somehow matters that she shouted.

Tess mouths *sorry* to everyone and asks Angelica, "Why?"

"It would have been awkward if on Gerard's way out he saw Tazio waiting for me. That week Tazio went to North Carolina."

But the way Angelica said it, Tess could tell there was more she wanted to say.

"And then?" Tess says.

"Around 3 a.m. everyone was gone except for Gerard, and I was wiping down tables and washing glasses. Gerard poured himself another martini. Not only was this his second drink, but martinis always signaled the beginning of something for him. Drinks all carried their own ridiculous symbolism. It had only been a couple weeks since the last time we'd slept together. I told myself that I would be the one to decide how this night was going to end.

"He asked if I wanted a nightcap. I'd been waiting for that word. I told him that he usually made us wait six months between our nights together, and he laughed it off.

"He made me a Cuba Libre: just rum, Coke from the glass bottle, and lime. It was my drink in those days, and somehow even that was better when he made it. I asked him if it was because Tazio had been hitting on me. He acted like he didn't know what I was talking about, but I could tell that he did. I told him maybe I'd work for Edwards, too. He said that as long as I showed up to work afterward, that could be a great idea. And then he said he wanted to go home with me that night. I asked him if that was all he wanted from me. Again, he acted like he didn't know what I meant.

" 'If we do this,' I said, 'we have to actually do this. It has to be the beginning of something.'

"He looked at me in that plain way of his, completely open with his motives but still inscrutable. He patted down his hair and seemed to consider it.

"But then he said I knew how busy he was. He couldn't be good to me in the way I deserved, but he wanted to be with me that night. He needed to be. I told him to go home—that I'd see him the next day at work."

"You turned down Tazio and Gerard in that same night?"

"Gerard motioned for me to come over to where he was standing, and I said no, that I didn't want it to be like that. He looked at me with a combination of desire and disdain. Like he found it impossible or funny that I might say no. He took his dick out and started playing with it. He'd done that before—in bed, I mean—but this was at the bar. I pushed by him, but he grabbed my arm. He told me he loved me. I screamed, but the place was soundproofed because the neighbors had complained when it first opened."

"I'm so sorry," Tess says, horrified that this man she'd been hearing about for years did whatever Angelica is about to tell her he did.

"What happened?" Tess asks.

"I told him to get the fuck off me," Angelica says quietly.

"He raped you?" Tess says, in her normal speaking voice.

"He fucked me. Is it rape if you're in love with the guy?"

"Yes! Sorry. I'll be quieter. But yes. Of course it is."

"I know. I know. *Stop*. A few minutes later, he kissed me with an Altoid in his mouth and told me how beautiful I was."

"Jesus," Tess says.

"Maybe he thought I was into it. I have no idea."

"You told him to stop?"

"I don't know."

"But you screamed?"

"Yes."

"And you kept working there?"

"For another month. I was scared to make any changes. I stopped feeling real."

"Jesus."

"Gerard stayed away from me, though."

"I bet," Tess says. But after a moment she says, "I don't know why I said 'I bet.' "

"I know. The whole thing," Angelica says. "I tried my hardest not to think about it for years."

Tess's heart is beating with anger and caffeine. "Why did you tell Tazio now?"

"Everything that's going on. I so badly wanted Trump to lose, and not only lose, but to get publicly embarrassed and shamed for doing and saying all those awful things so everyone would know how reprehensible he was and how his type of masculinity is no longer acceptable, and so he would know how terrible everyone knew he was and feel like the fucking monster loser he is, but instead, the opposite happened, and all those awful things Trump did, all the racism and misogyny and sexual assaults, were rewarded with the biggest prize in the world. I'd never wanted anything so much. For Tazio, of course, because he was working for Hillary, but for me, too. For the whole fucking world.

"So now with this rapist who hates blacks and immigrants going to be president, I just can't take seeing Trump's face or hearing his voice. It makes me physically sick. For weeks, I've struggled getting out of bed in the morning. And Tazio never noticed. So I told him what Gerard did to me. He tried to comfort me a little, but the next day he told me he was going to DC."

"You said you were raped, and Tazio left you?"

That couldn't be true.

"It wasn't that simple," Angelica says. "He tried to be nice, but I think Tazio just doesn't like talking about this other guy I had a thing for. He can't see past that part of it. He'd always been jealous of Gerard. And now I'd been keeping this secret. I know how you and David think of him, but Tazio can be an asshole. He's been caught up in his own misery after the election. I get it. His dad was an immigrant, too, and his mom is Mexican, for God's sake. I'm equally despised, but Tazio can't see past his own rage."

Everyone around Tess had been focused on what would happen when Hillary won. Tazio would make his mark on history. David would start feeling better. Angelica, Tess sees, was giddy at a repudiation of this type of man. Of men.

The three of them were shocked—overwhelmed—when Hillary lost.

But Tess wasn't. Tess knew to her core that the worst could happen and usually did.

Angelica sips her water. Sips her espresso. Sips her water again. Seems like she's about to talk, pauses, then says, "I've been Googling him."

"Tazio?"

"Gerard. With Tazio out of the house and more time to myself in the evenings. He sold the bar years ago. Now he teaches at a charter school in Harlem. He's a success story from that New York City Teaching Fellows program. There was a little paragraph about him on the site."

"No way."

"He's been teaching for, like, five or six years. I hadn't heard his name for a while, so I figured he was working at that Abel and Cain that opened in London, but no. He's just teaching. Tazio freaked out when I told him about it. He told me to leave Gerard alone. And I listened because what am I going to do? Fight this guy? Have Tazio come fight him? Call the cops with a story from over a decade ago?"

Angelica takes another sip of espresso, purses her lips.

"Even though it's all I can think about," Angelica says, "with Trump on TV all the time. Trump just has that same look. Like he can take whatever he wants."

"I'm so sorry," Tess says.

"Thank you. But there's nothing you can do."

Of course there is.

"Why not?" Tess says.

"Why not what?" Angelica says.

"Why isn't there anything we can do?"

10

David sits on the couch, recovering, with his virtual reality headset to his side. He is sickness made flesh: worn out, scared, with his head in his hands. He doesn't want pity or conversation—just a constant implicit acknowledgment about how terrible his life is. It seems important to him that his pain is always on her mind. Which is an insane thing to want because she shares his life. It's also her life. Though it's reasonable, too. He suffers alone every day. He wants a witness to his suffering.

Tess stands in the kitchen with a glass of red wine, wondering if she should bring a weapon. Angelica makes more sense to her now. Her self-protectiveness came off as superiority. Tess doesn't want to connect every personality trait to a tragedy in someone's past, though she's been self-diagnosing in this way for years. She focuses her thoughts on tomorrow.

Should she bring a baseball bat or crowbar? Where could she buy a crowbar?

Maybe just a bottle of wine.

A full one has more weight, but an empty one would be more likely to break and cut someone's skin.

As if Tess could wield a wine bottle, empty or full. As if she'd be capable of anything other than playing make-believe onstage.

Tess used to like going to the wine store and trying different bottles, seeing if David said anything. He always said how much he liked it. He always noted the wine's name in his phone for the next time he was at a restaurant. But he liked every wine, so he never bothered to check for one he'd had before. David had the zeal of a preteen who hadn't yet learned that open enthusiasm was something to hide. So much made him happy. She'd ask why he was smiling, and he'd say, "I guess I was thinking about the Knicks?" or "I love this couch!" or "Can you believe that by having sex we made two little people with their eyes and fingernails and everything?" Every morning when the alarm went off, he danced. The morning after that first night they'd slept together—that same night, it turns out, that Angelica was assaulted by the man they will confront tomorrow—David swung himself out of bed at noon, and he did a little knee shaking jig, like a dorky twist. She thought he was doing it for her, and she was half smitten and half embarrassed for him, but then he kept on doing that little dance every morning after. It was a wonderful thing, his dancing to Z100 at 6:05 when his alarm-radio clicked on. He must have stopped when he was living with Tazio and Angelica.

(So Angelica's position was that Tazio was ignoring *Tess* because Angelica told him about what had happened with Gerard? It was silly to think Angelica could translate Tazio. If there was a real reason he cut off communication with Tess, he'd have to tell her himself.)

Now David takes an exaggerated breath and puts the headset back on to start a new round of stimulation. He alternates between nodding and shaking his head, repeating, "I am learning that experience and change are good. I am learning that experience and change are good." And then, "I am improving. I am improving." She's happy he's trying something—that he's hinted at some optimism—but repeating hackneyed phrases and walking down virtual sidewalks and alleys as birds fly by seems like an unlikely way to regain neurological health. But he wants to put the work in, and Angelica vouched for Monica, and they can mostly afford it.

Tess pours herself another glass of wine. He still has insurance— David gave up most of a financial package from PepsiCo for two free years on the company insurance—so even if Trump lets Ryan repeal Obamacare they'll be okay for another year with Dr. Saltman, the neurologist. But unless she's cast in a commercial soon, they're not going to be able to pay for the new sequences for long. The insurance company doesn't have a code for virtual reality vestibular rehabilitation.

And they have no one to ask for help. Tess's mom is dead, and her father has been hiding out in the mountains somewhere since his release. David's parents are on a budget, and already it's evident how much being around David makes them suffer. In the hospital after the fall, David's father was silent, and his mother begged the doctors for positive prognoses. The one time they visited the apartment afterward, they brought bagels and smoked salmon with doughnuts and toy limousines for the boys, but after a few minutes, David had to excuse himself to lie down.

"Isn't he supposed to be better by now?" David's mother whispered while the kids played. Tess's own mother would have been tougher. She knew how to handle adversity.

"Your limousine is for Trump!" Ethan said to Max in the background. "Mommy says he says mean things to ladies. And girls. And babies who are girls."

"I don't know. Yes," Tess said, doing everything she could to hide her frustration and grief. "He's supposed to be. Being around a lot of people at once is tough for him."

David's mother's eyes watered, and she slowly put all kinds of things into her purse—tissues, her eyeglasses and cell phone, a bagel wrapped in a napkin, cough drops, vitamins she'd lined up to swallow during lunch—and told Ethan and Max that she was leaving. "I don't want to be too difficult for your daddy to be around," she said.

David's father, feebler than his wife and less comfortable around the boys, stuck it out for another hour before presumably meeting David's mother at the diner on Fulton Street.

"I'd do anything to make him better," his mother responded the next day to Tess's email apologizing for giving the impression that she wasn't wanted. "I just can't bear seeing him like that. I know it reflects poorly on me, and I should be stronger. If he ever wants to come out here I'll do my best to take care of him, but I'm useless in the city knowing my presence causes him additional pain. I see how worried Max and Ethan are. I can't hide my concern, either."

So, to introduce financial anxieties to them seemed both useless and cruel.

And David and Tess didn't have anything of real financial value other than her engagement ring. Her mother's, given to her by Tess's grandmother. Eight years ago, Tess handed it to David and said, "If you're thinking about buying one, there's no need." The marriage had been her idea. He cried, which made her cry. They hugged, and after they made love, he teased her about how long he'd wait before proposing. Six months? A year? The next morning he woke her up kneeling beside the bed.

So she'd rather starve than sell the ring, but they will need food, rent, and continued treatments. David has around eight grand in the bank. She has almost two. The apartment is small, equally far from the C and G trains, and rent-stabilized, so it only costs twelve hundred dollars per month, and his student loans are down to three hundred a month, which means there's no need to panic yet.

She considers rolling a joint, but she's been drinking enough and Ethan hasn't been sleeping well. She doesn't want him to catch her and think that smoking is okay. She could take the joint into the bathroom, like a junkie. She pours herself another glass of wine. When Ethan was young, she was anxious to give him everything she hadn't had, but when she saw how much love there was in her home—how David was as doting on the boys as he'd been on her—she settled into a pleasant routine of morning parenting and evening work. But she was exhausted. She'd been so excited to be offered work on *The Great Comet* just as Max transitioned to formula, but to be in the ensemble while understudying for the lead takes twice as much preparation. And that's become her niche. Of course she wants the lead roles—and the money that comes with them—but directors know her as reliable, flexible, able to retain staging, and eager for the bump in pay on the nights she fills in.

At all times, she was either parenting or working. Rehearsal weeks weren't awful, and she could sometimes get to see the kids before bed, but once tech and then previews started, days stretched beyond twelve hours plus the hour-long commute. She barely slept five hours a night, coming back from performances at midnight, winding down with a glass of wine, and then waking up with the boys, if she was lucky, at six or six thirty.

Jonah said that David only saw her as a mother, and she needed a man to see her as a woman. David was obsessed with the kids. But that wasn't why she ended up with Jonah. It was, she thinks as she helps David into their bedroom with his glass of water, that she simply seized the moment. Carpe fucking diem. After so many years. Nearly a decade and a half of David's jokes and love and morning dancing. Their relationship defined her life. Her family life, her sex life, her time away from work—and as she hasn't made it big, never knew when she'd be allowed, because of someone else's strep throat, to spend a few days disappointing audience members who'd months earlier bought tickets for the experience of a lifetime to see someone who wasn't her—her family life was supposed to be the source of her pride.

But there was the knowledge that she'd settled. Well, "knowledge" is too strong a word. Intimation. And still, she's never doubted that she settled for the right man. That she was right to settle, as no matter what, she'd have to choose someone to satisfy one half of her personality or the other. She's never doubted that she was right to err on the side of herself looking for safety, comfort, warmth, and love over the side that wanted only pleasure, because that second half didn't stop at pleasure. It also wanted uncertainty, the thrill of reliving the physical and emotional pain that accompanies loss at a young age and on such a hideously large scale. Ego, shame, sex, desire, hatred, and loss were all inseparable from pleasure. Jonah checked every box. And now—wineglass in hand, David and the boys in bed, Rachel Maddow on television telling a twenty-minute story that could be distilled down to two—if Tess is forcing herself through all this again, she has to stop pretending that Tazio doesn't check those boxes, too.

When she and Tazio made plans to meet up as freshmen at Cooper and he only showed up two times out of three, it was all the more thrilling when he did. When he snuck paintbrushes into her bag, she might not have known she was stealing but she felt something illicit between them. Something dangerous for the sake of danger. And she was attracted to it. She still is.

She felt a similar potential during the few days when she rehearsed with Jonah. The lead was sick or away for some reason, and there was a tug there that kept finding reasons for them to touch each other. There's craft to the performance of desire—she's learned how to fake that spark—but when she feels a true connection, the scenes become so much more alive. So much easier and more fluid. Then, that delicious week before it happened. When the unknown was all she could think about during the day and Jonah showed up in her dreams at night. When she got back onstage after what had turned into a three-year maternity leave, she and David weren't sleeping together as much as they did before they had kids, but that was natural and, she really believes, beside the point. She'd always liked sex: the game of it, the loss of control, the closeness, the substitution for violence, and how it made every part of her body feel alive and present. But she preferred acting and, especially, singing in front of a large audience. Which was why her closest friends other than the girls from high school it'd become too logistically difficult to see were fellow actors, and which was why, she thinks, when Jonah suggested they leave the party to get a drink somewhere quieter, she nodded and followed. He was famous and beautiful. Their bodies felt the need to experience in real life what they'd mimicked before an audience.

She didn't "end up" with Jonah. She saw available pleasure and claimed it before it could be taken away from her. She wanted him to touch her, and, even more, she wanted to have something she wanted. Something that was just for her. She let herself be selfish. Maybe that was a lack of strength, as David has accused her of, but she wasn't sure. It took strength to go from wanting to having. A weaker person would have done nothing and let her life continue uninterrupted. It would have been better, much better, if that's what Tess had done, but she took what she wanted. Jonah's body was powerful but relaxed. She'd felt it in rehearsal. Soft skin over hard muscle. She was overcome with the anticipation of yearning's release. Big picture, she had everything she'd ever wanted. Two boys, a loving husband, unlimited Diet Pepsi, and evenings onstage in front of crowds who, though maybe not there to see her, applauded wildly at the end. She loved her family and she loved winning over an audience that had initially been disappointed to see her onstage. But every day was so difficult. She was so tired. Every moment was so hard. Waking up was hard, getting the kids ready was hard, taking them on the subway was hard, rehearsing was hard, talking to David about how they didn't spend time together was hard, having no time to spend with David (or her friends or aunt or anyone other than her kids and castmates) was hard. Not hard like it has become after the accident, but still, unremitting. Even when David was healthy and dancing, Max screamed in his crib and Ethan refused to get dressed, and then David took off to work early—it was pleasureless, mostly, except for the moments onstage.

There was nothing she loved more than her kids. They made her life feel meaningful, connected, and worthwhile. Tess loves them both so much that she finds herself pitying the thirtysomethings she passes in Washington Square Park who are throwing Frisbees and eating fancy sandwiches. She doesn't understand how someone can live a life for those small pleasures without the kids and family that make existence important.

Tess used to think that having kids would be hard, but that the goods and bads would even out. She thought "evening out" meant that the tough times—the yelling, fear, and frustration—would be offset by the joyous times full of love and delight. She thought that the number of minutes would literally be the same: like for every hour of yelling there'd be an hour of cuddling. But that's not true at all. It does all even out, and more: children provide far more happiness than they do aggravation. But not day to day. On any individual day, it's more like 80 percent frustration to 20 percent joy. And that's on a good day. Days spent dealing with kids—no time to herself, constantly doing chores and having conversations she's not interested in—are far worse than days prekids. But in exchange, she has a sense of purpose, which is worth more than even any amount of cuddling. Having kids makes meaningful all the hours worked and good deeds done.

Also, how many people in the world does one actually, to the core of her bones, love? Two, five, eight if she's lucky? Having kids let Tess make more of these people. Make more of this love. She got to create human beings whom she loves and who love her. And that's something that has nothing to do with washing dishes or scolding Ethan that bedtime was an hour ago.

Nonetheless, she still longed for the small selfish moments of delight. Maybe Ethan and Max provided a greater existential pleasure, but the tedium was so hard. She found herself looking forward to Sundays' two performances, when she could take the entire day off from momming. Every moment she wasn't working she was with the kids, who were too young still for full-time pre-school, and she and David were paying back his loans so they only had babysitters in the late afternoon when they both had to work.

Subway commutes were the only true moments she had to her-self, and those were spent running through her lines or reading news on her phone to keep her angry and awake. That night when she was drinking with the cast after that first performance, she wanted to do something for herself. It had nothing to do with David or the boys. It was for herself. Like yoga, or a massage. Jonah knew about her husband and kids. Everyone did. The kids were all she talked about. It was her first role after giving birth twice, and everyone was impressed she still had it—the endur-ance, the voice, and, Jonah wasn't too polite to say, her body—so quickly again. Jonah was surprised when she bought him a drink. Which excited her. Afterward she felt guilt, terrible guilt, but once it was done, why not do it again? It felt so good. His power and certainty. The lack of gentle hesitation. They were selfish together, and watching a powerful man use her body as a source for his own pleasure was unbearably sexy. And then being onstage after-ward. Fucking Jonah made singing with him, even in the ensem-ble, even better. Not since her aunt had signed her up for voice lessons that first miserable year out in Jersey had she found such pleasure in singing. She told no one about Jonah and vowed never to tell David. She loved David too much, and he was too sensitive. If he could be made so happy by a meaningless Knicks win, she couldn't imagine the sadness that would come from finding out that his overall happiness was fraudulent. Except it wasn't fraudulent. It was real. And so were her moments with Jonah in his dressing room, extended-stay apartment, and expensive, cheap-looking Times Square hotel. Jonah helped her understand that instead of being weighed down by life's impermanence, she could embrace it, which, unsurprisingly in retrospect, increased the impermanence in her life.

Enduring David's current helpless and miserable state, Tess longs for the corny man he used to be, even though the corny man she longs for was the same man she'd cheated on. It wasn't his fault. It was hers. But David was maybe something like too comfortable to be around. Uncomplicated. Too quick to laugh or enjoy. Compared to time with Jonah (or, for that matter, with Tazio), time with David wasn't a challenge. She didn't feel she needed to earn his laugh or respect. David was smart and ambitious enough to get through grad school and find a good job at a good company, but he was constantly and unnervingly kind. Goofy. That was the word. It was Angelica's word for David, though Angelica hadn't read the journal. But still, goofy was better than corny. He was goofy. He chewed loudly. He made friends with waiters and bank tellers. He was almost too good with the kids, rolling around on the floor with them until they tired of it. He liked changing diapers and warming bottles. He liked how much they needed him when they woke up from a nightmare. Maybe it wasn't that David saw Tess as a mom instead of a wife, but that after so many years with Tess he saw himself as a father instead of a husband.

Or did it have something to do with Tess's father? With her consequently not trusting men? With coming from the most broken of broken homes? With seeing relationships as inherently unstable? With needing a powerful man in her life to replace the father she lost?

That's what David asked her after she confessed. And that's what he wrote in his journal. He asked if she'd done it because she was so fucked up.

Before then, she hadn't known he thought of her as fucked up. She was offended, but knew it wasn't the time to accuse him of insensitivity, especially when he was always so infuriatingly sensitive.

And maybe the answers to all David's questions were yes. How could she know? A lifetime of therapy couldn't tell her if she allowed herself to act on her attraction to Jonah because her father was absent, because her father was a murderer, because her father killed her mom specifically, because Tess lost her mom, or because of something else inside her, if there was anything inside her that wasn't a product of her father's insanity and violence and the repercussions thereof.

If Tess were not herself Tess, maybe she'd have the objective distance to ascribe action to psychology and create an if-A-then-B—if father murders mother then daughter cheats on husband—but all she knew was that she both loved her husband and cheated on him.

Though objective distance couldn't be the problem, as Tess has plenty of distance from *and* unanswered (unanswerable?) questions about Angelica. Is Angelica with Tazio because or in spite of the fact that he was friends with Gerard? Was Angelica's slight detachment from the world caused by her experience as a rape victim—survivor?—or was this quality something Gerard saw in her that made him want to victimize her?

Tess confessed the affair to David after realizing that a larger number of people were aware of it than she could control. She had friends who were friends with David or whose spouses were. She'd always known that, but now David was going to be at a party in celebration of the show's extended run. She couldn't bear his finding out from someone else. Jonah was too much a topic of conversation under normal circumstances, and he wasn't particularly discreet.

Or possibly it was just that the day before the party they never went to, after Tess dropped Ethan off at day care, he said, "Mommy? I really, really love Daddy."

She gave Ethan a big hug, told him that she did, too, and she sat David down that evening.

David is in bed, exhausted by the combination of his symptoms, stimulation from the VR goggles, and antidepressants. But it's not even ten, so Tess won't be able to sleep for a while. She turns up the volume on MSNBC and pours the rest of the bottle of wine into her glass. Bernie is Bernieing on with Rachel Maddow about the billionaires in Trump's transition team who will take money out of the pockets of working men and women. Tess is tense. She's always tense when she watches cable news, yet she always watches cable news. It's the closest thing they have to a televised Trump Show, and, as if she's watching some horror movie and waiting to find out if the protagonist gets killed, Tess can't turn the television off. America is afflicted with Trump, or Trump is a symptom of a larger American illness, and Tess can't turn away. She needs to know who's going to die. America, Trump, something or someone else. It strikes her that David's pain might be at least partially psychosomatic. That David is sick along with the country, that he spends his days watching the deterioration of America as he experiences the deterioration of his body and brain. Or that, even if injury initially caused David's decline, cable news has exacerbated it and kept David from fighting his way back. The escapes into virtual reality then might actually provide a useful break from MSNBC. But Bernie seems in great spirits. He's shouting and gesturing, telling Rachel about how the world can be.

Tazio noticed Bernie early on—after that first debate with Hillary, O'Malley, and those other two, which was months before Iowa—when Bernie's polls were barely in the double digits. Tazio warned Jennifer Palmieri, who had been John Edwards's press secretary and then ran communications for Hillary's campaign, but she laughed him off. It wasn't until after the Michigan primary that Jennifer asked Tazio to join. It wasn't until Trump ranted that Judge Curiel's Mexican heritage meant he couldn't be trusted to preside over the Trump University lawsuit that Tazio seemed to care.

Still, Tazio always liked Hillary more than he let on. He thought Edwards and Obama were frauds in a way Hillary wasn't. Tazio felt more comfortable with a capable woman in charge. Women, Tazio seems to think, are less likely to disappoint.

That was the other thing. How wrong David was about Tazio in his journal when he wrote about what initially led Tazio to drink until his liver failed. David is Tazio's best friend, the person who, possibly with the exception of Angelica, should know Tazio best, and David didn't know Tazio at all.

11

Three o'clock across from the school seemed right. Angelica arrives at two thirty, Tess five minutes later. In her crimson down puffer, Tess looks ready to go skiing. Angelica wears a simple dress and trench coat, and is cold. They hug. Tess seems off. Awkward and constrained. Like how Angelica felt in English class seeing a boy for the first time since making out with him drunk at a party. Tess's anxiety makes Angelica anxious, and Angelica doesn't want to be anxious. Doesn't want to be distracted. She is revved up. She's ready to cut this fucker's dick off.

"Whatever you need, I'm here," Tess says.

There's a chance it will snow. Angelica breathes in deeply. She tries to feel the cold air in her lungs. Her father—more cold air into her lungs—is always talking about isolating feelings. It's how he meditates. He told patients to do the same. Feel the needle go into your gums, he'd say. Feel it as a sensation. Understand the sensation. Don't feel it as pain. Feel it as something new and unusual for you to discover. Sometimes Angelica tells her own friendlier patients the same thing.

A Mexican or South American woman sits under blankets behind a small plastic table not far from them. She's cutting mangoes with a long sharp knife and selling plastic bags full of the chunks and slices.

"Mango?" Angelica says as a joke, because this isn't the time for mango.

"No, thanks," Tess says.

Angelica needs some space. She excuses herself and buys two waters at the Walgreens behind them.

"Thanks," Tess says when Angelica returns.

For twenty minutes, the two women stand together sipping their waters and breathing into their hands. At home that morning, Angelica thought about bringing along a sickle probe from the office, but she couldn't imagine holding the metal tip at Gerard's neck. Gerard. The image she keeps returning to is literally cutting Gerard's dick off. From what she remembers, he has a nice one—clean, straight, and circumcised—perfect for cutting off. The steak knife could do it. Professional-grade Wüsthof, actually, purchased just a few months ago from Williams-Sonoma. Angelica is making good money. She has a nice apartment. They've been starting to buy nice things.

"I know I should know this, but who's Ella Baker again?" Tess says to break the silence.

There's only one visible entrance to the school: four evenly spaced orange doors a half dozen steps off the ground. On both sides of the doors are columns topped with gargoyles sculpted to look as though they're holding up the five or six floors of concrete above. Grimacing, worried faces. It's an old building on the Upper West Side, gray except for the doors and, along a playground wall, a giant mural of Frederick Douglass, Martin Luther King, and Ella Baker with their names stenciled below.

Angelica is grateful for Tess. She wouldn't have been here without her. But has she seriously never heard of Ella Baker?

"Actually," Angelica deadpans, "she was my grandma's sister. Auntie Ella."

"Really?" Tess says.

Angelica laughs. She doesn't want to make Tess feel bad, so pretends she doesn't know, either. "My guess, if she's on the wall with those two, is that she was some kind of civil rights leader," Angelica says.

Just after 3:20, hundreds of black and Latinx students tumble out from the orange doors. Dressed in ski jackets and woolen pea coats, khaki pants and skirts with blue polo shirts and cardigans, they are laughing, shouting, and playfully shoving. They hold the door for one another.

Teachers then begin to exit in groups of two and three. Tess and Angelica have finished their waters. Tess reaches for Angelica's, takes a few steps toward the corner, and drops both bottles into a wire-mesh garbage can.

"Thanks," Angelica says. "What do we do if he's with other people?"

"I don't know," Tess says. "What do we do if he's alone?"

All the waiting has cost Angelica her momentum. She's too cold to feel anything other than general discomfort. She doesn't have the equanimity of her father. And what is she doing here? She's got patients to see. She'd moved on from Gerard until saying out loud to Tess what she'd been feeling since Trump became ubiquitous. That she was thinking about Gerard again. And that even the sanctity of Angelica's office—where she was in control, calm, respected—no longer felt safe.

So here she is, confused—clueless—about what to do next.

A woman buys a bag of mangoes. Late January doesn't seem like mango season, but the fruit looks delicious. Fleshy and sweet.

"I brought a knife," Angelica says, hoping to get back into the mode of cold-blooded, cold-lunged cock chopper. "The kitchen knife that—"

Tess looks over to make sure Angelica is joking.

"—Tazio bought. Just in case he gets violent," Angelica says sheepishly. "Gerard. It's in my bag."

Angelica glances down at her bag, which looks comically small. As if, at most, it could hold a mini Swiss Army knife.

"It's just, like, bouncing around in there?"

"I wrapped it in paper towels. A steak knife from home."

"So if things get violent," Tess jokes, "you'll go into your purse and start unwrapping the paper towels?"

Angelica laughs. "Okay, it's dumb. I just wanted to be ready. I couldn't sleep last night. Are you sure this is what we should be doing?"

"Not at all," Tess says. "It's completely up to you."

They don't need a plan. Angelica has the truth, a kitchen knife, and a sense of self that will allow her to do whatever she needs to when it's time.

A group of awkward kids—the chess team or math club—are affecting a lack of seriousness as they jog down the steps. One overweight girl, prizing her dignity, doesn't run after them. She is graceful on the stairs. Her friend waits for her at the bottom.

Tess jumps up and down a few times to warm up and says she has to pee.

"Hold it in," Angelica says.

When adults become parents, they start acting like children. They talk about peeing and pooping. They lose all sense of physical dignity.

"The idea," Tess says, "in my mind, at least, is to have a moment with him where you're the powerful one. The one with agency. That's the way I'm thinking about this. When it happened, he didn't treat you like a human being. Now we're going to force him to."

"Okay," Angelica says. Yes. This is exactly right.

"You sure?" Tess says.

"I don't know if I want to see him again," Angelica says. "But yes."

Tess has surprised Angelica. Yesterday, and again today. Angelica had thought of her as Tazio's wounded best friend. She created chaos and was lucky to have found someone as stable as David who could dampen and control it. Angelica didn't want to be friends with Tess. She didn't want to get involved with Messy Tessy. But now in the middle of exactly the kind of mess she'd always feared, she feels fantastic. Scared, confused, clueless, but fantastic.

"Of course you don't want to see him," Tess says. "Seeing him isn't the point. He should be forced to see you."

An old lady is yelling at the mango vendor. They're speaking Spanish, which Angelica doesn't understand, but the disagreement seems to be about hot sauce. Angelica didn't know people put hot sauce on mangos. Papaya, sure. *Som tam* is as spicy as anything. But papaya doesn't have anything to do with mango. Still, she can imagine the bite of hot sauce on the fleshy sweet fruit.

The mango buyer's Spanish seems bad. She is old-time formally dressed in a pleated skirt and heavy tweed jacket. The mango vendor is having trouble understanding her. "I speak English," the vendor keeps saying. "Talk to me in English." But the old woman is already making a performance of carrying the full bag of mango slices over to the garbage where Tess tossed the water bottles, and one by one throwing the slices out. She's yelling at the vendor in broken Spanish. A crowd has formed. The vendor is casually cutting mangoes with her long knife and watching from under her blanket as the woman screams and waves the empty bag around her head. Little drops of hot sauce splash on her hands and fancy clothes. Empty bag still in her hand, the customer walks away muttering. The vendor chuckles to herself and cuts into a new mango.

"How long do we wait?" Tess says.

"Did you not just see that?" Angelica says.

"Yeah. People are insane. When do we leave?"

"Five?" Angelica says.

"No later than five," Tess says. "It takes at least forty-five minutes to get home, and I have to be there by six to relieve the babysitter."

Angelica laughs.

"What?" Tess says.

"Does fifteen minutes give us enough time to attack the guy who sexually assaulted me? Let's say four forty-five."

"Good call," Tess says. "That will leave us more time to attack."

Angelica is not really sure if they're joking. Or rather, she knows they're joking, but she's not sure if they're serious, too.

"What are we actually going to do?" Tess says.

"Even if we do see him," Angelica says, "which we won't, because I probably have the wrong school or he's taking a sabbatical or he's in a bowling league or something like that, though the picture online is definitely him—he coaches the softball team—I don't know? We roll with it. We make him . . . uncomfortable. Worst case, we turn him in."

"Girls' softball?" Tess says.

"Oh my God, I haven't even thought of that," Angelica says.

There's no one to turn him in to. Even if the statute of limitations hasn't passed, the police won't be able to make a case from a decade ago where there's no evidence. She said as much yesterday afternoon.

Angelica sees someone who might be him. He's thin with a thick head of brown hair, and he's alone. Tess must see Angelica looking, because she says, "Yeah?" but Angelica shakes her head. People don't change so much in ten years. But maybe without the suspenders and slicked-back hair he'd be unrecognizable.

A young white man in a shiny suit buys a zippered sandwich bag filled with slices of mango, and pours in a few spoonfuls of sugar. The mango seller says, "Five dollars." The man pays, selects a plastic fork, and walks past Angelica and Tess in the direction of the 1 train.

"Have you ever thought about teaching?" Tess says.

"I think everyone's thought about teaching," Angelica says. "Before I went for my postbac, I thought about it. But do you know any teachers who are happy?"

"Is that a thing? Teachers aren't happy? Some of my teachers seemed happy when I was in high school. I've guest-taught a few times at LaGuardia and liked it," Tess says. "Are dentists happy?"

"Some are," Angelica says. "I am. I'm happier than I'd ever thought I'd be."

"Really?" Tess says.

The problem with Tess is that she won't take happiness for an answer. The opposite of David, whose first inclination was to find joy. When David lived with them for a month, Angelica wanted him gone. He made it impossible for Tazio and her to speak privately. But, even as he seemed constantly on the verge of tears, David managed to lighten the mood. He played up-tempo music and told them about uplifting stories. Dogs who saved their owners. A lioness, abandoned by her pride, adopted a baby antelope. Little-known facts about first ladies. (*Andrew Jackson's wife, Rachel, was a bigamist! Sarah Polk forbade dancing in her company!*)

But contrary to Tess's doubts, Angelica really was happier than she'd ever thought she'd be. While working, at least. She was a great fucking dentist. She helped people feel better. She made an uncomfortable experience comfortable. She liked leaning over an open mouth, the patient's trust absolute. She was happy for a good eight to ten hours every day.

"Tess," Angelica says instinctively.

He wears green corduroys and a herringbone sports coat with a striped shirt and white collar. He's balding, his hair trimmed tight on the sides, clean-shaven, gold wire-rimmed glasses. He is walking with a teenage girl, explaining something to her. He looks so much like a regular white-guy teacher. And then, proclaiming instead of talking, he looks like a Trump voter. The man's a chameleon. He spent years as a barman from the 1920s and now he's a middle-aged conservative academic. When they reach the bottom of the stairs, the girl seems to thank him, and he follows her for a moment with his eyes. He is not what Angelica dreams about, not what she remembers. He has lost weight. And charisma. He looks cold, which makes Angelica feel colder. She flips up the collar of her trench coat. Tess doesn't look at her. Angelica appreciates the privacy.

He sees them and is crossing the street purposefully to approach her, but no, he's just on the way to the 1 train. He's still far away, crossing the street, and then he's just a few steps from them. Angelica waits for Tess to say something, but she doesn't. Angelica doesn't know what to say.

She begins to unzip her purse.

He passes them, his eyes on the pavement.

"Excuse me," Tess says loudly enough for four or five people—him included—to turn around. His clothing is tailored. Golden thread gleams through the brown of his jacket, and his pocket square matches the blue vertical stripe on his shirt.

"Yes?" he says, eyes still on Tess. His voice is deep in a way that surprises Angelica. "Can I help you with something?"

He says it sincerely, not rudely. As if Tess might need directions.

"Do you recognize my friend?" Tess says, which makes

Angelica wince. Tess is using her acting voice, the voice filled with artifice that makes it impossible for Angelica to watch Tess onstage.

Despite how he has changed, Gerard is handsome. As much as Angelica hates him, she's still drawn to him. In the same way she's drawn to Tazio. Her body is. His face seems . . . significant. It has become a teacher's face, inquisitive and open but tired. When he shifts his gaze to Angelica, Angelica finds herself searching for something in his eyes. Kindness or cruelty. It will determine how she'll act. Her hand is still on her purse. She'll keep it there.

Gerard softens, approaches, and leans forward gallantly, unbuttoning his jacket. He says "Angelica?" in a sweet way, full of wonder or disbelief, as if she were some goddamn magic butterfly. The block is no longer crowded, but a few people enter and exit the Walgreens with frustration that they have to walk around the three of them.

"Hi," Angelica says, her voice professional. Tess has an acting voice, and Angelica realizes she has a dentist voice.

He chooses not to hug her, and then, lunging forward, he hugs her. Angelica hugs him back. For a moment—less than a second—her body responds to his. Through their jackets, she can feel the way he used to hold her. But then she's fighting down a wave of nausea. She backs away. He smiles. If she were already holding the knife, she'd slash his throat.

The two bodies separate. Angelica is shaking, but that might just be due to the cold. "It's good to see you," he says in his bartender voice. "What can I do for you?"

He's thin but his cheeks are flushed and his eyes are as alive as ever.

"How have you been?" Angelica says. She's speaking without thinking. She's waiting for inspiration on what to do, how to act.

"I've been well, thank you," he says. "You look lovely, as always. How have you been?"

A young woman approaches the three of them. Angelica can't understand what she's saying, but it becomes clear she's asking for money. Tess shoos her away but the sexual predator they are confronting reaches into his jacket pocket to take out his wallet. His wallet is elegant. Supple brown leather with blue stitching. He gives her a ten-dollar bill.

Everyone is just looking at one another. Gerard seems happy to see her. Angelica needs something more to happen.

"Do you remember what you did to her?" Tess says.

"Tess," Angelica says. It comes out critical but was meant to express gratitude.

People push past them to the Walgreens. Angelica sees Tess's breath in her periphery.

"I asked you a question," Tess says. The woman can't stop herself. This is none of her business, but as long as she's here and it was her idea, Tess must feel compelled to drive the interaction forward. Angelica adores Tess. She is doing everything right.

"Who are you?" he says to Tess, though he's still looking at Angelica. "Angelica and I worked together for years."

"You raped her," Tess says at the same moment he says, "Is it right that you're a dentist now?"

No one responds to either comment.

"Excuse me," a teenager says, jostling Angelica on his way into the Walgreens. "Oh, hi, Mr. P.," he says.

"Jasper," Gerard says, not breathing. "See you tomorrow in class."

Jasper laughs like he'd just been told a great joke.

"Sorry about that," he says once Jasper is safely inside the store.

"Sorry about what?" Angelica says. This is what she wants.

"Jasper," he says.

Not that. Angelica looks to Tess, who is staring down at the sidewalk.

"Is that what you think?" Gerard says.

Angelica looks at him and waits. They all wait.

"I've missed you," Gerard says to Angelica in what is nearly a whisper. "I think . . . sometimes I think I closed the bar because it wasn't the same after you left."

"After I left," Angelica says.

"It is good to see you," Gerard says.

"I was yelling for you to stop," Angelica says.

He looks around frantically for cops. But he's more likely checking for students or colleagues. He nods his head at the alley to the side of the Walgreens where there are some shopping baskets, empty cardboard boxes, and delivery pallets, but where nobody passing would likely look.

"You were not yelling for me to stop," Gerard says once they are in the alley. "Are you taping this or something?"

Angelica should have thought of recording the conversation.

"I told you to stop, you fucking asshole," she says.

"We loved each other. I loved you. You told me you loved me. You wanted to be with me. But we were both too messed up then. And I don't just mean on coke."

"That's why you held me down?"

"You smiled. I'm sorry if I hurt you."

"You did," Angelica says, feeling bigger and bigger.

"Okay. Okay. Then I'm sorry." He thinks this should be the end of it. Ha! He thinks she will forgive him! "What do you want?" Gerard says.

And now, watching him wait for his fucking reprieve and knowing how righteous is her indignation, how richly justified is anything she could yell into his monstrous schoolmarmy face, she finds herself taking her time, suspending the moment. She feels a pure, aching anticipatory pleasure.

"What can I do for you?" he says. "I don't have much money, but I can give you some? Or whatever you want? I'll turn myself in. No, I can't do that. It would be too horrible for the kids. But I'll do whatever else you want."

"You have kids?" Angelica says, shaken.

He pauses. "I meant my students. I'm not married. I just teach. I don't even have anything to do with Abel and Cain anymore. I turn down interviews. All I do is teach history. I don't go out. I barely drink. But I promise I thought that night was what would be best for us. You have to be spontaneous. Everything was always so planned between us, and weird. You mocked me for it. I thought you wanted it more spontaneous." He looks up at her questioningly, childlike, without any facade at all.

But Angelica won't concede. "More spontaneous?" Angelica says. "You know what you did." She won't concede control.

Gerard forces an awkward, pained smile and looks at Angelica with something like nostalgia. She has to end this, but she doesn't know how, so she says the first thing that comes into her mind: her initial reaction when she saw him.

"Who'd you vote for?" Angelica says.

"What?" he says.

"Did you vote for Trump?" Angelica says.

"Are you crazy? Sorry. I didn't mean that. Of course not," he says.

Angelica looks to Tess for affirmation. Tess is wide-eyed, embarrassed.

"You swear?" Angelica says, back on Gerard.

"Of course. You know me."

"I don't know you at all," Angelica says. "Say it."

"I swear I didn't vote for Trump. I'm not a bad guy."

"No, I mean say what you did to me."

"What? What did I do?"

"I'll go right to your principal now. Or worse. Tell me what you did to me."

"What are you talking about?"

"You know exactly what I'm talking about," Angelica says. She has regained her autonomy. Her adulthood. She is powerful. "You must think about it. I do know you. And people like you don't just do it once. There have been others since. And before. And then you acted like I was crazy?"

"You're not crazy. You're beauti—"

"Jesus," Tess says.

"Fucking say it," Angelica says, her hand reaching into her purse.

"I'm sorry," Gerard says.

"For what?" Angelica says. "I need you to say it. I don't want to feel anymore like I'm crazy."

"You were so beautiful," Gerard says. "You still are."

"This is your last chance," Angelica says.

"I forced you into sex," he says. "And I'm sorry. I held you down and pretended to think you wanted me to. I told you to smile. I'm sorry. I made a terrible mistake, but I'm not a bad guy."

"You are," Angelica says.

"Come on," he says.

"What?" Angelica says. And the word takes on more meaning. It's a challenge. *Defend your goodness,* she is saying. *I fucking dare you. Tell me why you think you're good.* Gerard steps backward and nearly bumps into a man crossing behind him.

Angelica restrains herself from laughing due to the release.

"Nothing. I'm sorry," he says.

"Good," she says.

Angelica straightens her back and walks away, the wrong way, away from the 1 train. She doesn't know if Tess is following her, so she looks and sees that Gerard is waiting, hiding next to the store, until they're gone.

"Are you okay?" Tess says, jogging after her. "Was that okay?"

"It was perfect," Angelica says, and passes Tess to buy a bag of mango.

12

Tess arranges for Pam, the babysitter, to put the boys to sleep so she and Angelica can share a bottle of prosecco at an otherwise empty French restaurant. Angelica is exhausted but calm.

The women recall the afternoon moment by moment. How Tess thought Angelica was going to pull a knife, and then how Tess didn't know what Angelica wanted from him, but he knew.

"It felt so good," Angelica says. "Or I feel good now. It was hard. I didn't cry, did I? In front of him?"

"You didn't cry at all," Tess says. "I'm kind of scared of you."

"Good! I mean, really? But good. I'm glad I was scary."

But now it all feels too easy. All it took was an admission and forced apology, and now Angelica feels relief or vindication or . . . whatever it is she feels. Tess is happy for Angelica and equally pleased that it wasn't a disappointment for which Tess was to blame, but Angelica is too relaxed, and for a moment Tess wonders if Gerard really had considered it consensual. But then she remembers his face as he was apologizing. He had known.

"I know Tazio thought he was protecting me," Angelica says. "But that was so . . . Gerard was so pathetic! Like that night hurt him more than me."

"I don't know about that," Tess says.

"I want to call Tazio, but I shouldn't. He should call me when he wants to apologize. Or at least let me know if we're still getting married. I told my parents we wanted to change the date because of venue problems."

"They buy it?"

"My dad was happy."

"I see that. Tazio isn't exactly the safest choice for your daughter."

"That's not what I meant."

"Oh. Sorry."

"Stop apologizing. You're always apologizing," Angelica says. "I didn't know what I wanted until I saw him. Did you see how he still thinks he's a player? How old is he? Almost fifty, or close? He still has that same bullshit suave demeanor, acting like it's a privilege to see him. I didn't know what to do until he started acting like that again, and then I had this sensory memory of my body shutting down and just letting him do whatever he wanted until it was over, and I had to make sure he knew what he did. You think he knows, right?"

"Totally," Tess says.

"I want to tell Tazio, but he won't like that I saw Gerard again. Especially without him there. He'll pretend it's for my benefit, but he'll still be jealous. Don't tell him, okay? I'm sorry to ask that of you."

"Tazio was that jealous of Gerard," Tess says, "even after you told him what happened?"

"Tazio?" Angelica says incredulously.

"Really?" Tess says.

"Tazio was jealous of everything. Is, I mean. I've always had to tell him exactly where I'd be and for how long."

"Tazio?" Tess says.

"And with the sobriety and all, I didn't want to give him an excuse to relapse."

"My whole life, I've never seen him jealous," Tess says. She'd never seen him care that much about another person. Art, politics—sure. But Angelica? Maybe they did have some real kind of connection. "Are you sure you're okay?"

"I've never been better. I promise. Thank you. Thank you for convincing me to do that."

"I didn't convince you," Tess says, then laughs in spite of herself, thinking, *How wonderful! To find your rapist and make him apologize!*

Angelica has been talking about Tazio, and Tess begins listening again: "I got used to it. The first time I came home late from a convention and saw him just sitting there, waiting for me . . . It was before I moved in officially. He had headphones on and was just staring at the door. For some reason his texts hadn't come through. It took him days to calm down."

"And he never called David? Or me? He just waited for you?"

"I assumed that was why we all never really got along. That you didn't like me because of it?"

"Because Tazio was acting crazy?"

"I didn't know that was what you'd think. You and David idolize him."

"We do not idolize him! And David was living with you for a month. He never saw any of that."

Sure, Tazio had trashed an art gallery, and worse—but that was all while he was drinking.

"That was during the campaign. Things were already different. Tazio didn't care enough to be jealous anymore. Or maybe he was hiding it from David. Or I've learned to be better about checking my phone? I think Tazio can only really focus on one thing at a time. And for the first few years it was me."

The man Angelica described was both like and nothing like Tazio. Tess refills their glasses.

"Are you sure you're okay?" Tess says, and when Angelica says yes, Tess can tell Angelica wants to talk about anything else, so she asks how Angelica and Tazio met.

"His professor or friend or something introduced him to Gerard. He came over to the bar one—"

"No. Sorry," Tess says. "I meant how you met up again. Like, years after?"

"I was working in pediatric dentistry at Mount Sinai and he was in for a scan of his liver. We saw each other in the elevator."

"You worked at a hospital?"

"For almost three years."

"With young children?"

Angelica's eyes meet Tess's.

"Tess—we really don't know each other that well."

"I know," Tess says.

"When I looked up, I saw it was him, and he saw it was me, and we both started smiling. Like we were kids. He gave me a big hug. Lifted me up in the air. And this is Tazio I'm talking about. He was so uncontrolled. He used to say it was love at second sight. We caught up. I asked him about politics, he asked me about Abel and Cain, and we both said something ambiguous. He asked if I wanted to go to Abel and Cain for old times' sake, and I told him it was better if we didn't, and he said he was sober anyway, and for some reason we both just started laughing.

"We ended up walking in Washington Square Park and then up to Union Square and Times Square. All the squares! He made us go back down to Madison Square Garden because we needed four squares for geometry. We were laughing at what the trees looked like with no leaves. We were laughing at everything. We ended up talking about politics mostly—what the Edwards campaign was like—and when he told me how disappointed he was, I thought he meant by losing, but it was more than that.

"I asked him about policy and Obama, and what could change and whether he missed being involved. He became so serious but, I don't know, optimistic. Like he could finally relax about politics with Obama in charge, and though there was still inequality and Abu Ghraib, wars, you know, and he never really trusted Obama, he still believed we were heading in a good direction. I hadn't talked about this stuff for years. But I loved hearing how optimistic he was, how excited. He seemed like a totally new guy. Serious and sober, optimistic, caring. He had a job at that kids' arts organization. He'd grown up. He told me he'd visited Thailand and thought about me the whole time he was there. I told him what I was thinking about how he'd changed, and he said he felt so relieved to be talking to me. He couldn't explain why, but talking to me made him care about things more. He said I reminded him about what he was like before the Edwards campaign, which was when he told me about his hospitalization. We ended up at his place really late at night, and he must have sensed I wanted to make a change, too. We talked about my taking over my dad's practice, something I always swore I'd never do. He said that something about me made him want to live a more important life, and I felt the same. It wasn't exactly love yet, but after a few hours together I felt excited for the first time since the early days at Abel and Cain. And the sex was unreal. For the first time since, you know, I wasn't thinking about Gerard. I was excited to be with Tazio, excited about the future for the first time in so many years. Maybe it was love immediately. For a long time, every time I was with him, even if we were just watching TV or doing errands, I felt excited."

Tess says, "When did that feeling fade?"

Angelica looks down to her glass and then takes a sip.

"It didn't," Angelica says.

"You still feel that way when you're around him?"

"But I don't think he does. I think he's so beat up by the Hillary loss and David's sickness or whatever it is that he doesn't feel it around me anymore. Or maybe it was just a phase of his. You know how he goes through phases. And I can't ask him because he'll deny it. There's no way for me to know."

"He wouldn't have proposed if he didn't still feel that way," Tess says.

"He puts on a show for David," Angelica says, "but he's been miserable. I told him that we had to spend more time together, to go on vacation, or work on our relationship, and that was when he proposed. Right after he joined the campaign. You remember. Like getting married would make me less needy. I turned him down at first, said he didn't mean it, but he said I didn't understand. I asked him what didn't I understand, and he didn't have an answer. He just told me that he needed to live a bigger life, that he couldn't keep failing. That he loved me but I wasn't enough to make him happy, and I had to understand that if this was going to work. I said that if he felt like that, we shouldn't get married. I couldn't sign up for a life where his happiness, and therefore mine, was dependent on some mysterious outside goal that might or might not ever be achieved. He'd turned his back on the art world a long time ago. And if it was politics, I don't think I could endure another campaign. Even—especially—if it's against Trump. When Tazio and I were talking about it then, my fear was that he'd insist on working at the White House.

"I hadn't planned on saying anything like this but I did. I told him that if he felt he needed more than me to be happy and that he didn't know what that thing was, we couldn't spend our lives together. All stoic and dead-eyed, he asked me if I was sure. I'd never seen him like that. Have you? It was ugly, brinksmanship, or some venal game of chicken that I didn't want to participate in. Or that I wanted to win. So I told him that no, I wasn't sure. He asked me to marry him again, and I said yes. I won, for all it's been worth. But I do love him. I want to be with him. But I told him about Gerard, and now he's in DC. Which might be a good thing because he'll accomplish whatever he needs in order to be with me. Or it might be a bad thing, because he's slipping away. And again, it's not like I can trust his answer if I ask him."

"I'm so sorry," Tess says, but she finds herself thinking about if Tazio needs her right now. If he needs someone other than Satin to rely on. She dislikes having someone else tell her about Tazio. Tess understands him. She always has.

13

Water tumbled down the black marble wall and slapped flat against the floor in time with the music. When the music sped up, so did the pulses of water falling, slapping, and disappearing as the next pulse fell and slapped. It was 2010. Just before her first pregnancy. Tess watched the water. She'd never seen anything like it. She sipped her vodka. She tried to get Tazio up from the little booth where they sat.

Tazio was less than a year sober, but he insisted that she drink. He didn't want to be the kind of ex-drinker who made people uncomfortable. And her friends didn't know. They assumed whatever they wanted to assume. They were actors, dancing wildly under the flashing lights, the candles, and the fire swallowers who dangled inside cages above.

David's father had slipped in the driveway and broken his collarbone, but doctors said that after a few months he'd probably be back to nearly 100 percent. David had gone to Jersey for the weekend to help. He said that there'd be nothing for her to do out there with him, and that she should have a night out with her friends. So Tess called a group of them and suggested a club she'd heard was in some way better than the others. She thought Tazio might hook up with one of the women. It'd be good for him. Tazio was single and, as far as she knew, celibate since his sobriety. She'd begged him to come.

He'd said he didn't want to go to a club, that he wasn't in college anymore, and even when he'd been in college he hadn't been interested in paying twenty dollars for a four-dollar drink so he could scream over music he hated. She told him to consider it an anthropological or artistic experiment, and he wouldn't be buying drinks anyway. He went along. He must have been bored with his life as an optics consultant or whatever he was at the time. Or he wanted to prove that the two of them could comfortably be out together without David.

But Tess quickly regretted inviting Tazio. She couldn't leave him alone at the table, he didn't want to dance, and she didn't feel like babysitting him while her friends drank and danced off the stress and exhaustion of a two-performance day. She'd never seen Tazio dance, and she couldn't imagine that kind of public loss of control when he was sober. She left him, danced with her friends, returned to him. This was long enough ago that tube tops were in fashion and the women were all wearing them in bold or neon colors. She returned to Tazio when it got late and told him to suck it up, and he could go home soon but just try to come out on the floor and have some fun. He brought his water glass. It had to be after two in the morning. Everyone was drunk, and Tess chastised herself for dragging him there.

The music was loud and awful but fun, and Tazio followed her into the middle of everyone. Tess rushed the remainder of her drink into her mouth. The ice clicked against her teeth. The music or falling water or sea of surging bodies affected him enough that he began dancing in self-contained, confident shifts of his hips and shoulders. He closed his eyes. It was only awkward for a second or two, as it always is when men dance without irony. One of Tess's friends made a *yee-haw* noise and backed up into him. Tazio spun her around, and her arms extended on and over his shoulders.

Tazio dropped his glass of water and it shattered. Shards jumped from the marble floor and settled. Someone screamed but nothing more came of it. It was beautiful, the glass needles creating a vanishing rainbow in the black and white flashing lights.

The woman—Tess can't remember her name now—dancing with Tazio leaned in to his neck, whispered something, and headed off to get a drink or find the bathroom. Tess waited to see who'd take the girl's spot. When no one did, she approached and asked where he'd learned to dance like that. Tazio couldn't hear her. They didn't touch, but she leaned closer to ask the question again.

"Oh! Ha! In North Carolina," he said. "Some of those nights there were insane."

Neither spoke as both realized what he'd accidentally referred to.

"Tess," Tazio said.

"What?" she shouted over the music because she wanted to know. What could be said? What did he want?

"We've got a long time left," he shouted.

"What does that mean?" she shouted.

"Life is long and things change," he shouted. "But for now, we're where we are. David tells me you're going to try to have children."

"We've been talking about it."

"That's great," Tazio shouted. "David's a lucky man."

He squeezed her hand and she tried not to think about what they were talking about. A parallel world where she was with him. And the possibility that she still might be one day. His implying it was impossible made it possible again. That was the first time in a decade that she really thought about it. Leaving David. Ruining David. Where instead of imagining having kids with David, she imagined having them with Tazio. It couldn't work. Tazio was too unpredictable, too selfish and grandiose.

She couldn't rely on him. David would lose his wife and his best friend. She might be selfish, but she tried not to be cruel.

Tess's friend, whoever she was, returned with two drinks, one for herself and one for Tazio. He declined. She was offended or walked away to find someone else to give it to or to drink them both. Tazio asked Tess if he could go home now. He left. Tess drank and danced. Everyone else in the club watched them— the group of actors, most of them professional dancers—as Tess drank and drank and danced.

14

She planned on not telling David about Gerard, but when she strips off her jeans and lies down next to him, he says, "White wine?"

"Prosecco," Tess says.

"What's the occasion?" David says.

"Did you know Angelica was assaulted?" Tess says.

"At NYU?"

"Abel and Cain."

"You talked to Tazio?"

"No, just Angelica. She wanted to talk about Tazio," Tess lies.

"With you?"

"I know."

In the dark room, David is in bed on his stomach, his face between two pillows. Tess straddles his lower back and leans forward to rub his big shoulders and neck. He groans with pleasure as she kneads and pulls at his muscles and skin. It is the most physical intimacy they've had since his disappearance five weeks before. David's illness must in some way be exacerbated by America's. Just as Trump made Angelica feel as though her sexual assault was inescapable, his constant, grinding presence is making David unable to heal.

Tess tells the whole story, from the conversation about Abel and Cain and Gerard through the events of today, and when David says, "She asked if he was a Trump supporter, and when he said no, she forced him to say he raped her? Jesus. I feel terrible for her, and for Tazio that he felt he needed to keep that secret from me, from us, I mean, but that's . . ."

Tess says, "I know. The whole thing, right?"

"She's always been weird," David says. "Not weird, I mean, it makes sense, but—"

"We didn't know her."

David says something she can't hear, and she plows her knuckles down both sides of his spine. His body provides more resistance than she expects. She is warming up to him. She needs to wake him up. Taking care of David as if he were a third child has killed all desire for him. Mothering—caretaking—is the opposite of sex. Spending the day on an adventure with Angelica has made Tess want a physical connection. With a kind man. She reaches over and begins playing with the hair at the back of his neck.

"And you think today helped her?" David says.

"I do."

"That's amazing!" he says. "That's so great. Fuck that guy. He deserves worse. Good for Angelica." David's voice is muffled into the sheets and pillows, but she senses a glimmer of real enthusiasm.

"I guess you're right," Tess says, and she doesn't know what to say next. So she says, "How was your day?" a question that for the most part she'd stopped asking.

David says something like, "You know how my day was. I napped and watched MSNBC. I'm so proud of you."

"What?"

"Nothing," David says. "Sorry. I'm tired."

Tess exhales, unstraddles her husband, and begins to prepare for bed.

"Wait, come back," he says into the pillow.

"One minute," she says, brushing her teeth. She's still a little drunk.

It's ten o'clock, much later than he can usually stay awake. Maybe the virtual reality vestibular rehab will work. He has rotated onto his back, and she curls up against him.

"I want you to be happy," he says.

"It's a tough time," she says. "But I know you're trying. You're doing your best. I know that. We'll get through this."

She runs her fingers down his chest.

"It is a tough time," he says. He swallows. "Which is why I think you should try to do for yourself what you did for Angelica."

"I don't follow," she says, withdrawing.

"I can't make you happy right now."

"That's not the point," she says. "Our goal is to make you better, and then we can figure out luxuries like happiness."

"We don't know how long it's going to be like this."

"I know that," she says.

"Don't get angry," David says.

"I'm not. But I know that this could be our life for a while."

She doesn't want to fight. At the very least, she wants to rest. To fall asleep feeling good about her day for the first time in a long time.

"I couldn't go with you," he says. "That trip to DC took too much out of me, and Monica is going to upload a new VR progression tomorrow. A walk in the park, I think, with people everywhere. But I think you should go to Pennsylvania. I thought you'd only do it with me, but maybe Angelica can repay the favor you did her today. I don't think you should go by yourself, and neither of you should bring a weapon." David laughs. "But . . ."

Nausea floods into her stomach and throat.

"Absolutely not."

"But why? Why not?"

"Because I haven't spoken to him in twenty years, and there's no reason to do so now."

"What's the worst that could happen? And then what's the best? Like Monica says, 'You have to feel everything you want coming true. It is innocent to have what you want.' I've been thinking about this for a long time, and I never thought you'd consider it, but now that you're suddenly convincing *someone else* that in order to feel better about a traumatic incident, she needs to confront the perpetrator?"

"That has nothing to do with me," she says, but she slows down and lets herself consider the possibility.

"I thought you'd only do it with me, but Angelica is perfect," he says. "She's faced adversity. You've seen her vulnerable. She's tough. I'm sure Tazio has told her almost everything about our lives, so you don't need to worry about explaining. You could both use a friend, even if she's got her own demons."

"She doesn't have demons. She was raped." *Angelica isn't guilty of anything.*

"Of course. That's what I mean. And you just did the exact same thing for her."

"But this is my father. My parents. It's . . . it's worse than what she went through. Much, much worse."

"I know that," David says. "Or at least, I know it feels much worse to you. I just want you to consider it."

"And I don't even know where he lives."

"Google his name and Greeley, Pennsylvania. It's listed. Just over two and a half hours with no traffic, Google Maps says."

She's crying, he's holding her.

"Just think about it for a day or two. My mom can come over. I need to talk to her anyway, and it might be easier if it's just me and her. She can see how well the kids are really doing."

"Are they doing well?" Tess says.

"I think so," David says. "Max is starting to feel more confident. Pam told me he was jumping off the side of the couch today. He wasn't scared at all."

"Yeah?"

"He and Eath were both doing it. And as I was rubbing Eath's back after Pam got him into bed, he was telling me how he hopes I get better. He's starting to understand things. The kids will be okay. They have you as a mom. And with the VR stuff from Monica, I'm going to get better. But you have to look after yourself, too."

"You think your mom will come over?" Tess says.

"Of course she will."

"I don't want to see him," Tess says.

"You don't have to, but you can choose to. You can have what you want. Like Angelica. Except in your own way. You'll talk. You two can go around the country confronting people." Tess doesn't laugh. "Sorry. Dumb joke."

"I like that you're joking. It's been a long time. I'll think about it," Tess says, but it's too hard. She doesn't want to think about her new knife-toting friend or her violent father.

She also doesn't want to think about her wounded husband or delicate kids.

Her mind, as always, goes to Tazio. Why hadn't Tazio found and confronted Gerard? Maybe his tendency was to always look forward. Always find the next battle to win. Maybe it was a way of not drinking again.

When Tazio told her he'd designed a poster for John Edwards, she assumed it'd be witty or snide, but when she first saw the tagline in big, bold letters—Make America Proud Again—under Edwards looking out at a sea of workers, teachers, and families, she shivered. She'd never seen Tazio so sincere in his work. Tazio had heard Edwards tell a reporter that Americans weren't proud to be Americans anymore, and that he was going to change that. So Tazio sketched something in red, white, and blue. Just Edwards's back and hair, with ordinary-looking Americans and the slogan at the bottom. Tess felt moved by it in a way she'd never been moved by any of Tazio's other work. Elizabeth Edwards saw a copy at a New York event. She tracked Tazio down and asked his permission to print thousands more. Make hats. Three months later, Tazio was living just outside of Raleigh.

15

The Inman Park Apartments offered four hundred dollars off rent for referrals to new occupants. So one by one it filled with Edwards staff. Members of the leadership team, mostly former Gore people, occupied their own one-bedrooms. Tazio was assigned a roommate. The only piece of furniture in Tazio's room was a battered mattress, which he put sheets on and pushed into the corner farthest away from the door. He congratulated himself for thinking to bring sheets. He'd stored his books, art supplies, and CDs in his mom's Long Island basement.

His roommate stumbled in, wearing pleated khakis and a baggy dress shirt, carrying a case of beer under his arm. Tall, pink, and pudgy, he introduced himself as Satin, "like the fabric." Over the first few beers, Satin asked Tazio standard questions about how he ended up on the campaign, but he became spirited about the changes Edwards would bring. Satin—on his own bed, Tazio on the carpet with his back against the wall—spent hours laying out for Tazio the strategy to stop Howard Dean, who was only speaking to northeastern Bush haters. Tazio asked questions, trying to get caught up as quickly as possible.

Knocking back and then for some reason crushing cans of Bud Light, Satin called Edwards a cunt but agreed with him about almost everything. Tazio felt oddly eager for a chance to live a version of the American college life he'd been missing at art school. It had been great to get out of Long Island, out of his mother's house and away from the diners and movie theaters he'd gone to with his father, but Cooper Union was just as unsettling. Nobody wore normal clothes. Gray hoodies were matched with fanciful scarves. And nothing anyone said was real. It was all about art. Everyone except Tess talked about art like it was necessary, or valuable, or anything other than the thing that this group of kids happened to be best at. Politics done correctly could measurably improve lives.

Satin, with an effeminate flourish that occasionally reminded Tazio of his own habits of enunciation, told Tazio about the campaign's plan to have Edwards stay positive and speak exclusively on behalf of the disadvantaged. Refusing to denigrate Dean or Gephardt, Edwards was the good guy. Like George W. Bush, you'd want to have a beer with him, but unlike W., you thought he was smarter than you. He could finish third behind Dean and Gephardt in the first caucus and primary, and then win in South Carolina, which would make it Edwards vs. Dean to decide who'd take on Bush. Dean was too unconventional to beat Bush. A win on or before February 3 would be enough to make Edwards emerge as the more charismatic, less angry, quasi-Clintonian option. They were hungry, and Satin had food. They ate big mixing bowls of raisin bran with M&M's and globs of peanut butter, mini bags of Doritos, Fritos, pretzels, and Cheetos, a tube of Pringles, defrosted chicken pizza rolls and meatballs, a dried chorizo sausage that Satin swore he'd never seen before, and fistfuls of still-cold mozzarella from a red plastic pail.

The North Carolina office, housed in freestanding new construction off to the side of a strip mall, was divided between the policy staff—including Satin—in a dark series of small rooms off a fluorescent hallway, and the media team in a single large room with floor-to-ceiling windows. Even in winter, they kept the windows cracked open to stir the fetid smells of pizza, anxiety, coffee, and beer.

It was a month or two before the Iowa Caucuses and, in an office down the road from Inman Park, Tazio spent the first few weeks monitoring the media for any mention of Edwards, and anything significant involving Dean, Gephardt, Kerry, and a few of their less prominent rivals. Tazio watched TV, read newspapers, and scanned the Internet, which meant newspapers and a few political blogs: Andrew Sullivan, Drudge, Instapundit, Talking Points Memo, Gawker, Matthew Yglesias. He translated releases for Spanish-language media and represented the campaign at one poorly organized roundtable in Texas for groups that spoke on behalf of nonunionized Latino construction workers.

Gephardt's, Kucinich's, and Kerry's representatives wore suits and carried binders. They passed out materials and spoke English in a louder and more formal way than they would have if speaking to a group of, say, autoworkers in Michigan. Tazio wore the gray pants and white dress shirt. He was typically ashamed of his Spanish because it was Mexican accented even though he'd never been to Mexico and he'd only met his Mexican American relatives a handful of times. But this time, instead of hearing his mother's voice in his own mouth and resenting it, he spoke up loudly. "Hi! My name is Tazio Di Vincenzo, from the famous Mexican state of Vincenzo," he said in Spanish, and people laughed!

He hadn't planned it. He'd never spoken Spanish in front of more than his mom or a couple of people asking for directions in New York City. He continued in Spanish, "Listen. I know you're skeptical. And not a lot has been accomplished here today. But I'm here to tell you that we at the Edwards campaign honestly care about you," he said. "I'm one of you. John cares about you. We want you to be as much of an American as Dick Cheney and Donald Rumsfeld. We want every member of your community—our community—to have a good, stable job. This is our country, too!"

Nothing came of the meeting. There was no follow-up or donations or even mention of it in the press, but Tazio was speaking about workers' issues and rights of citizenship that would have made his mother proud. Finally. If he could ever really help their people, she would approve. His mother's standards were high, and not only high, but also specifically unreachable for Tazio. If she'd had high standards for sculpture or AP scores, she'd have been satisfied. But she demanded something else—an altruistic elegance, a noblesse oblige or ability to follow an almost chivalric code of conduct—that Tazio had never been interested in. He didn't call her to tell her about the meeting because it wasn't significant enough yet. She hadn't approved of his delaying graduation. But he reveled in this new sensation of believing in what he was doing.

Tazio initially shared a desk in the media room, but after Edwards finished a surprise second in Iowa, the campaign began having trouble keeping the necessary pace of issuing press releases, scheduling interviews, and framing their message. New staffers arrived, and Elizabeth Edwards insisted Tazio be used to punch up some of the language across all communications. Jennifer Palmieri, Edwards's press secretary, agreed after Elizabeth let Tazio pitch her a new slogan.

"America deserves a president who believes in you."

He'd run it by Satin as "America deserves a president who believes in Americans." At two in the morning, listening to R. Kelly's "Ignition (Remix)," stomping around their kitchen/living room, they began replacing "America" or "believes in Americans" to avoid the repetition. Satin screamed out, "America deserves a president who will lick my cunt!" which wasn't really funny but seemed hysterical at the time, but then Satin stopped laughing and said, "What about 'America deserves a president who believes in you'?"

Christina Reynolds, who was a communications advisor, liked the phrase, and though Jennifer said it might be too soft or sentimental, Elizabeth Edwards felt it was the best distillation of Edwards's message they had so far. Because of "America deserves a president who believes in you," his conscientious work as a media monitor, fluent Spanish, a mixed-race "face of the future" biography, and Make America Proud Again, Tazio was promoted as a kind of intermediary or unofficial lower-level chief of staff/ copy editor through whom all documents passed on their way to Jennifer or the candidate's wife. Tazio wasn't resented because he didn't take any credit for himself, improving work and passing it along as though the initial draft had been as good as the final.

But it took Satin to convert Tazio from believer to fanatic. Satin was always going on about how George W. Bush didn't give a horse's cunt about anyone other than white people in Connecticut and Texas, while the Edwardses had faith in Americans. "Imagine living in this country if you're me. Neither political party is willing to discuss my right to basic property guarantees if I fall in love." Satin talked about love when he was sober and sex when he was drunk, and, like everyone else, he was drunk a lot. "Elizabeth Edwards might be a bitch, but at least she tells me that under her husband, being gay won't be any different from being straight. And I grew up with money. Imagine if you're gay and poor, didn't graduate high school, if you have a conviction. And I'm not talking race here. You could be from Detroit or Appalachia. Would you want Dick Gephardt on your side? John Kerry? Jesus Christ. Edwards is our only hope."

The two fantasized about what they'd push for when they got jobs in the White House. Satin would lobby Edwards to come out immediately for gay marriage and gay soldiers' right to serve openly. Tazio had started to read more deeply into options for a true path to citizenship. At first, Tazio found himself saying what people expected him to say. "Comprehensive immigration reform that fixes our nation's broken immigration system *and* improves border security." "A path to citizenship." "At minimum, temporary status that allows children of immigrants to study, work, pay taxes, and contribute to the communities they grew up in." Tazio believed these were probably good ideas, but he wasn't sure if he really cared. Before the campaign, what had he cared about? Being left alone to paint? Doing something important, which was just another way of saying "having control over other people." Affecting invincibility. But now he found he believed in what he was saying and doing. And he saw his life laid out before him. He could do good and do well.

Tazio's gift was his ability to distill the core of an argument to a few words. Thinking about what Satin said as well as what Tazio's Mexican American mom, Italian American cousins, and suburban friends would respond to—and what his father, if he hadn't abandoned him, gone to Italy, remarried, and promptly died of a heart attack, would have wanted—Tazio continued fine-tuning press releases, pushing the campaign's message toward the dignity of work and the average American's declining resources, options, and safety net. Edwards's win in the South Carolina primary was the best night of his life. They gathered in the Five Spot, the local bar, as numbers came in from Greensville, York, and finally Charleston counties. It was really going to happen. Tazio would work in the White House. Make decisions that would change the world. The next week, he was officially named deputy press secretary. Gephardt had already dropped out, and Dean's scream appeared to cripple his chances. Elizabeth Edwards was against the war in Iraq, so no matter what her husband was saying on the stump, a John Edwards presidency would mean more life and less death. Elizabeth had been meeting with Satin to propose something about gay rights to John that would be morally and politically palatable. And John and Elizabeth were both for raising the American poor out of poverty. At twenty-two years old, Tazio was overcome with the conviction that this was where he was meant to be, at the center of the movement that would redefine the United States.

He suddenly found himself devoid of cynicism. Uninterested in the spotlight for himself or in anything, really, other than getting Edwards elected, Tazio channeled what Satin had instilled in him: that Tazio's grandmother had been a Mexican immigrant who cleaned office buildings at night so Tazio's mother could go to college and sell Long Island real estate so Tazio could be in this place at this moment in American history, as Elizabeth Edwards's boy on a campaign she not-so-secretly ran.

Elizabeth Edwards was the one who coined that phrase "the face of the future." It was Elizabeth Edwards who sought to harness Tazio's implicit authority. Tazio understood that his approachable otherness was—had to be—an important part of his appeal. But that wasn't a problem. It didn't feel like selling out. It felt logical. The campaign was proud to have a Mexican out on the front lines, and he was proud to be that Mexican. Tazio couldn't get enough of the sincerity: his own, Satin's, and especially Elizabeth Edwards's.

Between her son's fatal car crash, her husband's infidelities and love child, and the cancer that took her own life, it's difficult to remember Elizabeth Edwards as anything more than a victim—a tragic figure whom life happened to—but at the time, she was the engine of the campaign. Her husband had the charisma, the accent, and the beauty. He was an outlet for authenticity. Well before Mayor de Blasio talked about "A tale of two cities," Edwards warned of "two Americas." Edwards talked about what "I can do for you." And well before Trump said he'd "make America great again," Edwards had said, "We are going to make America proud again. I can't do it by myself, but we can do it together, and America deserves a president who believes in you." He spoke out against the outsourcing of high-tech jobs and for getting young people into science and math. He was all about hope, while Dean's campaign was about how much everyone hated George W. Bush, and Kerry was as boring as Gore had been four years before. "Choose a president America will be proud of," he said. "Believe in what is possible. FDR and JFK both came to the office in difficult times, and they brought laws that changed society for the better. I'll use the power of the presidency to help where people need help. I'll create an American government that never looks down on anybody."

But it was Elizabeth Edwards who framed policy and political strategy, having only a few years earlier—in the private room at the Fig Tree with their best friends and first donors—convinced her trial lawyer husband that the US government could be a force for good and that he was the one to transform it. She made sure people were doing their jobs, reaching out to superdelegates, planning events, lobbying local officials. John was a beautiful windup doll that Elizabeth kept wound and running.

"What a team the two of them make! I've never met anyone as effective as Elizabeth Edwards. And I've never seen anyone glow the way John does," Tazio told Satin after the first time he met the candidate. They were drinking at the Five Spot, where the campaign team, pent up and exhausted, spent their evenings. 50 Cent's "In Da Club" pounded in the background. "Everyone who meets him wants to be around him. You're in love with him—don't deny it!—and I think I might be, too!

He's a beautiful southern man who happens to be totally right about what the country needs. It's amazing."

"I know," Satin said, glowing. Satin's pink skin got pinker around his lips and eyes. Tazio, drunk and happy, looked at Satin and wondered. He'd never been good at differentiating between drunken enthusiasm and lust. He'd never been able to connect with any of the girls he'd slept with. He'd never felt as alone as when trying to fall asleep next to a girl in his college twin bed. He felt safe with Satin. He felt good in the bar. But even if Tazio could want it, his body wouldn't.

Tazio shook off the thought.

"I can't believe my friends are still taking classes from professors who act like they matter. They don't matter. This matters! Sorry. That's not what I mean. I'm trashed."

"No," Satin said. "I know exactly what you're saying."

Over the first few weeks, Tazio called David most nights to fill him in and ask for advice. David was finishing up his degree in economics with a minor in philosophy, and Tazio liked knowing what Voltaire or Kierkegaard would say about a subject. Tazio told David that Edwards was hitting the idea of two Americas as often as possible, and David told him that Kierkegaard would stress the language of alienation when it came to that underserved second America. Tazio was excited to go back to Jennifer to stress the importance of empowerment when speaking about the two Americas, and Jennifer either listened or pretended to listen and carried on either illuminated or having humored Tazio. Tazio wasn't sure, and he didn't really care if his bosses thought he was naive. He believed in what he and David came up with on those calls.

Sometimes Tess answered David's phone. Tazio was happy that the two people he loved most were having fun with each other in his absence. He was confident that he'd always be a first priority for both of them, so he let them do their thing. But he could never shake the surprise. It made sense that David would want to hook up with Tess. But Tess with David?

Tazio realized one night after he'd ended a call with David that he'd been saving Tess. For himself, for after he grew up more. The weight of her family history, and the fact that she was only the second person he'd ever felt like himself with while talking to, made him not want to waste their time together before he was ready. But now it was too late. After David and Tess broke up, he'd have to choose between them. How could he look David in the eye after sleeping with his ex? So he'd have to choose David. Because David was—another realization—the most important person in Tazio's life, and it had been that way for a while.

Which was why it made him feel all the more ashamed for being so surprised that Tess went for David. David was charismatic, funny, industrious, and, especially, kind. Tazio hadn't ever met anyone else whose kindness approached David's. But he was a physically unattractive bozo. The perfect best friend. Reliable and selfless. But to fuck? To straddle? To blow? Tazio had thought better of Tess. But good for David. And good for Tess. Their relationship spoke well of them both.

Tazio was awake at seven, at his desk at seven forty-five, and, if John or Elizabeth wasn't around, downing his first beer at four or five as call time began. Everyone stopped work to call registered Democrats in Iowa, New Hampshire, South Carolina, all the way through the Super Tuesday states, trying to convince every Democrat on any list that Edwards was the only path forward. Trying to convince them to donate, to organize for the campaign, to share John's vision of the future. Tazio broadcasted the message, went off script, explained to voter after voter that if she wasn't happy with the direction of the country, if she thought her world had nothing to do with what people cared about in Washington and on Wall Street, John Edwards was inimitably suited to change all that. Edwards had spent his life fighting for people who'd been screwed over by big powers, and he would do the same for the American people.

The entire team was at the Five Spot by seven thirty. Tazio, Satin, and the rest of them ate wings and curly fries, and drank pitchers of Miller Light. Tazio was getting noticed—by his colleagues as well as the organizers and fund-raisers who came through the office—for Elizabeth Edwards's approval of his work, the dapper clothes he wore in comparison to everyone else's pleated khakis and baggy shirts, and his ability to hold his liquor. His first campaign fuck, a week after his arrival, was his fellow media monitor, a tall local with big bright red hair. After three nights in a row of them getting drunk, fucking sloppily, and passing out by ten, she told him she was still in love with her boyfriend. Tazio spent one night in his small room alone, and then he brought back a policy girl three years out of Georgetown who was mousy and brilliant, and who could orgasm, she claimed and then demonstrated, just by his teasing her nipples. On the nights he wasn't with girls, Tazio and Satin gorged themselves on junk food and fantasized about the future.

Tess told him she didn't like it. It was one of the nights when Tazio called David, and Tess picked up the phone.

"I recognize your work drive," she said, "how you always throw yourself into everything. But you've also always kept life—whether art or politics or girls or even our friendship—at a distance. You always framed everything in its context. But you're so eager now. It's weird. I just want to make sure you're okay."

"What're you talking about?" Tazio said.

He was outside the Five Spot motioning to Satin that he'd be back inside in a second. He tried to focus on Tess.

"David thinks I'm crazy, too. But you just seem so weirdly eager these days. To drink, sleep with girls. To win an *election*. It's all so bald, so raw and desperate, and unlike anything I've ever seen from you."

Tazio realized Tess was scolding him, and he laughed her off. "You've only known me for two years," Tazio said, and thought he heard her gasp. "At *art school*." Admittedly, he was drunk, but what a crazy lecture to be receiving from someone still painting the same portrait over and over again.

"I'm happy," Tazio said. "That worries you? I've found a place where I can trust my instincts and be myself. I have friends, even. Other than David, and you, I'm not sure I've ever had friends before."

"What's the last time you went to bed sober?"

"Is this about drinking or my 'critical distance'?" Tazio said. "I drink. I've always drunk. What's bothering you? I like what I'm doing."

"I know," Tess said. "I guess. I just want to make sure you're okay."

"I'm fine," Tazio said, but he suddenly didn't feel fine. Tess had never been angry with him before. Well, fuck her, Tazio thought, for trying to bring him down. And fuck David for fucking her. Tazio went back into the bar furious with Tess for talking to him like that and with himself for letting her sour his mood. He found himself telling Satin things about his life that he'd never told Tess.

Tazio's father married a high school classmate soon after he returned to Rome, Tazio said. They were sitting alone at a table at the Five Spot, just the two of them. Satin listened actively but not eagerly. Tazio liked Satin. Tazio's father called on a couple of birthdays and Christmases, but Tazio didn't have much to do with him after that. Tazio attended neither his father's wedding nor, a year or so later, his funeral. But lately Tazio was relating more to his father, as someone incapable of satisfying his mother or, really, anyone.

Sometimes Tazio imagined that his father left because he'd known he was sick. That he wanted to spend his remaining years in Italy, but also that he wanted to spare his wife and son his deterioration. But Tazio understood that the reason he hadn't tracked down the hospital records was because there'd have been no benefit in discovering the truth. And if his father had wanted to spare his family that kind of pain, why would he remarry?

Satin didn't know.

Tazio told Satin that the question was rhetorical.

Maybe he said all this to Satin in order to spite Tess, because part of him knew she was right that he wasn't acting like himself. He thought of that later that night, lying in bed, when he couldn't stop the room from spinning.

After South Carolina, a virus went around the office, and of the people who hadn't fallen ill, Tazio was the most trusted staffer not on any particular assignment, so Elizabeth Edwards asked if he wouldn't mind driving John to a TV studio in Richmond, Virginia.

For an hour of the drive, the candidate was on the phone. At first, Tazio had thought it was with his wife, and he was worried that so vicious an argument might derail the momentum of the campaign. But then Edwards started saying things like, "You know I can't see you for the next few weeks," and, "Baby, I have to be here." In retrospect and from Googling around, Tazio is pretty sure Edwards wasn't with Rielle Hunter yet, but it was clear that he was having an affair, and that he was comfortable speaking about it in front of Tazio. Which meant that Edwards was either sloppy about his affairs or comfortable with his wife's knowledge of them.

When the call ended, Tazio expected either an explanation or some kind of sign that what Tazio had heard was expected to remain between the two of them. He hoped that at least this might bring him closer to the candidate and was indicative of a growing trust, but instead, Edwards fell asleep. An hour and a half later, on a local road into Richmond, Edwards spent twenty-five minutes primping in the sun visor's little vanity mirror. He straightened his tie, removed two miniature hairbrushes from the glove compartment, and after a few minutes of brushing, he made invisible changes to the front of his hair with the index and middle fingers of both hands. He applied hairspray and straightened the front again with his fingers.

Tazio's initial reaction was fury that this man who could be so good for so many people was careless and deeply self-absorbed in a way that had the potential to ruin everything. But what nauseated Tazio afterward was that Edwards was less a cipher than he was a con artist. He talked about the two Americas, but really that was his wife's issue. He made speeches about how he was going to be there for other people, but he was obsessed with himself. He talked lovingly about his wife—how he'd be nothing without her—but was in what sounded like a relationship with another woman.

Let him be obsessed with himself in the mold of a Kennedy or a Clinton, as long as he had core beliefs. Vanity and machismo came with the political territory, and they'd all spent their high school years defending Clinton by convincing themselves they believed that what happened in other people's marriages was nobody else's business. What bothered Tazio was that in private Edwards wasn't interested in anything he pretended to be passionate about in public. Clinton famously wouldn't shut up about policy and politics. Edwards didn't seem interested in either. The problem wasn't Edwards's vanity. It was that vanity was Edwards's only characteristic. He was so much worse than a beautiful, hollow vessel. He wanted power in order to be on television and cheat on his wife.

That night when Tazio returned to North Carolina, he sat down with Satin and gravely reported what he'd heard. Satin burst out laughing.

"Everybody knows," Satin said. "And Edwards knows that everybody knows. That's why he didn't give a shit about talking to her in front of you. And can you blame him? With a wife who screams at you for a grammatical mistake and who seems to only be with him to become First Lady? Let the man have an outlet."

Tazio didn't find any of this funny. "Then why are we all still here?" he shouted. "All the talk . . . if this is true, he's doomed. If the Dems don't get him, you think the Republicans won't unearth this like a stinking fucking corpse?"

"This stuff is off-limits. You can't honestly believe Republicans want a world where sex is fair game?"

Tazio didn't buy it. And he didn't like that Satin hadn't told him about Edwards's affairs. Satin's cursing was boring and juvenile, and he seemed to resent Tazio's sex life. Fuck Satin, fuck Edwards, fuck all this shit. The problem wasn't just that Tazio had been left out of the big secret, or that Edwards was a piece of shit, or even that Tazio had cared so much about ensuring that this piece of shit would become president. It was that he'd allowed himself to focus on being good when there *was* no such thing. Sure, Tazio believed in a path to citizenship, and in an ideal world he'd be able to work to accomplish it, but in this world, come on. There was nothing worse than pretending to be good. Tazio got drunk enough off a handle of Duggan's Dew—*America deserves a president who believes in Dew*—to eventually fall asleep.

When Edwards lost big on Super Tuesday, Tazio wasn't surprised. Still, he didn't understand Kerry's appeal, and in spite of everything he knew, argued that Edwards had to stay in the race for as long as possible because allowing Kerry to run against Bush would be to give Bush another four years. "Americans will not vote for John Kerry," Tazio repeated to anyone who would listen. Most people at the office thought Tazio was crazy, that Bush had been a disaster and voters knew it. Jennifer Palmieri suggested Tazio take a few days off while the candidate thought through his options. With nothing to do in that dull complex of small apartments, Tazio floated in the overchlorinated half-heated pool by the parking lot. Edwards dropped out of the race as Tazio swam, drank, floated, and drove to the Five Spot in order to keep on drinking. He'd already slept with most of the single women, and no one was in the mood for anything like that anyway.

Elizabeth Edwards called Tazio into her office during that time and told him she'd heard he was struggling. She said that all people make themselves miserable. The difference, and why Tazio was going to be okay, was that he and she were miserable over something that mattered. The two of them will bounce back to undo the misery. "As long as you're miserable about something that matters, as opposed to the bullshit ephemera that get in the way of real life, then you're doing it right." Tazio almost told her about her husband's phone calls but decided not to, as much in fear that she already knew and would laugh at him as that she didn't know and would be doubly crushed now that they'd lost the campaign.

After Edwards dropped out, Tazio and Satin still had a month of rent paid on their apartment. Tazio was pissed at Satin, but the only other option was returning immediately to the vacuous world of art school, and he didn't want to lose this guy who'd become important to him. He swallowed his pride and asked if Satin wanted to hang out and blow off some steam for a week or two, maybe continue working on local Latino issues, or to keep the concept of two Americas in the press.

Satin said, in the voice that Tazio would have used if he'd told Elizabeth Edwards about her husband, "I've already got a job with Kerry."

"Why? When?" Tazio said, sincerely confused. Kerry was going to lose. He didn't believe in anything that they'd been fighting for. He was the antithesis of Edwards: a man of substance, sure, but also an elitist, prowar, indifferent, homophobic prig.

"I'm going to be assistant director of research!" Satin said.

"Fuck Kerry," Tazio said. "And fuck you, too."

Satin laughed as Tazio slammed the door to his room.

Tazio didn't move his mattress into the larger room. He didn't do much of anything. He woke up, ate breakfast at Denny's, swam, napped, and ate dinner at the Five Spot. Senior year was still months away. He was furious at Edwards for cheating on Elizabeth and for losing the race. He was furious at Satin for pretending to care about Edwards when really Satin was no better than a mercenary lawyer or investment banker. He was furious at himself for having fallen for any of it.

16

When Tess arrived to drive Tazio home, he looked better than she'd thought he would. All the swimming and fresh air partially compensated for the drinking and junk food. David was finishing a draft of his senior thesis, so he couldn't come along as planned, but they both wanted Tazio back in New York. It wasn't healthy for him to be out there indulging in the loss.

"You two spend a few months together," Tazio said at the local dive, "and become my parents?"

The place was dark and loud, and the tables were sticky with spilled drink. Cigarette smoke hovered over every surface.

"What are you still doing here?" Tess shouted over "Crazy in Love." "Most people would kill for your life. Finish school. Choose painting or politics or anything. Anyone would hire you."

Tazio nodded dismissively and kept drinking Bud Light, but then he focused on what Tess had just said.

"Choose painting?" Tazio shouted.

"Sure."

"The sad thing is, I probably will."

"Okay?" Tess shouted. She didn't want to parse his riddles.

"Outside of those involved in the art world," Tazio said softly, sipping his beer, talking as much to himself as to her, "no one cares about art. Especially contemporary art. We might as well be composing Gregorian chants."

She wasn't sure she heard everything he said.

"So what?" Tess shouted.

"Those who do follow this stuff, they see the work that has filtered down into something approximating the mainstream, which leaves the art world to cannibalize itself out of view of anyone not involved. It's just people wallowing in their own self-indulgent metacritical bullshit."

"Metacritical? You don't believe that. You've always cared about your work."

"You're still in it," Tazio ranted. "Art school: the sophomoric being led by the slightly older but equally sophomoric. Take the Richter retrospective last year at MoMA. Everyone, you and me included, found the blurry images captivating. I stared at them for hours. But that's not what we talked about after, remember? What we were supposed to take away from it was some academic treatise on the 'Nature of the Image and, hence, the Image Maker.' I had no idea what anyone was talking about. What managed to make it into the classroom was mostly that we all had to have an artist's statement that explained our paintings and why we made them. Their place in the great artistic narrative."

"But that's what you're good at," Tess shouted. "Creating work with a perspective. I was just painting my parents in different ways."

Tazio laughed. "That's what I'm saying. What's wrong with what you were doing? Nothing. Their expectations are all just bullshit. At least you know what you're trying to get at. I don't know why I do what I'm doing or even why I'm painting to begin with. I just have an image I think will be captivating or funny, and I produce it. Those fucking buffoons Close and Hirst—Jesus, Hirst, the worst of them all—we talk about them because they prattle on about why they've created what they've created. The fucking logic behind the art. But the reasons they give for their work are horseshit. They paint or sculpt what they're capable of, and then they spend as much time fashioning a narrative to suit it. It's all pretend, vapid, and so easy to reproduce. So I did that series on George Bush and everyone loved it. And then that one on crossing the border. It's easy to do, but it's fucking meaningless."

"Okay," shouted Tess, unsure as to whether or not she was supposed to take him seriously. Tazio hadn't written a word about art in all their emails, and now he was lecturing her like a desperate adjunct who'd just been denied tenure. "Then just paint what you want. Like you said you did in high school. Don't work for them. Do it because you've always done it."

"Over and over and over," Tazio shouted. "Over and over and over we asked each other why I was making the paintings I was making. My answer, as you say, at least until I started with the political stuff, was that I always had. Since before I could remember. But it was always unsatisfactory. To my classmates and professors for sure."

Tazio did the shot of whisky or bourbon that had appeared in front of him.

"Since working on the campaign, I've begun to ask myself that same question, why was I making these paintings, and I found no answer, and the fact that I had *once* believed it to be my nature isn't enough. I think it's better not to be a painter. I think it's better to do anything else. People here, we lost an election, and most of them probably knew we were never going to have a president who cheated on his wife and didn't give a shit if people found out, but at least it's possible in this world to help real people, make a real difference so people don't lose their jobs and gays can get married and families can be reunited or whatever. Be known for something more important than cutting a hammerhead fucking shark in half."

"Stop. You're just all mixed up," Tess shouted, though she agreed with a lot of what he was saying. She'd started pursuing theater more seriously while Tazio was gone. David had been encouraging her.

"I'm just saying that it's possible to live a life that matters to more people than the twelve obsessives who spend their weekends gallery hopping. What is art? It's entertainment. Just like music. Or *Seinfeld*. Or *Sesame Street*. But we have to talk about it like it matters in a way *Seinfeld* doesn't. It doesn't matter. And I'm not sure it should."

But to Tess's surprise, Tazio agreed to return home with her the next morning. He seemed okay—just drunk, disappointed, and with nowhere he needed to be. He wasn't even drinking much more than she'd seen him drink at Abel and Cain. She was relieved and looking forward to having him back in their life. Things weren't as exciting without him around.

Tazio insisted on sleeping on the carpeted floor next to the mattress. He and his bed both smelled of beer and sweat, and she slept poorly with her face close to the wall. It wasn't until the sun woke her through the curtainless windows that she felt him sleeping beside her. An hour later, she woke again to the pressure of his chest against her back. She turned toward him. He still smelled sour but not bad when they kissed. She gasped, laughed, told him to stop it, and pushed him away. He groaned and rolled back over, pretending that he'd innocently and instinctively reached out to her body for warmth.

She turned back toward the wall, trying to calm herself. Steady her breath. When she'd pushed him away, she'd felt his body, which was harder than David's and less welcoming. She was disgusted, then angry, then something between guilty and ecstatic. She had thought that by choosing David she'd missed her chance with Tazio. Tazio was sharper, grittier, and more important than she was, and she'd chosen his less extraordinary best friend. She couldn't remember why. For a moment, or maybe for much longer than that, she wanted to live in a parallel world just to see what it was like. To open up options she believed had been closed. This was her opportunity.

Their two bodies reached for each other, his powerful and hers thrilled to be feeling, not thinking. He held her harder than David did, more firmly, licked her back and front, desperate to get every part of his body inside hers. She tasted his mouth, probed his chest, and reached down until she felt for and wrapped her hand around him. For a long moment, she held and felt him pulse. He said something about a condom but she didn't answer. The nausea and anger never fully left her, but those emotions were subsumed into the ecstasy and guilt. She was fighting him as she loved him. It might have lasted two minutes or twenty. She rolled back to face the wall when it was done.

Afterward, she drove him to Brooklyn. They listened to a series of NPR affiliates and stopped for fast food. When they reached out at the same moment to open the door to the Arby's, his hand touched hers. He flinched and pulled back. Tess was disappointed but relieved. That's understating her emotions when Tazio, in that act of jerking his hand away from hers, made it clear he didn't want to touch her again. She was devastated by the loss and overjoyed at the reprieve. There wouldn't be any conversation or decision. She and David had sex later that night as they did almost every night back then. She'd showered beforehand and primarily felt relief to be back in David's arms, the most comfortable place in the world.

Tess didn't get pregnant or contract an STD. When Elizabeth Edwards called asking if Tazio would consider joining her husband's VP campaign team, Tazio politely declined. He told Tess he didn't want to work for anyone pretending to be good, even if his wife was a saint. If you're an asshole, you should own it. The good-guy smile that obscured the rot beneath: he'd seen that before and didn't want any part of it. Which was a shame, because, Tazio said, he could have helped Kerry and Edwards streamline their message. Bush seemed vulnerable for the first time.

Tess thought that Tazio should have told Elizabeth Edwards about her husband. He had a second shot at the conversation, and it was selfish not to have. Worst case, one or both of them would have been a little embarrassed. Best case, he could have saved the woman years of humiliation and pain. But Tess kept her opinion to herself. Things hadn't gone back to normal for them yet.

Tazio returned to Cooper in the fall and, in spite of his disdain for his classmates' work and even, or especially, his own, he started painting again, but he also started drinking in a way he'd never drunk before. He smelled of whisky by lunchtime. Tess told David to tell Tazio to stop, and David did and reported back that Tazio said he knew he should drink less. Tazio was painting wonderfully sinister works depicting Kerry, Bush, Saddam Hussein, and Osama Bin Laden all dressed in shorts and T-shirts at parties that looked awkward, but no more awkward than a normal awkward party. These were images that spoke—powerfully—for themselves. Tazio didn't want to discuss them, with Tess or anyone else. When Kerry lost to Bush, Tazio didn't make a big deal of it. He even accepted some freelance design work. He kept painting and drinking. He graduated and became more volatile. He stopped seeing his mother and therefore the rest of his family. He stayed at bars until closing and took home whatever woman was waiting around for the same. One was a prostitute, but Tazio didn't realize. He'd gone alone to a strip club in Queens and then found his way to a nearby dive. He didn't remember how. He refused or was too drunk to pay the woman, and she punched his face with her keys sticking out between her fingers. While he was trying to splash water on the cuts, she took his wallet. It could have been much worse. He clearly avoided being alone with Tess but, when David was there with the two of them, they all hung out like nothing was different. Tess knew Tazio's self-destruction was about that night they had together, but she couldn't find a way to talk to Tazio—let alone David—about it. She saw a psychologist who insisted that Tess couldn't help her friend if she didn't help herself and she couldn't help herself if she couldn't see the connection between her father's actions and her own.

A small gallery in Williamsburg devoted a show to Tazio's political work, which, as part of a group review, received a positive few sentences in *Time Out NY*. At the end of his next opening in Bushwick, Tazio trashed the gallery. He handed out paintings to people as they were leaving. Work he'd spent six months on, he took off the wall and shoved at strangers who'd stopped in for a free glass of prosecco. Some paintings were large and heavy. The show was supposed to run for a month. The gallery was supposed to earn 50 percent of sales. Tess asked David to stop him, but David said Tazio was too far gone.

Tess wore one of her more delicate dresses. Her arms and neck were exposed. She was twenty-four years old and feeling glamorous. Even beautiful. Tazio wore his typical uniform of a white dress shirt tucked into pressed gray pants. She was about to tell Tazio to knock it off with the gifts, but his cheeks were red with burst capillaries and the exertion of lifting large framed canvasses off the walls. He was smiling but looked miserable. She tried to smile calmly, to make a joke. He just looked at her, and then he looked with more focus, as though she'd succeeded in waking him from his half-conscious craze. She relaxed, but his face, after seeing hers clearly, filled with such loathing that she had to clench her teeth in order to stop herself from crying. Tazio again smiled that drunken, manic smile and turned and tore another painting down, wall-mounting hardware and all. Where the hanging hook had been anchored, a matte square of drywall broke the wall's glossy plain. It was past midnight. Hardly anyone was left. The one horrified gallery assistant had long before departed in tears. The cops were on their way. David tried to grab Tazio's arm, and Tazio balled his fist like he was going to hit him. David left, Tess followed, and, she found out later, Tazio slashed up the walls of the gallery with a box cutter he found in a supply closet. Police never arrived. Tazio photographed the vandalized walls and developed the photographs and sent them to *The New York Times*, which either never received them or did nothing with them if it had. David and Tess didn't see Tazio for a week, and then David got the call from Columbia Presbyterian that Tazio's liver had failed.

Tazio only alluded to their night in North Carolina twice in the intervening years. The second time was at that club. The first was just weeks after he got sober. Obama's general election campaign was revving up, but Tazio didn't respond to the couple of soft-offer emails from his team. Tazio told Tess that he had to work at his recovery. He thought the return to politics might fuck him up after all the hard work of getting clean. But also, he didn't trust Obama. Obama had that same cocky smile as Edwards. Like he was doing the world a favor. Like only he could bring back what was hopeful and right.

It was the summer between David's two years at business school, and he was interning in the food or farming division of PricewaterhouseCoopers. Something like that. Either way, the job demanded long and unpredictable hours, David was called away for work, and Tazio was the only one Tess knew at a small gathering of David's and Tazio's high school friends.

"I'm sorry," Tazio said.

"It's a dumb job. He's not looking for an offer from them anyway. And they don't call him back to the office so often."

"No. I mean I'm sorry."

"Oh."

"I'm not sorry for you. Or that it happened. I'm happy it happened. I'm sorry for him."

"Okay."

"Okay," Tazio said. "Okay."

But it wasn't okay. She didn't want this secret from her husband, but she didn't want to ruin David's friendship with his best friend. She knew she should have thought about that before sleeping with his best friend, but Tazio was her best friend, too. And there was no point in thinking about it any further.

And there still isn't. It's not like Tazio's in love with her. Though if she can love Tazio and then also David, why can't Tazio love Angelica and then also Tess? And just as the worse David's condition was, the more she obsessed over her parents, Tess has to admit that the worse David is, the more she sees the degree to which her feelings for Tazio have been left unresolved. How the pain in her present illuminates those in her past. She's been wrong to think it was possible to compartmentalize pains. The current stress is a sledgehammer that has cracked wide open the protective shell around her anxieties, traumas, and grief.

But that doesn't mean she wants to leave David for Tazio. She has chosen David. Before the kids, maybe it was still an option. Or at least a fantasy. But now, she couldn't do that to Ethan and Max. She couldn't break their childhood even if only a fraction of how broken hers had been. And she loves David. She wants to be with him. Especially when he gets better. The kids will be so happy. They all will.

17

"So I spoke to Tazio," Angelica says.

Angelica is driving, Tess choosing the music.

"Yeah?"

Vents blow heat at their faces and feet, and they're listening to sappy, gut-twisting songs that remind them of being teenagers. "Anna Begins," by Counting Crows. "Losing My Religion," by REM. Nirvana, Madonna, Green Day, Indigo Girls.

"He was serious," Angelica says. "Sober. He said he was, at least. It was weird talking to him on the phone. We've never really done that."

"Is he working at that think tank thing?"

"He didn't want to talk about work. He was pissed at me for seeing Gerard."

"He didn't think you should have?"

"He didn't understand how his apologizing changes anything."

"How does it?" Tess says.

"I don't know. After living without anything tangible for so long, I know he knows he did it now. Before, I wasn't sure."

"Okay," Tess says. "But—did Tazio say why he's in DC? Why he doesn't want to talk to me or David?"

"He's going through something. I don't know. I think he wants to do something alone before we move forward. He told me he was happy I felt better."

"Good," Tess says.

"He said everything would be okay."

"Okay," Tess says.

"Because we love each other," Angelica says, but she sounds uncertain.

"Okay," Tess says. "Do you?"

"Of course we do," Angelica says.

"Then that's great," Tess says. "I agree with him. Some time apart will do you good. A happy ending is inevitable." Tess is lying. About Tazio's relationship with Angelica, time apart being valuable, and inevitable happy endings. But Tess wants to be the type of person who finds these things credible.

"Inevitable?" Angelica says. "He'll still be detached half the time. I can imagine it. Months of bliss alternating with years of feeling ignored and wondering if I should leave him. Probably kids first, for better or worse? You don't understand, with a guy like David who adores you."

"Trust me," Tess says.

"What?"

"I don't know," Tess says, and sighs, because she doesn't know and because even if she did, she wouldn't want to talk about this with Angelica.

"Come on," Angelica says, which is all it takes.

"It's a responsibility when his happiness is reliant on you. If I were the one who was weaker and hopelessly in love, then I could just desire and have my desire satisfied or not. There wouldn't be any pressure. I could just want. It sounds so liberating not needing to be the source of the other person's happiness. Love him when he's home, and cheer him on when he's off fighting dragons."

"Is that an expression?" Angelica says. "You're really telling me that you'd rather be vulnerable? To have your happiness dependent on the whims of a less interested partner?"

"I think," Tess says. "Yes."

"Not cared for?" Angelica says. "Noticed? Made to feel important?"

"And stuck with a gooey, needy dependent while thinking the whole time that there's someone else out there you could feel gooey about?" Tess says.

"That strikes me as the teenager's answer," Angelica says. "You'd rather spend every day feeling unworthy, yearning, unhappy, unappreciated?"

"I think I would," Tess says. "I'd rather be in love than be the object of someone's love."

"Well, you're lucky not to have that problem. You clearly love David as much as he loves you. Staying with him through all this. Right?"

"Of course," Tess says. "But I have to care for him, be responsible for his . . . I don't know. It's too much. It's hard."

"Are you guys okay?"

"Yes, we're okay. We love each other, but you know what happened. What I did. How he's been. It's hard. And hard in a way that has nothing to do with how much I love him. I get so little back. And I want to give, I do. I want to care for him. It's just not the life I thought I was signing up for.

"I keep thinking about the wedding. Years ago. My aunt was so happy. 'Now there's someone to take care of you. You can have a life now,' she kept saying. Like her job was done, and she was passing responsibility over to David. Which made me understand how much of a burden she saw me as for all those years. Raising her dead sister's little girl. It was a job she hadn't chosen. She never had time to meet anyone. Especially when I was twelve, thirteen, and I could hardly get out of bed for months, and when I finally did, I called everything awkward or boring. I must have been hell to live with.

"And then David chose it. Chose me. My aunt's responsibility was over because my life was all set. I was acting on Broadway! I had fans who emailed my website! And I chose David, too. It all seemed so settled and official. Like I could relax. I would take care of him, and he would take care of me. But I thought 'taking care of' meant soothing him if he got fired or nursing him when he was sick with, I don't know, bronchitis or something. I love him, and I'm happy to do all of that, and more, clearly. Or if not happy, at least I don't deny that it's my responsibility. But there's nobody left again."

"I'm not sure I understand," Angelica says.

"To take care of me." This is the first time she's said it out loud. She's been caring for Ethan, Max, and now David. No one is able to look after her.

Tess isn't accustomed to this level of sincerity, and her words hang in the air, competing only with No Doubt's "Don't Speak."

"But there must be meaning to that, at least?" Angelica says, stuttering a bit. "There must. Even if every day is difficult. There must be meaning or importance—a kind of deeper pleasure or satisfaction or lack of yearning, at least—in knowing that you're helping someone you love, and that he'd do the same for you? I'd trade places with you in a second."

"Deal," Tess says. "Let's do it."

"I'm being serious," Angelica says.

Route 6 winds up and down hills past stone repositories and gas station convenience stores. They pass an occasional bar and grill. Naked trees bend heavy with ice.

"I don't know if he works or what he does all day out here in the woods," Tess says. "He used to be so busy."

"What's the last time you saw him?"

"You're Still the One" transitions to "Truly Madly Deeply."

"Savage Garden?" Angelica says.

Tess's stomach has felt in the midst of an hour-long roller coaster plunge, but she forces herself to talk, because silence makes the time pass too slowly.

"I asked my aunt to take me for my tenth birthday. She refused, said it wasn't good for me. That we could go on a trip instead. She didn't have much money, but this clearly meant a lot to her. Disney World, she said, or England. But it was all I wanted. For four years, I'd been telling myself that I'd see my father on my tenth birthday. I think I got the notion in some kids' book about forgiveness. It made me feel good to think about forgiving him."

"What happened?"

"I don't know."

"You don't know if you visited?"

"I visited. He looked different. The only pictures I had of him were ones from when he and my mom got married. Their wedding. I should have been able to remember what he looked like in real life, like in my memory, I mean. But I couldn't. I could only remember his face from those pictures. I was scared when I saw him in prison. He smiled weird. We were in the same room with all the visitors. He hugged me and smelled weird, too. Though I wouldn't have thought about how he smelled before then. He also cried, which I'd never seen before. He'd always been so controlled when he wasn't acting wildly. He was always put together. But crying and wiping his eyes with his sad blue uniform or whatever it's called in prison, he just seemed like some guy. Like he had nothing to do with the man who'd lived in my house for the first six years of my life."

Angelica turns off the music.

"I was wearing a frilly fancy dress that he crumpled when he hugged me. I cried, too, more out of self-consciousness than sympathy or hatred. I didn't forgive him. I was too young. And too old. I had all these thoughts and feelings but I couldn't express them. For years, therapists have been trying to get me to remember more. But I can't. It's so grave. What happened is so terrible that sometimes even now it's all that matters. It's my reason for everything. I can't remember more, but I also can't escape it. Like it has always just happened, but I can't get my mind around it. I don't know. I never figured out how to think about it, let alone talk about it. Sorry."

"Stop apologizing. The last time you spoke to him was twenty-five years ago?"

"Twenty-seven, but yeah."

"And he's been out for years?"

"Awhile. He was released when I was in college."

"He murdered your mother and was out thirteen years later?" Angelica says.

"From what I understand," Tess says, "the prosecutor didn't want to take it to trial in case something went wrong. The idea in his plea was that he wouldn't get released until I was away at school."

Tess doesn't want to talk anymore. She has tried her best. David should be there with her. She wants David. He knows all this already. He'd make her feel okay. He'd take her hand and make her smile. If he were healthy, at least. She wouldn't need to talk or to go into this without support. She barely knows Angelica. He'd talk and joke, and time would pass that way.

"I don't know if this is a good idea," Tess says.

"Do you want me to turn around?"

Tess doesn't answer. There are five, ten minutes of silence, except for Google Maps directing them left and right.

"Do you?" Angelica says.

Again, Tess doesn't answer.

"Tell me if you do, okay?" Angelica says.

Angelica removes the iPhone wire from the console and finds a radio station playing high-energy pop. Justin Timberlake, Pharrell, Bruno Mars's "Uptown Funk."

Tess tries to remember what he looked like when she was six. Then what he looked like when he was stabbing her mom. Then, what he looked like in jail. And she can't summon up anything other than his face in the photograph taken at their wedding. Tess's mother is wearing a traditional wedding dress with frills and lace, except it's pale yellow.

"That was just your mom," Tess's aunt said when she gave Tess the photo. Tess had asked for one to look at when she got sad. Tess's aunt first gave her a photo of her mom on the beach, but Tess asked for one of both her parents. Her family.

In the photo, Tess's father wears a black tux with a pale yellow bow tie. He's looking at his new wife and smiling like a big, dumb kid, while Tess's mom is smiling at the camera. They're both a decade younger than Tess is now. Her father, with big brown eyes, curly brown hair, and a wide smile, looks like no one she's ever met.

"You okay?" Angelica says.

"Definitely not."

"Fifteen minutes," Angelica says.

"Please slow down."

The house is small, not dissimilar from how Tess imagined it. It's at the end of a long, recently plowed frozen dirt driveway. A purple car is parked on a rectangle of gray pebbles. It's almost six o'clock. The idea was to arrive when her father was done working for the day. If he worked.

Angelica turns off the radio and heads toward a spot of frozen dirt beside the parked car. Four bikes lean against the house under the overhanging roof. Lacrosse sticks and a skateboard have been planted in the snow.

"No fucking way," Tess says.

"Can I help you?" a woman says. She's in her late forties, has one foot in and one foot out of the front door. She's not white, but she doesn't have an accent. Tess can't tell if she's Hispanic or from the Middle East. "Can I help you with something?" she says, more firmly this time, as Tess steps into the glacial air.

"Maybe we have the wrong address?" Tess says to Angelica.

"Who're you ladies looking for?" the woman says.

"Um . . . Andrew?" Tess says.

"He expecting you?" she says.

"What's going on?" a man says. He is old, bald, wearing a crisp white dress shirt tucked into pressed khakis. He's neither thin nor fat. Bent just enough to accentuate his age. Dark crescents shadow his eyes, and his forehead is scrunched and wrinkled.

Though Tess doesn't recognize anything in him, she feels like her heart will explode. She breathes deeply.

"Are you Andrew?" she says.

"I am," he says, or almost says.

"I'm Tess," she says, but her father is already crying.

"Is this . . . ?" the woman says.

Tess's father is crying too hard to answer. Crying like Ethan cries when he gets hurt: unrestrained, relieved to have an excuse to let it out.

"Dad?" Tess hears. She didn't say it.

One boy, followed by another. Maybe thirteen and fifteen years old. Both thin, lanky. They don't look like anyone she recognizes. They're just American boys. One's in gray sweatpants and a white sweatshirt, the other in jeans and a Penguins jersey.

"Dad?" the taller boy says again.

"Let's all go inside out of the cold," the woman says.

The six of them sit around a kitchen table. Something with cheese and tomato sauce is baking in the oven, and four plates, napkins, cups, and forks have been set. The women drink red wine, and the boys and Tess's father drink lemonade. Everyone is sipping slowly, waiting for Tess's father to settle. He's blowing his nose in a paper towel. His wife has a hand on his forearm. The kitchen is clean. Dinner smells good. The kids look healthy.

"You have a family?" Tess says.

He takes a deep breath. "Tess," he says. "I'd like to introduce you to Susan, my wife, and Levi and Teddy," he says. "Your brothers."

The boys look younger now that they're sitting at the table.

"Did they know about me? Do you know about me?" Tess asks Levi, the older one.

"You're Tess," Teddy says. "Pop says you wouldn't want to see him, but that he loves you anyway. We can look at pictures of you on Facebook, but we're not allowed to friend request you. And you're not on Instagram or Snapchat that we could find. And a few times Pop showed us articles that mention you in shows. He always said we can see a show you're in and maybe meet you when we're eighteen and old enough to make choices for ourselves. But then he changed his mind and said we can both go when Levi is eighteen because it wouldn't be fair for Levi to meet you and not me."

Teddy's tone is that of a student racing through an oral report.

"Well, it's nice to meet you two," Tess says.

Levi is silent. They all are. No one knows what to say next.

They look at Teddy, who seems the least uncomfortable, or the most excited. But now he's waiting, too.

"I'm Angelica," Angelica says. "I'm just Tess's friend. I'll wait outside."

"No!" Tess cries. "Sorry. Whatever you want."

"Whatever Tess wants," Tess's father says. Angelica doesn't go anywhere. Her glamour is out of place here. She's smiling, dressed casually in jeans and a slim dress shirt, but Tess sees Susan judge her for putting on airs. Like this new wife is anyone to judge.

Tess is cold. Windows are cracked open.

She's angry with him for having a family and she's angry with his family for getting in the way of this confrontation. She doesn't know what they know or what she can say in front of the kids. Her brothers.

"I've spent years imagining this day," her father finally says.

"Why?" Tess says.

"Let's all maybe head into the other room to give them a chance to catch up," Susan tells the boys. *This one probably used to be locked up, too*, Tess thinks.

"I don't want to," Teddy says.

"I'll meet you more properly later on," Tess says.

"Okay," Teddy says.

He follows Levi to the next room, more the other half of the kitchen than a room unto itself. There's a small couch and small TV. A family nook.

"Bedroom, guys," Susan says. The boys comply. Susan follows them in, and Tess can hear her trying to calm them down.

"I'll be in here," Angelica says, pointing and then moving to the couch in the nook. She begins paging through a super-market circular.

"Tessie," her father says.

"Hi," Tess says. "How are you?"

"I've been keeping track of you, keeping you in my heart," he says. Video game music muffles the voices in the bedroom. "I check Facebook almost every day to see if you've posted anything. Those boys! My grandsons. Ethan and Max. I sometimes let myself hope you've left your profile public because you wanted me to be able to look in. I imagine that you post pictures knowing I'll see them."

"No," Tess says.

"Well, still. Thank you for coming. I didn't think you'd ever want to see me again. I didn't want to disrupt your life. After you stopped coming to visit in prison and . . . I just figured . . ."

"I don't know," Tess says, forgetting why she's come. What had David said? Confront him. And then she'll feel better. But now that doesn't seem right.

She could get answers, though. To questions she'd never thought she'd be able to ask. When she got down to it, there really was only one.

"Why'd you do it?" Tess says.

He doesn't immediately speak.

"I've never been able to conjure up a good enough answer. You married her, presumably you loved her, I bet you thought at least that you loved me. She was a good person, right? She tried to love you, to protect me from you? That's what everyone says. That's what I remember. So why'd you do it?"

"Which part?" he asks with an openness that reminds her of David. There's a guilelessness that surprises her and makes her feel that though this is obviously her father, she's talking to the wrong man.

"Mom," Tess says, not wanting him to see her cry.

"Cutting right to the chase."

It's supposed to be a joke, Tess thinks.

"Sorry," he says. "Of course you are. I had schizophrenia. Have it. Or a version of it. Doctors aren't sure what I have, because most people who have schizophrenia aren't violent. But I was. I don't fit most of the criteria—maybe it was the drinking, too—but Seroquel takes away the violence as well as the delusions, so I stick with that. They prescribed it to me in prison. I was hoping when you visited that you could tell the difference, but you were so young, and what, what happened was still fresh."

"Fresh?" Tess says.

"Too recent," he says.

He looks well cared for. Shaved, with tightly cropped hair on the sides and a shiny bald head. She remembers her aunt saying that talking to him was like living inside a book. This old man in the woods with a wife and two normal sons is the reason for everything. For her entire life.

"So that's it?" Tess says. "You were sick, so you stabbed Mom? And now you're better?"

"Stabbed?" he says.

The way he says it makes Angelica turn around, but Tess hears Angelica move and gives her a look that makes her return to the circular.

"Yeah, you have an excuse now? Like you had to stab Mom because you were sick? And now you aren't guilty of anything? You killed my mother." This felt like something. Not good, yet, but getting there. Let her pain hurt him.

"I'm not saying anything like that," he says. "I was in prison for what should have been the best years of my life. I lost a wife and daughter I loved very mu—"

"You're comparing your loss to mine?"

"I'm not comparing anything. I am asking forgiveness. Right

now. I did a horrible thing. I ruined my life and yours. It's all my fault. But what do you mean by 'stabbed'? No one was stabbed."

"What?" Tess says.

"You said 'stabbed,' " he says.

"You killed Mom. And went to jail for it. And left me orphaned. Was the drinking also a symptom of your disease?"

"No. You're right about the drinking. Self-medication is what doctors call it. I'm sober since going on the Seroquel. Twenty-six years. I had impulses. Regardless of why I had them, I did something terrible. I live with that every day. You have no idea."

"I have no idea?" Tess says. "You seem to be coping just fine."

Tess is furious. She wanted to let him know how much pain he'd caused, but instead of owning any of it, he's going on about his own fucking suffering. His disease. His cure. What about her pain? Her ruined life? He doesn't have the right to air his grievances. This isn't about his catharsis. His new wife and sons can provide him that.

"But I got very lucky with Susan," he continues. "I don't deserve her." He smiles in a way that makes him look happier than he has any right to be. Happier than Tess is.

"I can see that."

"But I didn't stab anyone."

"What do you mean?" Tess says.

"I . . . I guess I punched your mother. Twice. We were fighting, and I punched her."

"This is what you tell them," Tess says. "Your new family?"

"Julia's heart gave out. She was on all those medications, beta blockers, uppers, and blood thinners, and she went into cardiac arrest."

Tess is dizzy. She feels a heart attack of her own coming on. Tess recalls Angelica's face when Gerard had initially insisted that the assault had been consensual. Tess had lived her life analyzing the emotions of her father's crime. But now he was challenging the facts. Angelica had made Gerard admit it. She had dared him to keep on lying. Tess could try the same.

"Tess?"

She holds the table to steady herself.

"Then why did you go to jail for so long?" she says. "What you're saying doesn't make sense."

"Because I'd been abusive," he said. "I had a record. I'd been arrested before for . . . for fighting, and the court-appointed therapist claimed I was abusive with you, and I didn't fight any of it in court. I wanted to die. I didn't care about going to prison. I deserved worse than that. I loved your mother, and I lost her. And you. Until the Seroquel I didn't think I could continue living with the pain."

"You killed her. You stabbed her. I remember it. I can see it right now."

"That's just not what happened," Susan says from where she'd been listening in the hallway.

Susan joins them at the table. The boys stay in their room.

Tess wants to yell at this woman that she shouldn't be here. But Susan reaches out and takes Tess's father's forearm.

"Before we married," Susan says, "Andy had me look into all of it. He wanted me to know everything. I saw the police reports. It's all public. Anyone has access. He struck her, and she died. It was his fault. But there were no weapons or anything like that. We've always been honest with the boys. We talk about the mistake that ruined Pop's life for a while—"

"For a while," Tess says bitingly.

"Yes. For a while," Susan says. "We tell the boys how their pop did a terrible thing, and they have to know about it. And how the actions they take are so important. Because Pop lost two people who mattered so much to him."

Susan is talking like a kindergarten teacher. That's probably what she is.

"He did an awful thing, but he's not that man anymore," Susan says.

"So he's said," Tess says, but the memory of the stabbing is already growing murky. She remembers her mom on the floor, but now she doesn't see any blood. She tries to shake off the dizziness.

"Wait! You threw a full can of soda at my head!" Tess yells.

"I would never!" he yells back at her, and from this outburst, she recognizes him for the first time. Tess thinks she sees Susan flinch, too. Tess feels his old self there in the room with her. It's still him. He's still what he was, even if medication fights against it.

He regroups. Softens his voice. "I'm sorry," he says. Indistinct memories flood her brain. "I did something terrible, but I never in my life hurt you. Physically, I mean. I must have been hell to live with. I didn't make enough money. I could be cruel to your mother, and to other people. I regret it all more than you could ever know. But I wouldn't have ever hurt you."

"Maybe you don't remember because you were drunk all the time. You smacked me across the face. I was scared to go to school because people might see the mark."

"I would remember that."

"Let it go," Susan says to her husband. She turns to Tess and stares into her eyes. Tess feels the ache she always feels when confronted with someone maternal.

Susan says, "He's a reliable father to Levi and Teddy. But you're absolutely right. Maybe he doesn't remember, and he did do some of what you say. Right now all he wants is to have you back in his life, in whatever way it might be comfortable for you."

"It's not possible," he says.

He means it's not possible that he hit her. He's a maniac. He seems to really believe what he's saying.

"It's not possible? You hit me. A six-year-old girl. And fine, if you don't want to have stabbed her, you still murdered her."

"I killed her. There are no excuses."

"That's it?" Tess says.

"It?" her father says. He reaches for her hand, but the round kitchen table is large enough that Tess would need to lean forward across it to meet him, so she doesn't need to pull back in order to signal her anger. After a moment, he retreats, but with no visible shame.

"I understand," he says.

"Stop talking like that," she says.

"I served my time. I'm trying to make up for what I've done."

"You won't even admit that you hit me!"

"I didn't."

"Andy," Susan says.

"Okay," he says, slumping deeper into his chair. "I probably don't remember. I probably did. I was drinking so much back then."

"You're humoring me," Tess says.

"I love you. I'm telling you the truth. I don't remember hitting you. But that doesn't matter."

"It doesn't matter?" Tess says.

"I'm sorry," he says.

"You're sorry," Tess says with sarcasm.

Susan stands to take a lasagna or baked ziti out of the oven. It smells good, like the kind of thing she could be cooking for Ethan and Max if things were different or she were someone else.

"Can I make you a plate?" Susan says.

This isn't Susan's fault.

"No, thank you," Tess says.

A breeze crosses them from one window through another. Nobody moves to pick up a paper towel that has drifted to the linoleum floor.

The buzz of an electric heater is replaced by the sound of a truck passing nearby.

"Would you like to see the boys' room?" Susan says.

Tess isn't finished with her father. She feels worse, lost, scared, and shaken, but she stands and follows Susan into the boys' bedroom. She's surprised that her father stays behind. The boys' room is small but nice. Red carpeting. Beds on opposite walls. Jackson Pollock posters above one bed and athletes above the other.

"You like Pollock?" Tess says.

"Who?" Teddy says.

"The guy who painted these," Tess says.

"He's the shit!" Teddy says.

"Language," Susan says.

"On YouTube," Teddy says, "there's this thing of him painting you can watch. You like him, too?"

"I do," Tess says. She sits on Teddy's bed. "How old are you guys?"

"I'm ten and Levi's twelve," Teddy says.

"No. I'm serious," Tess says.

"They're tall," Susan says. "We have no idea why."

"I've got two sons, too," Tess says. "They're not much younger than these guys. But mine seem like babies compared—"

"They grow up fast," Susan says.

Tess feels better now that she's away from her father. She has a life away from these people. Kids of her own. For a moment, she'd forgotten.

She sits next to Levi on his bed.

"Hi," she says.

Levi pretends not to hear her.

"Levi," Susan says.

"It's okay," Tess says.

"Levi can't save," Teddy says. "So if he stops he'll go back to Level One."

The four of them watch the screen. A small green man is jumping over large yellow men, but the graphics are so good that the men really look like men. She'll have to get something like this for Ethan soon. He already refuses to watch Elmo, Daniel Tiger, Thomas, Dora. Even *Paw Patrol* and *PJ Masks*.

A large yellow man stomps on the small green man. "Fuck," Levi says.

"Language!" Susan says.

"Fuck fuck fuck!" Levi says.

"Levi! Stop it right now or remember what we said about soccer."

"Fuck soccer," Levi says.

"Levi!"

Levi is acting younger than his ten-year-old brother, but Teddy is brilliant or precocious or something. Having flung down the controller, Levi grabs his sweatpants at the knees and squeezes tightly.

"Levi," Susan says. Tess thinks Levi might have some kind of developmental disability that she hadn't recognized, but Levi relaxes a bit and seems normal enough.

"Do you want to ask your sister anything?" Susan says to Levi, trying to calm him out of a fit.

"She's not my sister," Levi says.

Susan cringes but recovers. "Teddy, do you want to ask Tess anything?"

"Do you live in New York City?" Teddy says.

"You know that already," Levi says.

"I live in Brooklyn, which is a part of New York City," Tess says.

"We know that," Levi says.

"Levi," Susan says. "Soccer."

"Fine," Levi says.

"When Levi is eighteen can we visit you?" Teddy says.

"I'm not sure," Tess says. "We still have a lot to figure out here, your father and I."

"I don't want to visit," Levi says.

"Levi," Susan says. "Stop it."

"No. I don't want to stop it. I don't want her here. She can't come back after a million years and act like he's her father. Pop wants to move on. He doesn't want her here. She's a . . . a . . . bitch."

"Levi!"

"Pop has never even wanted to talk to her all this time. I said I don't want to visit her and I meant it."

"I'm sorry," Susan says. "I know this is hard enough without that." Susan doesn't know anything.

Tess wants to say it's okay, he's only a kid, it doesn't matter, kids are possessive, especially about their parents, she didn't mean to intrude.

But instead she says, "I should be going now anyway."

"No!" Susan says. "Really. Your father. You have to at least stay for dinner. I made ziti for the rest of the week. There's more than enough for two extra plates. I'll serve it right now. Just before you head out."

"No, thank you," Tess says.

"Please," Susan says. "Please."

"No," Tess says. "I want to go home."

"Please—"

"Why would you marry him?"

Susan says nothing. Then: "Okay, go."

Spring

18

At first it's nice, going to bed with David, with his front to her back like they used to. Kids down by eight, an hour to eat delivery, watch the news, in bed by nine. Neither of them is interested in sex now, though they don't discuss it. They don't talk about much after Tess briefly tells David that she shouldn't have seen her father, that he has a new life and family. David asks questions she can't or doesn't want to answer. Instead, they talk about politics, wonder what kind of person would have voted for this terrible man. How angry or broken someone must be to think Donald Trump is right for this or any moment.

They fall asleep quickly but can't stay asleep. David says it's the antidepressants that give him nightmares. He clenches his muscles, grinds his teeth, sweats, wakes, and tells half-coherent stories about protecting her and the kids from invaders, getting stabbed and stabbing, running into Tess and the boys, who recognize him but can't remember where from.

Tess is awake for much of David's thrashing and grinding, but she doesn't interfere. She stares at the ceiling, trying to form patterns from the cracks in the paint she can barely see or that she invents, or she is sleeping and dreams the patterns form some landscape. David wakes her with a sudden movement. She mistakes the sound of a stopping bus for the cries of one of the boys.

Between fits of sleep, she remembers more clearly than she ever has before. The wide-plank wooden floors of the apartment. An easel for what must have been her fifth birthday, one side chalkboard and the other for clipping paper. She spent years at her aunt's house with that easel, but she'd forgotten it had been at her parents' apartment the year before. At her aunt's house, she drew with markers. Birds, trees, the sun, a rainbow, flowers, ponies, a stream. Tess lost her virginity at fifteen. The boy was fourteen. It was late in the afternoon in the stairwell of her Jersey public school, and they did it three times in a row. It was just after she started to feel less depressed. She was getting out of bed every morning again. She graduated from markers to watercolors and oils, from pretty drawings to paintings out of her subconscious. She was eating without being forced. Or maybe it was the boy's attention that broke the depression's spell. It excited her and she couldn't be excited and depressed at the same time. Sex unlocked a new category of ache and release. Soon after, alcohol did something similar, and then theater.

On her first non-Equity tour, the three combined: sex, drinking, and acting. Topeka, Portland (Maine), Santa Fe. She was theoretically with David at the time, but the tours didn't count. She wasn't sure yet if she loved David, and those boys had nothing to do with her real life or with anything, really, other than the ache and release. She was so empty and then so full. Sometimes she wanted to get back to David, where she felt a less satisfying but constant contentment. Itchy stability was usually better than the oscillation between hunger and gorged overabundance. There were moments, though, when she wanted to stay on the road forever, sleeping in motels and buses with one of the actors—Billy—when he wasn't too drunk or too self-important on his first taste of adulthood. She hasn't thought of him in more than a decade. He was short, cute.

Why did she cheat? With Billy, Tazio, and Jonah? It'd be easy to explain these men away as three different cases. Billy was for pleasure, Tazio for love, and Jonah, she now sees, was a way to try to re-create Tazio. But Billy didn't feel meaningless at the time, she didn't love Tazio, and Tazio and Jonah are different people. She cheated because in those moments with those men, the moment became more powerful than the larger trajectory of her life. Her body wanted another body, David's wasn't there, and everything in life can vanish at any moment, so she seized pleasure where it was available.

Also, there was something delicious about the shame. She refuses to listen to another psychologist hypothesizing about how her sexuality was a reflection of her nonrelationship with her father, but in all three cases the anticipation of shame was inseparable from the pleasure of cheating. The two mixed together to create a deep, nearly unfulfillable hunger that was stronger than her self-control. Lying in bed now, she can't make sense of that longing. It seems impossible. It must have taken so much energy.

There's nothing to do with these memories except indulge them. Sometimes, from three in the morning until the kids wake up, she makes patterns in the cracks above her bed and falls in and out of her childhood. Her father is a shadow and then the sun itself, before he recedes again. Did he hit her? She can feel the slap across her face. She'd never considered a sibling until a therapist hypothesized that it might have helped her share her pain during the worst couple of years. Imagine that: inventing someone just to make that person suffer. To wish for a sister so she could have been hit, too. So she could also watch her mother be murdered. So they could cry about it together. Even when a sister would only add an additional untrustworthy perspective on her childhood. It's not as though memories can be disproven. Just, for better or worse, reshaped.

David can't get out of bed in the mornings, and after a month or two Tess can't, either. At first it's merely difficult. She has to push herself, she is late dropping off to school, to day care, and she can tell she's getting strange looks, but she doesn't know why, and she doesn't care. The boys don't think it's funny, how Mommy and Daddy stay in bed and roll over when they stomp in in the morning.

Ethan says, "It's daytime, Mommy! Daytime, lights are on, it's not time to sleep, it's time to wake up and eat breakfast!" while Max does a dance with a balloon.

"No! You can't have that, never! That's my balloon!" Ethan says.

Max says, "Ba-oon!" so Tess rouses herself to try to scold Ethan for talking to his brother like that.

She thinks but doesn't say *You're not Max's parent, Eath*, and *A time-out next time you use that voice*. She wants to say these things, knows she should, and in another life is saying these things, but in this life she doesn't. And it doesn't matter. It's liberating to know what she should be doing while not doing it. Pressure begins to dissipate and is replaced by a comfortable slowness. She should be doing all sorts of things for David, her sons, her new brothers, and probably for many other people she can't think of. Tazio. David had a reason to leave. She hurt him. But for Tazio to abandon her and David? This is the longest either she or David has gone without talking to Tazio for close to twenty years. She doesn't understand. But pleasure comes from her realization that she doesn't need to understand. Tess relaxes, curls up against a pillow, and lets the world rotate and revolve.

Ethan tires of scolding Max. The two boys jump on the bed between their parents. When Tess and David allow them to jump and crash without scolding or comforting them, the game becomes more fun and then less fun.

Ethan jumps, purposely landing on Tess.

"Gentle," she murmurs.

"Boys," David says, holding his head. And then he says, "I can't, Tess, I'm sorry," and Tess says it's okay, but she doesn't reach out to him.

"It's okay," Tess says. "It's all okay."

David continues with the goggles on his face multiple times a day for longer and longer each time. Monica has found something that really works, he says. He thinks that the psychological respite combined with vestibular stimulation creates a kind of "healing zone." He and Monica have been talking about how more people should have access to this kind of technopsychological approach. He hasn't fallen in months. In virtual reality, he wanders a beach alone, watching seagulls swoop to snag fish from the ocean. It's six hundred dollars per month now because he's reached the end of stage one. Monica is "amazed" at his "progress." She says it will never be more than twelve hundred dollars per month. Tess laughs at the thought of such a sum. But she doesn't really laugh. She just feels latent laughter. David is relieved, or at least he says he is. He can walk from the bed to the table, from the table to the kitchen. In real life, not just in virtual reality. She can't remember if he could always do those things or if this is progress.

Tess goes to bed hoping to sleep forever. The morning sunlight sneaks around the curtains, and she is miserable. She's never not miserable, and the misery is so heavy that she can't escape it. The misery overpowers her and makes her feel as if she has disappeared. She's felt like this before—when she was thirteen and fourteen—and then again in moments throughout her twenties. The first time, a boy got her out of it. The other times it was

having kids. She never had postpartum depression. Only the opposite. But now she doesn't mind feeling like this. She accepts it.

Ethan stops asking for his breakfast. He takes for himself
and his brother the yogurts that David sometimes stocks in the
fridge. One yogurt each. Ethan has already chosen their clothes
for the day. He can't handle opening or pouring the juice, so he
asks for help from his parents, who don't respond. Tess imagines
the kitchen as she lies in bed, sees her older boy growing up,
becoming someone who can encourage his brother to pee in the
potty, take a yogurt for himself and his brother, get spoons, and
open the yogurts just like an adult.

"No, Max! You put yogit all over. Not nice!" Ethan yells at
Max with a viciousness that does not at all correspond with the
pride Tess was just feeling over how her boys are becoming so
mature and independent.

"Nakin? Nakin! Nakin peas!" Max begs.

"Maxy wants a napkin, Mommy! I can't reach even with
the chair!"

On this morning, David lurches out of bed, fetches paper towels, and cleans the boys up. He pours them juice. But when it's
long past time to go to day care and school, Tess is still in bed.
For a week, nobody mentions school. When administrators call,
David tells them the boys are sick. Or he and Tess are. Tess doesn't
really hear, as David needs to whisper on the phone in order to
maintain his equilibrium.

When she loses focus, her thoughts tilt toward her father's new
family. Her brothers. Teddy seems great. Levi is angry. But so is
she. That's genetic from their father, or just comes from spending time with him. Probably nature and nurture both. The wife
seemed kind. If careful. Possibly broken? She must be responsible for Teddy's sweetness. But then why wouldn't Tess be sweet?

Tess had a kind, careful mother. The answer—that Teddy lives with his mother, while Tess's mother was murdered by Teddy's father—is obvious. Or it's possible that Tess is sweet. Is capable of being sweet. When she feels good.

Tess hasn't checked Facebook in weeks, but her plan was to remove all the pictures of her kids, or at least make her account private. It's too late now. He could have taken screen shots. He could have done anything. The man murdered her mother.

But just in case, she deletes the photos. They're backed up somewhere in a cloud. She lands on her father's page and looks at picture after picture of his two boys. In photos, they look like older versions of Ethan and Max. Not exactly, but so much more than it seemed when she was with them in person. Both of her boys are like Teddy. But she's like Levi. Teddy looks like her boys. It's in his eyes. She messages *Hello* and Teddy writes back instantly:

Hi.

Why aren't you asleep?

Erly hockey practise. Some nites I sleep but others I cant

How are you?

Good u?

Good

Tess and Teddy exchange brief notes like this some mornings at four or five o'clock. She feels guilty that the kid is staying up late or waking up early. She asks him if he's tired because of it, but he says no. That hockey gives him extra energy. They don't discuss anything personal. Just that it's hard to sleep. Teddy writes her what he will eat for breakfast. Tess pretends that she is hungry, too. He fills her in on the hockey team. He was on the third line and now is on the first.

Congrats! Tess writes.

Thanks

They text more than they email, but mostly they use Facebook

Messenger. Teddy's parents won't see it on a phone bill, and it's easier than emailing. It makes Tess use her phone again, which pleases David. When David asks what she's doing, she says she's chatting with her high school friends.

Teddy asks questions about what their dad was like when she was growing up, and Tess answers as honestly as she can. She tells her brother about how their father always ironed his own shirts and Teddy responds that his mother irons them for him now.

Teddy asks what Tess did when he got mad.

Tess asks if his dad gets mad a lot.

Teddy answers that he gets mad only sometimes.

Tess asks what happens then.

Teddy answers that usually his mom can calm him down.

Tess asks what happens when she can't.

Teddy answers that their father hit the wall once.

Tess asks if he ever hits people.

Teddy writes *hardly never.*

Tess asks Teddy whom their father hits when he hits people.

Teddy answers Levi because Teddy knows how not to make him angry.

Tess asks if Teddy is scared.

Teddy answers that he's not scared because he knows Pop loves him.

Tess asks what his mom thinks.

Teddy answers that his mom says not to make Pop mad. Pop used to be violent and now hardly ever is, and she explains what triggers him.

Tess asks what triggers him.

Teddy responds: *when we interrrupt him at nite or ask about your mom, ask quebtions in general about b4 he met mom my mom or just when he has a bad day at work*

Tess asks Teddy to call her next time it happens.

Teddy responds that he will.

Tess helps him with math homework.

Teddy asks if David is feeling better and how Ethan and Max are. If they know about him.

Tess admits that they do not. That it'd be too complicated to tell kids so young that their grandfather was around but they couldn't see him.

Finally, Teddy asks if he can visit. He wants to meet his nephews. He thinks it's funny that he's an uncle.

Tess cries for a while and then responds that Teddy can't visit. She hasn't told Teddy about the state of her life. Her apartment smells bad, and she looks sick. She doesn't have the energy to pick him up or meet him out somewhere fun for a ten-year-old. And she feels guilty for giving Teddy more attention than her own sons.

She tells Teddy he can't visit because their father hasn't given Teddy permission and she'd prefer not to involve their father in her life.

If David was able to survive a five-hour drive to DC, to take subways to and from Monica's apartment, he can surely take his kids to school. Especially if the virtual reality vestibular rehabilitation is actually improving his equilibrium some. But maybe he can't. Maybe the stress of the kids and all their movement and requests and discomforts, all the yelling and needing to control one on the subway platform while the other is wandering toward the tracks—maybe the fear of all that, of having Max fall again, is too much for David. She gets it. That makes sense. The kids stay home. Max seems to have recovered physically. His head looks fine and he's not far behind any developmental milestone. There's that to celebrate. Even when David goes to see Monica and stops on the way home for bread, milk, juice, yogurts, Diet Pepsi, and sliced meats, he doesn't take the kids outside with him. They are home every day. It doesn't matter. In the face of murder—of losing her mother—nothing is important. Her children have not seen real violence. They are loved. It's spring and the windows are open. Gates are still on from last year so there's no way the children can fall.

Ethan invents games to play: increasingly violent versions of hide-and-seek. Hide-and-hug, which really means tackle. A lamp falls and glass splinters across a corner of the room, but no one gets hurt badly. Ethan helps Max with a Band-Aid. David makes them all eggs for lunch and sits in front of the TV watching MSNBC until the kids eat dinner, which he is usually able to order or prepare. Sandwiches. PB&Js for Tess and the kids. Supermarket chicken on gluten-free bread for David. When he asks Tess what's wrong or how he can help, she tells him he's doing great. She's proud of him. He finally cleans up the glass shards from the lamp. When he says she needs to see someone, she laughs or says she doesn't want to, or she pretends to be asleep.

She is lonely. She used to have David, Tazio, friends, children, and a career. Now, though, she interacts with no one other than in these occasional conversations with David, and though she messages with Teddy, she is drained of energy. And when she feels the misery deeply, she doesn't want to let it go. She hides under its weight and breathes it in. It's warm and cozy. She fosters it, nurtures it, falls asleep in its fog.

"You're depressed," David says.

"You're one to talk," she says.

"Tess, please," he says.

"Please what?" she says.

"Nothing. I love you," he says. "It's just that it's never lasted this long before."

"I love you, too," she says, and doesn't bother telling him that it has.

It's as difficult to get out of the shower as it is to get out of bed. Tess luxuriates in the lack of responsibility. She has nowhere to go. Nothing to do. The shower is warm. Minutes or maybe hours ago, she used soap and probably shampoo. She starts with the water warm and makes it just a little bit hotter every five or ten minutes, until an hour has passed and the thought of abandoning such heat for the cold of real life is too daunting. But then she's exhausted and dehydrated. She gives herself until the count of ten to get out of the shower, but when she gets to ten she makes it fifty and when she reaches fifty she starts again at zero.

No word from Tazio. What did she ever see in Tazio? Power? Volatility? Is it just that Tazio reminds her of her father? That Jonah reminded her of Tazio who reminded her of her father? And then how to explain her love for David? She's gone over this before. David is the opposite of her father. Or he was? People marry either their father or the opposite of their father? That's what David said Carl Jung said. Marry or fuck, that is. Tess isn't (David wasn't?) sure.

David spends a lot more time on the computer. She doesn't know why. Then they're in bed together and he starts reading out loud from a message board for people suffering from vestibular disorders. He shows it to her when reading gets too hard.

Hi I've been feeling dizzy & off balance, head & pain behind my eyes, feeling blurry all the time & find it so hard to eat & been in a confused state since this happened almost 2 weeks ago. I've had my blood tests taken but came ok. anyone else been feel8ng the same & if so what could it be? I'm feeling so low & depressed as I hate the confused feel8ng as I have two young girls and a baby to care for ☹. anita

"Two weeks," David mutters. She wants sympathy after two weeks.

They sit in bed and read the responses:

Hi anita ive been feeling like that for a year even lost my job over it have you seen e.n.t or a neurologist ive had an mri scan nothing showed i am now on notriptilene and prozac as it made me go into depression i like this site cos it made me feel alone till i found this site chin up hope you get better soon x

These two go back and forth until another joins in:

Hello I know this is an old post but I am very fed up today. I also have been suffering from dizziness for 3 years. I have had to give up work and I was just wondering how you are now and if there's hope, I mean. If you have gotten better. Kind regards Jenn.

There are hundreds of responses from the invisibly ill. David starts crying. She holds him against her.

"Three years?" he says. He sees a life where he will accomplish nothing more, and experience nothing more than pain. She sees it for him, too. For both of them.

Hi Jenn and anita if you're still there. This sickness or disorder or whatever it is has totally changed my life. I have 3 kids too and have gone from a healthy active dad to a dad that is like a 80 year old grandpa. I am not confident in my mobility and feel constantly dizzy and weak. They say it's vestibular or anxiety, but they don't know; no one does. I also am suffering from an upset stomach for almost a year and often get a feeling as though the earth moved under my feet, my body constantly twitches in weird places as well. I have had extensive investiga-

tions (ct of head, chest and stomach, endoscopy, ultrasounds, sleep study, X-ray, echo scan, Mri and holster test of heart, multiple bloods,) chiro 2x per week and have seen a psychologist and tried anti depressants for months with no results. Am now trying gluten and lactose free diet as well. Ive basically come to the conclusion I am gonna just feel crap forever.

And then:

Wow. Reading this post is like reading my life story for the last 5 years. I have never posted on a forum but I went from a healthy guy (I'm 28 now) to feeling just like an old man. I have no energy, my neck and back hurt, my bones hurt at times, I have this weird off balance feeling all the time. I could go on and on and like you have had every test under the sun and according to my doctor I'm the healthiest SOB on the planet. My body twitches and I get heart palpitations. The only reason I have a job today is bc I work for my family, and my mom in particular has been very understanding. I have a 7 year old daughter and I'm a single dad and it's brutal bc she wants to play and wrestle and sometimes I just feel like crap and I can't play. I have tried everything from antidepressants to low carb/no gluten diets but to no avail. I've thought I had every disease known to man but every morning I wake up and I gotta keep going. I've come to the conclusion it's gotta be candida or Lyme or something weird. Im looking into taking Iugol's iodine as a supplement. I would really like to hear back from you man. I'm in your boat, brotherman.

"Stop," Tess says. "Stop reading these. This isn't going to make you feel better. Let's see what they suggest. I mean, if there are any concrete suggestions that have worked for people."

David compiles a list:

MASSAGE

CHIROPRACTIC

ACUPUNCTURE

ELECTROACUPUNCTURE

BLOOD PRESSURE MEDS

TRIGGER-POINT DRY NEEDLING

HYDRATION

CUPPING

THE ALEXANDER TECHNIQUE FOR BREATHING

SCRAPING

ANTIPSYCHOTICS

ANTIANXIETY MEDS

TINCTURES

TONICS

CRANIOSACRAL THERAPY

OILS

HERBS

AROMATHERAPY

VESTIBULAR THERAPY

HOMEOPATHY

MEDITATION

DIETS BASED ON BLOOD TESTS

DIETS BASED ON THEORIES ABOUT GLUTEN AND DAIRY

DIETS BASED ON STUDIES OF SUGARS AND FATS.

"Which one do you want me to try?" he says.

"I don't know."

"Of course not! It's all just guessing! But massage isn't going to fix my brain! Meditation might work if I was too busy or stressed out. Massage probably does help muscle tightness, and everyone should eat less sugar. But other than the vestibular stuff, this isn't real medicine. It's what people become addicted to when medicine doesn't work and they're not ready to give up hope . . ."

David keeps talking like this, and Tess focuses as much as she can. She loves him and shares his pain, but what she thinks about is how the world of people like him must be so much larger than she's ever imagined. People look at David and see a healthy person. Even Tess does. There must be hundreds of thousands of Americans like him. And like Tess, too. But Tess is different. There's no reason to conflate the two. "Is it any consolation," Tess asks, "that people all over are hurting like you are?"

"I don't know. Maybe," he says. "Yes."

And imagine, she thinks, if she extends the suffering beyond those with faulty neurology. Everywhere people are afflicted with arthritis, cancer, nerve damage, sciatica, Lyme, whatever candida is, and who knows what else that makes every day impossible. People tell them to relax or to drink more water or to take some time and just get away for a while, when it should go without saying that the pain follows you on vacation and that if water helped they'd know it by now. They're preyed upon by hucksters, con artists, crooks, and swindlers who peddle all kinds of alternative methods that "the scientific community doesn't want you to know about," or that "people in China have been using for thousands of years," or that "just haven't caught on" or been "adequately researched" yet.

She tells David to stop reading the message board. He has access to a real neurologist. He has a loving family. It's not going to last three years, and if it does, she'll be there with him. She doesn't say that she'll be with him no matter what, but she wants to.

On Tess's birthday, Angelica visits and strokes Tess's hair as Tess cries, and then Angelica begins taking the boys out to the park most afternoons after finishing with her patients. David often asks Tess what he can do. He gets her water and yogurt. He does the dishes when there are too many in the sink. He even asks Angelica, in front of Tess, what he should do for Tess. What David and Angelica can do together. Tess wonders if they're sleeping together, but that's absurd for every reason. Angelica isn't interested in David, and they're never alone without Tess there, too.

Angelica is interested in the kids. The kids seem a little too interested in her. But Tess watches happily as Angelica massages moisturizer into their skin after giving them a bath.

"Did you have music today?" Angelica asks Max. "No, sorry, Thursdays is movement, not music, right?"

"Ha-ha-ha-ha!" Max laughs. "Tursday no moven! Friday moven!"

Angelica laughs with him. Gives him a hug.

"That's not fair, Aunt Angie, you hugged Maxy and not me," Ethan says, so Angelica hugs Ethan, too.

David sits with that machine on his face, no longer ashamed of it in front of the boys, who play with their limousines and Legos. He says that in virtual reality, he is at the circus, the park, a Yankees game. He prefers the virtual world to the real one. Sometimes the boys repeat with him, "I'm learning that change is safe," or, "I am imagining everything I want coming true." The three of them seem to enjoy it. Ethan says the news is boring. Max sits close to Ethan. When Ethan goes to the bathroom, Max sits next to the toilet, on the floor. Sometimes Ethan is vicious with Max, but usually he is sweet. Ethan helps Max with his pull-ups and tries to get him to use the potty. They start sleeping in the same bed. They ask to take baths. They cry for a while, but then they stop. Tess loves them so much. She loves them as she didn't know herself capable of love. The most powerful emotion she feels is love for her boys. It's over-whelming sometimes, their fragility and her love. She lies in bed at eleven in the morning, before or after her first or second shower, at two in the afternoon without having eaten, at one in the morning listening to David moan in his sleep, and she thinks about how much she loves her boys. How they are everything to her.

That she can't let her children starve is the clearest thought she's had since she visited her father. She needs money, and credit card debt is impossible with all the additional money they'll need in the future considering neither of them are work-ing. She's back to her old self, or at least it's a good sign that she's planning ahead. They have to retain good credit in case of an emergency after this emergency. That's the important thing. Life is a series of emergencies. Or at least a life is defined by its emergencies. Some moments are so important and all the rest don't matter at all. She's flooded by nuggets of pseudo-wisdom as Google teaches her about pawnbrokers. The moral seems to be that it's better to sell valuables than pawn them. You make more money and are no longer psychologically attached to the items. You sell them and move on. Whatever it is, it's just a thing. Even if it's a symbolic thing.

The question is whether to tell David, and the answer is obvious. If she tells David, he'd forbid it. He'd be simultane-ously failing his wife and her late mother. He'd try to go back to work or find another way to make money. Put himself in danger. Whereas if she just goes ahead and sells it, all he can do is be angry. But he'd get over it. They have their wedding rings, too. It's not like the engagement ring is the only sign of their love. What's the point of passing down value from gen-eration to generation if, when that value is needed to save one generation, it's not taken advantage of? She has twelve dollars in her bank account, and David has two hundred. Rent is due, though Google says that in New York City she can live in an apartment without paying rent for a few months. It's very difficult to evict. But imagine the kids going through that.

"I'm going to take a walk," she says.

"That's wonderful!" David says.

There's something lovely about how delicately he treats her in spite of his own fragility. He's making this easy for her. She panics on the stairs that she forgot the ring, but it's there on her left ring finger where it's been for eight years.

There's a store on a side street just north of Times Square. The cramped jewelry store she's walked by a thousand times on the way to work is dense with watches, necklaces, and rings. Real diamonds and gold. Prices are attached on little tags, even on the pieces in the window: $22,000; $19,500; $6,000; $920; $51,000. She's always wondered who comes here—to the theater district—to spend fifty-one grand on a bracelet, but the answer must be tourists or connoisseurs or very rich men looking to impress their girlfriends or wives.

It takes an hour to get there. The C train is ten blocks from her apartment and drops her a few blocks from the store. It's the first time she's been outside for weeks, but she's not blown away by the wind or scared of the crowds. The weather is good. It's late spring. She's comfortable in a T-shirt, jeans, and a hooded sweatshirt. She showered and shaved her legs and under her arms. She's a New Yorker. Nothing here is new to her, but seeing a dirty white guy with a cardboard sign saying Bus Fare Home to My Family in Kansas reminds her that she almost certainly qualifies for disability or Medicaid or welfare or food stamps or some social program that provides a safety net for people whose lives have been crushed by illness. She knows she's depressed. She'd consider antidepressants now. Meds work for her father, or so he says.

But everything costs money. They've had great health care for years, and doctors still cost hundreds of dollars. She presses the diamond with her middle finger on her right hand, then presses harder until it hurts, and she wants to keep pressing. She closes her right hand over her left and presses the soft underbelly of her middle finger as hard as she can into the diamond. She can take the pain. She separates herself from it. It's the fatigue that stops her. Two or three minutes of such a tight grip, and she no longer controls her fingers. They are their own entity and too weak to keep clenching. She discovers herself in a crouch up against the wall of a Citibank. She stands, shakes blood back into her hands, jumps up and down a few times.

She avoids the worst of Times Square instinctively, uses scaffolding to create some extra walking room, avoids Forty-second for the crowds and Forty-fifth for the memories. The tourists are friendly. They always are. So are the people selling them souvenirs. The T-shirts look like they're made from good-quality cotton. The little baby onesies have witty phrases on them. Someone in New York Loves Me, and Mommy Is Way More Fun Now That She Can Drink Again. Tess buys a chocolate bar at a newsstand and eats the whole thing. She'd forgotten how delicious chocolate is.

The jewelry store is even smaller inside than she imagined. An obese, intelligent-looking man reads *The New York Times*. "Lemme know if ya need any help," he says without glancing up. Tess studies the cramped glass cabinets for rings that look like hers.

"You buy?" she says.

"Always willin'a take a look." It's as though he's a regional theater actor playing an old-timey New Yorker.

Tess removes the ring from her finger. It's easy to do. She's lost weight.

He rotates his stool and reaches for the ring, but, locating a magnifying glass, he doesn't look up at her.

"What'd'ya know aboud'it?" he says.

"It was first bought," Tess says, "as far as I know, in the thirties or forties, but I don't know its origins before that."

"Okay, miss. Gimme a moment?"

He alternates between the jeweler's glass and his laptop. Her diamond is a little bit larger than average, but doesn't compare to the ones with the fifty-thousand-dollar price tags. Tess is determined not to take less than ten thousand dollars. She will leave, have it appraised, and return if necessary.

Now she's so tired she can't stand, so she sits against the base of a display case. The sugar from the chocolate, that she hasn't been out of the apartment for so long, the musky smell of cloth, metal, polish, and carpeting—she needs to sit and hope it's a number bigger than ten thousand. Or that it's not. Then, either way, she can go home to David and help him get better. Do something about something. At least take the boys to school. She desperately wants the money, and she desperately wants the ring. This is the meaning of have your cake and eat it, too. She wants to have her ring and sell it, too.

"I'm just gonna make one quick call and I'll le'cha know what I can give ya," the man says. "Hang tight. Can I ge'cha a bottle'a water or some'n?"

"A water sounds great, please," Tess says. Sometime later she's holding an unopened bottle of Poland Spring.

"Mommy is up in heaven with the other angels," her aunt repeated until Tess asked her to stop. It wasn't her mom she was worried about. She wanted her mom back for herself. She wanted to hug her mom and be held by her. She wanted to have her mom rub her back at night and cook the meals she used to make. Tess didn't care if her mom was in heaven waiting for her. Tess wanted her at that moment, as a seven-year-old. The thought that her mom was somewhere up there was too tantalizing. Tess could never get any closer. If Tess's mom was gone, Tess wanted her to be gone. It was terrible to think that she was up there, accessible only in death.

Nevertheless, thirty years later, Bible quotations helped Tess build the courage to sell the ring. "Set your minds on things above, not on earthly things" from Colossians. That makes sense, even if heaven doesn't exist. It makes sense to value higher-order principles like the well-being of her sons over any earthly object. "But the day of the Lord will come like a thief. The heavens will disappear with a roar; the elements will be destroyed by fire, and the earth and everything done in it will be laid bare" from Peter also has a useful logic to it. There won't be any end-of-days rapture, but she will die, and death will come like a thief, taking everything away from her. If she has something of use now, she should use it.

"Sorry to keep ya waitin'. Y'okay?" Their eyes meet for the first time. His, behind glasses, are professional, not personal. This comes as a relief.

"I'm fine, thanks," Tess says, and stands, unzips her sweatshirt. She opens the water and takes a sip. She wasn't thirsty, nor does she feel more stable after drinking.

"It's a nice piece," he says. "I can give you eleven five and probably sell it myself for close to twenty. I wanna tell you that now so you don't pass the store and think I ripped y'off. That happened recently. Some guy comes in yellin' that now I'm sayin' it's worth twice what I gave'm. Let him try'a sell that watch for ten grand. With the risk I'm takin', and the money I'm shellin' out up front, eleven five is the most I c'n'offer. And I don't bargain. That's what I c'n'offer. Is that in the range you are comfortable with?"

"It is," Tess says. "Thank you."

19

The Brooklyn Courtesy Dental Clinic is staffed by CUNY students and DDS volunteers. For the past month, Angelica has been spending three or four evenings a week there, monitoring and mentoring, jumping in when necessary. At 11:00 p.m., after fifteen hours of dentistry broken up only by subways and salads, Angelica leans over a middle-aged woman's mouth. Angelica could live a hundred more years, and her teeth would never look like this woman's, though the woman—Polish, Angelica guesses—is probably only five or six years older than she is.

It's obvious once you think about it, but most poor adults haven't been to the dentist in years. A tooth rots, they feel pain, and only then do they find someone to repair or pull it. Of course there are exceptions. And maybe it's the minority Angelica sees at the clinic, and most poor people prioritize their oral hygiene. The point is that if you're poor and have bad teeth, you have really bad teeth.

Treating such dire cases has made tending to patients with good insurance who come in for semiannual cleanings and checkups seem kind of absurd. But even at her private practice, Angelica spends most of her time working on alleviating pain—root canals and extractions. Her hygienists do the cleaning, scheduling, even fittings for mouth guards and superficial fillings so Angelica can focus on those in serious need. Medicine can be miraculous. For weeks, a man can't sleep or laugh, can hardly talk, can't chew on one side of his mouth, and after two hours in her care he is healed.

Angelica can't get enough of it. Until Tazio left for DC, she'd been dependent on his whims, waiting for him to settle down as if she were some kind of 1950s secretary courting her Brylcreemed boss. And before that, she was desperate for a permanent place in Gerard's fully formed life in order to escape the aimless, lonely, and, in retrospect, depressed existence she'd been working (and snorting) her way through.

But now—surrounded by white-coated dental students, and tenderly tapping with her mirror on a corroded molar porous as a coral reef—Angelica has more clients than she has time for. She took out a small business loan, bought out her indolent partner, and hired two dentists on salary. She's planning to expand into the adjacent space. Falling asleep, she fantasizes about the bigger office, the bigger practice, the patients coming in in pain and leaving able to live their best lives.

Her apartment in Fort Greene has great natural light, and all the appliances are stainless steel. She makes more money than her father did, and is able to send cousins in Chiang Mai all sorts of American crap—PlayStation games, barbecue sauce—they love her for. She has friends from her party days, and from high school, college, and dental school. She has family she loves. Parents who still love each other. And she'll be able to remove this patient's molar and save the woman some pain.

She loves Tazio, but he isn't her life. Without him, she isn't lonely. He isn't her meaning. He's her boyfriend. Her fiancé. Or he was. She's not sure—they haven't spoken in weeks—but either way, she'll be okay. She'll marry him, or find someone else. Or she'll be happy alone. Likewise, she wants kids, but she doesn't need kids in order to be happy. She's frozen her eggs, so there's no rush. If Tazio comes around—becomes a different person?—or she finds someone else, or if she decides she has it in her to parent alone, she's only forty. She has a good five years to figure that part out. She is, for the first time she can remember, relaxed.

It's not only distance from Tazio that has allowed Angelica to focus on what makes her feel good—it's also having seen Gerard so weak, sorry, tired, old, sad, and scared. There have been so few unsullied victories. David and Tess got back together, but they seem to be irreparably damaged and causing each other increasing levels of anguish. Dozens of women accused Trump (and Cosby, Ailes, O'Reilly) of sexual assault, and even if the accusers made some money out of it, the men (except for the dead one) are still rich and denying what everyone knows to be true. And then, Tess, in trying to reproduce Angelica's success-in-confrontation, left her father's house with more questions than she'd had before. This wasn't just a typical case of Messy Tessy. It was the emotional nucleus of a woman's life exposed and then denied. Tess left her father's house doubting her own memory. But Gerard had substantiated, authenticated, corroborated her pain.

"Ow!" the woman says, her tongue frantically caressing the suction tube.

"You'll be okay," Angelica says. "I promise."

After returning from their trip to Tess's father's house, Tess doesn't bother to acknowledge weeks of Angelica's emails and texts. Then one morning Facebook reports that it's Tess's birthday, and Tess doesn't respond to any of the birthday posts by lunchtime, so Angelica takes the afternoon off and brings flowers. She leans on the buzzer for twenty, thirty seconds before the door clicks open. She walks up the three flights. Knocks. It's Ethan who greets her.

"I can't reach the button without 'tanding on a chair!" he says.

Max cowers behind his brother's leg. Angelica is relieved they're okay, though it's the middle of a school day, and they're home in their pajamas.

"I'm Angelica, Tazio's friend," she says.

"I *know* that!" Ethan says. "Silly."

"Tazo and Angie?" Max says.

"Just me. Angie," she says. "Where are Mommy and Daddy?"

"Asleep," Ethan says.

"Dey *bery bery tired*!" Max says, and then he laughs and sings "Ring around the Rosy." The song takes a long time, and Ethan waits patiently. Max doesn't fall down at the end. He just looks up and says "Yay!" and claps his hands, waiting for the others to join him, so they do.

Angelica hugs the boys. It feels good to have them in her arms. They trust her with their bodies. She opens the door further, and the apartment confirms her fears. What must have been a large pool of milk has dried on the rug and floor, construction paper is scattered in the corner with a bottle of Elmer's Glue glued between two sheets, crusts of sandwiches litter the table, sippy cups are everywhere, and yellowed diapers—four or five of them, and that's what she's been smelling—have been shoved under the TV stand.

"Tess? David?" Angelica calls, and when they don't answer, she approaches their bedroom. The boys follow her. Tess and David are in bed. David might be sleeping, but Angelica doesn't think so. Tess's eyes are wide open and unfocused.

"Come on, Ethan," Angelica says. "Let's get this place cleaned up."

It takes a while, but Angelica and Ethan fill up a few garbage bags. Max has a great time waving around a broom. He's giddy for the attention. Ethan is serious about the work. They don't discuss how the apartment came to look like this. Angelica sets the boys up in front of a cartoon where the girl is an owl, and the villain wants to steal the moon.

At first, David's eyes are closed, but he says, "Thank you," and then shifts his weight to his feet on the floor, stands slowly, and gropes his way to the bathroom.

"I'm going to help," Angelica says, stroking Tess's hair. "I'm so sorry. I didn't realize."

"It's okay," Tess says, but she's already crying.

Angelica lies down and hugs her. When David comes out of the bathroom, he leaves the two women and sits with the boys in front of the television.

Angelica is going to talk to him, but he's wearing virtual reality goggles. She laughs. She can't help herself. It's all too horrible. And now with the goggles? David is this big guy in a humungous yellow New York Urban Professionals Basketball T-shirt. The villain isn't trying to steal the moon. She gets her power from it. Tess is still in bed. It's a miracle these kids are alive.

What a world! Angelica was jealous of Tess, that Tess was and will always be David's first priority. And sure, Angelica can admit that she's been jealous of Tess for her kids, too. But what the fuck is going on? How is it possible that all this love isn't more powerful than whatever the fuck is happening here?

She spends the evening making calls and Googling. The next day she returns in the afternoon.

"Sign this," Angelica says.

"What is it?"

It's lunchtime, but Tess won't eat. She's having a bad day. The kids are devouring slice after slice of a pizza Angelica brought. She'd forgotten that David can't eat gluten or dairy.

"I need your signature. As your mother's next of kin," Angelica says. Once she found the right department—the Office of the Chief Medical Examiner—everyone she spoke to was lovely.

"The cause of death is public," Angelica continues, repeating what she'd memorized the night before. "Heart failure. Plea-bargained down to criminally negligent homicide. But in order to know if there was a knife involved, I need the autopsy report."

Tess rolls over away from her.

"Tess?"

Tess curls up into a ball.

"Jesus Christ," Angelica says. "Sign the fucking paper."

"Why are you being so nice to me?" Tess says.

Angelica almost respects Tess for letting herself appear so pathetic in front of, well, anyone.

"Stop it," Angelica says. "I like you."

Two weeks later, Angelica has been coming over almost every afternoon. She brings groceries, takes the boys to the park, cleans.

David thanks her. He tells her that Tess came back from their road trip nonfunctional. That he was wrong to have encouraged Tess to go. Angelica learns that David's parents don't know what's been going on. She calls his mom, and the two of them begin alternating mornings and afternoons. The boys are so grateful to Angelica and their grandmother. They run to Angelica and hug her each morning. Angelica changes Max's pull-ups, wipes Ethan, bathes them, hugs them, feeds them. Their school is on the way to Angelica's office and, the truth is, she likes taking them on the subway, people standing up so they can sit down, dropping them off with their teachers. The boys hug her before they enter their classrooms. She reminds them to take their water bottle or art project or sneakers out of their backpacks. Angelica finds she loves it, taking care of the boys. It is good, and she is good. She feels almost as if she's stepped into another, better life, until one morning a teacher refers to her as the boys' nanny and the whole day is spoiled. But that night she thinks it over. Even if this new life with the boys is really just her old ugly real life, all the same, it is good, she is good. She's tired, sore, but happy. Happiness has snuck up on her.

"Stop that," Angelica says. "Eath, stop. Try to find a way to be nice."

It's the afternoon, she's given them their snack. Ethan drops pieces of construction paper on the floor. Tenderly he takes Max's hand and leads him out of the room. Tess and Angelica watch them go.

"Thank you," Tess says.

"For what?" Angelica says, stooping to pick up the largest scrap of paper. She smooths it out on the coffee table. Angelica peers into the next room, where Ethan seems to be teaching Max a game that involves pulling Kleenexes from a box.

Angelica sits back down next to Tess and looks at her, the laugh lines around Tess's mouth, and is reminded that Tess is an adult, too. Without warning, Angelica is livid. "For what?" she repeats.

She wants Tess to thank her for mothering her children. More than that, she wants Tess's children to have a mother.

Tess hunches down, nosing her way onto Angelica's lap. Angelica strokes her hair.

"It turns out you're my best friend," Tess says, her eyes filling with tears. "You're so good with them."

"I love the boys, you know that," Angelica says, still stroking Tess's hair and now also thumbing her tears away as they swell up from her eyes. Tess purrs.

"David never touches me."

But as much as Angelica feels for her, some part of her wants to withhold this comfort. She wants Tess to earn it.

"My mother used to do that," Tess says, her eyes closed.

Angelica's breath catches.

It was Angelica's father who worked long days, came to every parent-teacher conference and softball game, and put her to bed every night. Her mother didn't see the value in making a big deal of everything. But she managed to speak Thai fluently just six months after moving to Chiang Mai a few years ago. What could her mother have accomplished had she been a white—or even Thai—man?

But then: "Sorry," Tess says. "I'm sorry."

"Are you actually?" Angelica says. She'd planned on telling Tess today, but now she doesn't know.

"What?" Tess says.

"Are you actually sorry?" Angelica says. She stops stroking.

"What do you mean? Of course I'm sorry," Tess says.

"Fine, then," Angelica says. She shifts her legs sharply away from Tess, and Tess has to sit up to avoid clunking her head on the carpet. Angelica knows Tess is suffering and deserves assurance and relief, but she doesn't know if that's what's best for Tess. She wants what's best for Tess to be a scolding, because she wants to scold Tess. Wake her up.

" 'Fine, then'?" Tess says.

"*Fine, then,*" Angelica says. "You say you're sorry, you're sorry."

"Uh, my father killed my mother?"

Christ.

"Everybody's got issues," Angelica says.

She can't look at Tess now. She's picking up the smaller pieces of ripped-up construction paper from the carpet. Angelica feels guilt, but that guilt is tinged with disgust—the kind of disgust she sometimes felt for the alcoholics and coke zombies at Abel and Cain.

"Well," Tess says, "everybody hasn't gone through what I've gone through."

Angelica forces herself to look at her.

"And everybody hasn't gotten married and had two kids," Angelica says. "Figure it out. Why do you get to hang on to your excuses forever? You *don't* get to hang on to your excuses forever. And I found out. There was no knife. Your father told the truth." All the anger drains out of Angelica as she's reporting the news. She hadn't stopped to think about what it meant that Tess misremembered the most important day of her life.

Angelica tries to explain: "You must have conflated two instances, or said something to the detective and kept on repeating it. I'm sorry. I shouldn't have snapped at you. I care for you and want you to feel better. I'll email you some articles, but this kind of memory mix-up is super common. People spend their whole lives . . . Like I heard on the radio about this one girl who refused to accept that she hadn't seen her brother get hit by a car, when really he was murdered while she was sleeping. The brain is good at turning stories into memories."

"But I was there. I saw the blood. David remembers. I told him I saw the blood. And now you're telling me that's not right?"

"I don't know," Angelica says. "I'm just telling you what the report said."

"But . . . Fine, even if that is the case, it doesn't change anything."

"You mean—"

"He still hit her. And me. He denies that, but I remember it. Unless I can't trust anything I remember anymore."

Angelica doesn't know what she's done. No. It's still good that she knows. In case she sees her father again, she should know what happened that day. Just for herself. This is better.

"Fuck," Tess says, all mixed up.

"Mommy said a bad word," Ethan says. He is watching from the doorway. Max is still pulling Kleenexes out of the box.

"Mommy's sorry," Angelica says, setting the little pile of shredded paper on the coffee table and crawling on all fours toward Tess's boys.

"Aunt Angie's right," Tess says. Ethan and Max look up at her. "I'm going to do better."

"Okay, Mommy," Ethan says. Angelica has already picked up Max, who is giggling and oblivious again.

Ethan's eyes are on Tess. She is still their mother.

"I promise you I'll try."

But next time Angelica visits, Tess looks worse. Her collarbone presses more prominently against her skin, and her dark hair and light eyes are both so dull they've begun to meet somewhere in the graying middle. Tess says she's been trying. She doesn't want to see someone about it. She'll do more, Angelica will see.

Angelica makes some calls. One morning when the boys are at school, Angelica and David and David's mother all sit Tess down in the living room. They demand she see a psychologist. Angelica has found some names. There's a woman who focuses on depression, a patient of Angelica's, whom she confided in when she was worried about Tazio. The patient was kind and seemed smart. But Tess is incensed.

"Another patient of yours? I'm sorry," she says. "You guys stage an intervention and *I'm* its target? David spends his days in those useless fucking goggles imagining he's skiing down an empty mountain! How do we know that all this money is actually helping him? This is all such bullshit. Yeah, I'm depressed. Wouldn't you be? I've spent my life seeing psychologists. Generalists and trauma specialists, and they all say they can help me and none of them do. Just like David and his doctors. But at least I admit it. All these doctors have answers, but there is no answer. My father killed my mom and is off living his best life. My husband is an invalid. I quit. It's a rational decision. My kids are taken care of. And thank you. I'm grateful for you two. But this shit with the goggles? We don't even know if it's working!"

Angelica stares at Tess, not knowing whether to indulge her. David's mom has closed her eyes. David is crying.

"I admit I've been wondering the same thing," David's mom says gently.

Maybe, Angelica thinks, she likes being around David and Tess for the same reason she likes being around her patients. She can relieve them of their pain.

"Dave," David's mom says. "Does Monica do any tests with you? Something she could show us?"

"She just"—David pauses, rubs his temples, swallows—"asks me to rate on a scale from one to ten how I'm feeling. She can show you the record of that. And in the beginning I was at a one or two every time, but now it's threes, and even a four or five sometimes. I've been going to the store more. There are always bananas and eggs here now when Tess wants them."

"No. I mean anything objective?" his mother says.

David's mom is smart and helpful. Helpful with the kids, incisive now when she needs to be. Tess retreats to the bedroom. She tends to avoid David's mom.

"Fine with me," David says. "Ask her. I'll try everything. I want to try. I'm trying."

. . . .

Monica agrees to an objective measurement. A simple balance test, the results of which are written on the whiteboard mounted on the fridge. First thing every Monday morning, David balances on one foot on top of a stack of books, and he records how many seconds it takes before he falls off.

WEEK 1: 10

WEEK 2: 22

WEEK 3: 25

WEEK 4: 12

WEEK 5: 15

WEEK 6: 67

WEEK 7: 20

Angelica arrives to pick up the boys and take them to school right before the week eight experiment occurs.

David falls after sixteen seconds.

"Fuck!" David says. "Let me try again. Just once more."

The boys are in the bathroom brushing their teeth and turning the faucets off and on.

"David," Tess says.

Angelica microwaves frozen peas and chicken nuggets for the boys' lunches. She fills up their water bottles. There's a bit more water in Max's, so she evens them out.

"I don't want to stop," David says.

Since giving a set of keys to Angelica, David and Tess no longer guard themselves in front of her. They cry, argue, walk around in towels.

Sometimes all three at the same time.

David is pleading: "She's helping me, even if the goggles aren't working yet. We talk about strategies to manage symptoms. She taught me how to control my breath."

"We can't afford this," Tess says. "We have to save money for whatever the next thing is."

"It's your money. From the commercials. I know. But we're still married," David says.

"Still?" Tess says, tying her bathrobe tighter.

"We are still married, aren't we?"

"Yes," Tess says. Now she does lower her voice, though not enough to prevent Angelica from hearing. "Of course. I told you I'm not leaving you. Stop worrying about that. It's not my money. It's our money. But it's time. You've been doing this for months and it's not working."

"It is working. Slowly. It can't be for nothing," David says. "I'll work harder. Monica is helping me work harder. I'll feel better."

"You've been trying, and things are getting worse."

"They're not getting worse. You're not noticing it, but I'm improving. Or not improving. But I'm doing more. I'm trying so hard."

"I'm trying, too," Tess says. "But look at our life."

"That's you—not me. I've been better over the last couple weeks. You're the one who's changed. Sorry. It's not about that. The last year can't have been for nothing."

"Not nothing," Tess says.

This is the longest Angelica has heard them talk for weeks. It's, well, thrilling. She's sure one of them will break down, but they keep going.

"It's a process of elimination," Tess says. "You tried four people. One might have helped. She didn't. It's been, what, six months? You move on. Throwing good money after bad isn't going to help. When's your next appointment with Dr. Saltman?"

"Two weeks," David says.

"He'll change your meds, then. That could do it."

It won't, Angelica thinks. She's behind the kitchen island, trying to make herself invisible.

"It won't," David says. "You know that. A different SSRI? A higher dose? You—"

"What?" Tess says.

David is silent. He looks up at Tess.

"You can't have sold your ring for nothing," David says.

Angelica looks at Tess's hand and sees the diamond missing. *Fuck*. She could have lent them money. She would have said yes in a heartbeat had they asked.

"You know?" Tess says. "You knew?"

"How could I not have known?" he says.

"You mope around dizzy and a mess, not noticing anything, not noticing that the kids haven't bathed for a week, and I'm supposed to think you're focused on my fingers? You fucking fucker fucking knew and left me in the fucking dark?"

Angelica, terrified, cranes her neck to look for the kids, but they are still in the bathroom, not hearing, or pretending not to hear.

David is panting and holding his head. He's always holding his head. They're both having difficulty catching their breath. Angelica has finished packing the boys' backpacks and is cleaning off the counter, finding ways to stay away in the kitchen while they talk this through.

"I thought that's what you wanted!" he says. "The one day you leave the house, mysterious commercial money finally comes in? Come on. You didn't think I'd ever notice?"

"Why—?" Tess says.

"What was there to say? Thank you? I love you? That you would do something like that, and not tell me, but just do it? In your condition? I was ashamed!"

Angelica feels hope for them, and with it, jealousy. He's kinder than Tess is and Tess is more attractive; she's more selfish, and he's more . . . doofy, but—even the way they're able to fight—they're still so in love with each other.

"I want to see Monica," he says. "I'll stop doing the goggles if you want. But she's the only one who makes me feel any better."

Angelica flinches, Tess freezes.

"Other than you, I mean. And the kids."

"Fine," Tess says.

"You sure?" David says.

"It's two hundred a week for just the sessions?"

"Yes."

"Fine," Tess says. "She really makes you feel better?"

"I don't know! I think. I've been doing more lately. I called school and explained why the kids hadn't been going. I was able to make it through the call without getting too blurry to think. But there are too many factors. The kids, your mood, how I sleep, what I eat, nightmares, meds. My brain is broken. I want to keep seeing her. I think I'll get better."

"That's fine," Tess says. "I understand."

Angelica doesn't understand.

That Friday, David's mother is sick, and Angelica has a patient she can't reschedule.

When she arrives in the afternoon, David meets her at the door. He's smiling. "I did it. I was able to do it. Ethan sat on my lap on the train, and Max just played. It was so great. I was symptomatic. Really dizzy for a bit. But Ethan understood and held Max's hand. Nothing bad happened."

David begins taking them to school every Friday, which allows Angelica an extra morning to get to work before seven. David does seem a bit better. Well enough at least for Angelica to take occasional afternoons off away from him and Tess. But she's gotten into the habit of taking a couple of hours between work and the clinic, so she has started to run on the treadmill in her building's basement gym. The screaming television is always on MSNBC, and it takes as much energy to ignore the news as it does to get through three miles.

And then one afternoon Tazio is on the screen. "I can't guarantee anything," he says. "All I can do is let the American public in on what everyone is saying inside the beltway, which is that Donald Trump, in spite of his inclinations to infuriate many of my ilk, or perhaps because of those inclinations, is doing a much better job than anyone expected."

Tazio is talking to Andrea Mitchell. He wears a crisp white dress shirt with the sleeves rolled up and his grandfather's watch displayed prominently on his wrist. The chyron beneath him reads, MEXICAN AMERICAN DEMOCRATIC STRATEGIST: TRUMP DOING A GREAT JOB.

"That's quite the claim coming from someone with your background," Mitchell says. "You worked on the Hillary Clinton campaign against President Trump, and you ran John Edwards's press operations on his first run back in 2004?"

"I was a part of both teams, yes. But I'm sick of all the partisan deadlock. Look at what President Trump has done. He might be unconventional, and maybe he's a jerk, but he has moved us beyond the Second World War, finally encouraging our allies to think about how to protect themselves. He has rolled back needless red tape without our seeing any drop in GDP, the stock market, or productivity. Money is finally coming back from illegal tax shelters overseas. Factories are staying. And, most important, he's gotten politics out of the rut it's been in since Watergate.

"Listen. I'm no fan of the misogyny or race baiting. I have no love for Vladimir Putin. But after working with John Edwards and the Clintons, I've learned to judge a politician by what he or she does. Not by what he says. The truth is, President Trump and President Obama have a lot in common. They're both brilliant, charismatic leaders who lean too much on the propaganda of change in the campaign and then follow it up by keeping *some* of their promises. We *should* have more comprehensive border control. Europe *should* take charge of its own destiny. Taxes *should* be simpler. Nearly everyone agrees on these points. It's time for Democrats to acknowledge that even if we didn't initially like him, President Trump is doing an excellent job."

"What is this guy going on about?" says a man in his sixties who lifts giant weights. Andrea Mitchell asks, "So you feel his presidency has been successful thus far? The *Access Hollywood* tape, the Gold Star families, Judge Curiel: None of this gives you pause?"

"I just said it does. But these are words—before the election, mind you—not actions. On the ground, he's kept us out of new wars, improved the economy, and is solidifying the borders. He is keeping his promises. No presidency is entirely successful, but I'd say that many of us in DC are very pleasantly surprised."

Over the next week, Tazio is everywhere: MSNBC with Chris Matthews; CNN with Jake Tapper; and then Fox News in Tucker Carlson's A-block. Angelica continues taking care of the boys, but she won't talk about Tazio. She doesn't trust that Tess or at least David didn't know about this. But they ask her the same questions she wants to ask them. She doesn't respond to the calls and texts from her parents, friends, colleagues. She wouldn't know what to say.

And she doesn't call Tazio. If he doesn't reach out to her to explain whatever the fuck is going on, then it's over. He will have become something she'd need to try too hard to love.

Trump tweets the next day that Tazio has been put in charge of a task force—"Major Taskforce"—that has been charged with finding jobs for "LEGAL Americans." Later on, Tazio explains to Tucker that it's a way to show Mexicans and Latin Americans that the administration works for all Americans. The administration is only interested in combating criminals who have entered this country illegally. "My father had to wait on line," Tazio tells Tucker that evening. "So did my great-grandparents on my mother's side. It's only fair."

Tucker is trying to get Tazio to admit he's a fraud, that there's no way someone who worked for Edwards, who was basically a communist, could feel that Trump is doing a good job.

"President Trump has kept us out of new wars, improved the economy, and is solidifying the borders," Tazio says. "Sure we might disagree on the highest tax bracket's marginal rate, but that's all hashed out in committee anyway. I will try my hardest to find Latino and Latina Americans good, high-paying jobs. You're the problem if you think a lifelong Democrat can't have an open mind. Isn't that the purpose of Fox News? To make sure America is getting all sides of the story? Trump himself was a Democrat. He has asked me to work with my Latino and Latina brothers and sisters to reach full employment in their community. I am going to do just that."

Angelica finally asks what their best guess is about what Tazio is doing. Both David and Tess say they have no clue, but Angelica doesn't believe them. She leaves the apartment understanding why she has been keeping Tess and David close, why Tess and she were never friends before, why everything is as ruined as it is: all three of them are in love with Tazio. Angelica, Tess, and David, all in their own way. All in much the same way. So this feels like an equal slight to all three of them. They are all in love with this man who hasn't been worthy of anyone's love for years.

Tazio appears on Hannity's radio show, then with Mike Huckabee in conversation, and then on Tucker Carlson again. The Tuesday that Tazio's op-ed comes out in *The Washington Post* headlined, "On Wars, Economy, Borders: Trump Keeps His Promises," he is an in-studio guest on *Fox & Friends*, where he is laying out his task force's plans to work with Latinos and Latinas across the economic spectrum. From medical doctors to unskilled laborers. Tazio intimates that Trump will soon be doing the same for African Americans.

On Sunday, Angelica is about to take the boys to the playground when Chuck Todd asks Tazio repeatedly how he can so publicly support a president who said he couldn't trust a Mexican American judge when Tazio himself is Mexican American. With the travel ban and the wall . . .

"I'm certainly not a spokesman for the administration. I believe that I can serve our country by serving some of the most needy in it. Of course I think he shouldn't have said that about Judge Curiel. And I have reservations about the travel ban. But, especially after working with Governor Edwards and President and Secretary Clinton, I've learned to judge a politician by what he or she does, not says. President George H. W. Bush lied about raising taxes. President Clinton lied about his extramarital affair. President George W. Bush lied about the reasons behind the Iraq War. President Obama lied about closing Guantanamo and being able to keep your doctor on the Affordable Care Act. I have found that listening to politicians' words doesn't get you very far. Follow what actually happens. Wars, the economy, foreign terrorist attacks on US soil, solidifying the borders, fall in violent crime . . . I can go on and on."

"What about all the damage the president's critics say he has done?"

"Damage?" Tazio says. "The only real effect the president has had is that liberals in New York City and San Francisco are freaking out. Show me the actual negative effect. Where are real Americans suffering? My job is to mitigate suffering and help those in need. That's my concern. And that's President Trump's concern, too."

"Do you have any experience creating jobs?"

"For years, I've been a chief architect of Democratic jobs programs," Tazio says. "For Senator Clinton and, before that, as director of an education nonprofit. So yes. I'd say I do."

"We'll have to leave it there, but this has been an enlightening conversation with Democratic strategist and newest member of the Trump administration, Tazio Di Vincenzo. I hope to have you on again soon."

"Thanks, Chuck."

"Thank you."

Tess answers her phone and stands.

"I'll be there in between two and three hours. Calm down. In three hours or so," she says. "Stay strong until I get to you."

Summer

20

Tess drives and David sits in the passenger seat.

Teddy called her.

"I need your help," he said.

A tremor spread from her brain through her body.

"I'll be there in between two and three hours. Calm down. In three hours or so," she said. "Stay strong until I get to you."

"Yeah," he said. "Sounds good. Thanks. Thanks."

Tess ran her fingers through her hair.

There was joy in being told she had to go to the one place she most wanted to be. She wants to be with Teddy—to protect him—and she wants to return to the place where the hole opened inside her in order to try to find a way to fill it back in.

The last time she took this trip five months ago, David couldn't have done it. Now he can. Or maybe he could have then and just didn't want to as much as he does now. They are borrowing a neighbor's car because this is an emergency. The ride feels shorter than last time. They don't listen to music. They drive in silence for the first hour, and Tess imagines what she's going to find when they arrive. She's happy to have David with her even if he's incapacitated. She's happy to get them both away from home.

She can't think of a situation Teddy would need her there for, but that also could wait three hours. And she's too anxious to ask.

She'll be too late for imminent violence. He was accustomed to yelling and threats.

Tess blames herself for not having been more proactive, for not pressing Teddy when he told her that their father was still abusive. Her father appeared to be telling the truth when he said everything has been different since he's been medicated, and his wife confirmed it, but what if she was just protecting him?

She was obviously just protecting him. Tess has allowed her father to keep doing whatever it is he's doing because she's been too weak to get herself out of bed. His wife said that he was nonviolent and calm. Teddy wrote Tess that their father still hit them. Tess did nothing about it. He lied, his wife lied, and all Tess did was tell Teddy to call her if it happened again. She's thirty-eight years old. She could have—should have—called the police or gotten in touch with his parole officer or whoever is in charge of recidivism in domestic abusers and murderers. She could have stopped him as soon as she found out. Instead, she waited for Teddy to call.

So either she has enabled abuse by the same man who abused her, or Teddy is lying.

"Is Teddy lying?" she says.

"Why would he be lying?" David says.

"To see me?"

"He would have just asked."

"He has. Asked. A few times."

"When?"

"Over Messenger."

"Yeah?"

"So he could be lying?" Tess says.

"Sure. He's twelve, right?"

"Ten."

"You've been messaging with a ten-year-old?"

"He's my half brother."

They pass a field, a barn, and then a fallen crane on top of which two large birds are fighting. Tess shudders.

"At ten, sure, he could be lying. I don't think anything Ethan says is true, and he'll be ten in a few years."

"More than a few."

"I'm just saying that kids lie. But it's still worth going. I'm happy we're doing this."

"But he used the word 'trigger.' He must have heard someone say that. His mom said not to 'trigger' his father."

"So he probably isn't lying," David says. "Have you been talking to the other one, too? Levi?"

"No."

"He's twelve?"

"Yes."

"Have you been talking to your father?"

"No!"

"I'm just asking."

"Sorry, I know. I know I haven't been talking about this. About anything, really."

"It's okay. I'm just trying to figure out what we're walking into."

"I know," Tess says. "Me, too."

"I guess we hope that Teddy is lying just to see you. That would mean nothing worse is going on."

"But how messed up would that mean he is if he got all specific about abuse, waited months, and *then* called me? He's ten."

"Better than if he's getting hit. Kids imagine things."

Tess forgives David the reference to her own childhood mis-remembering. He hasn't directly brought it up or asked how it affected her. He hasn't wanted to upset her.

How has it affected her? She's less sure of everything now. Her memories. And therefore what she wants in her future. For now, it's easy. She wants to help Teddy.

She focuses again on the conversation. "I know," she says. "I'm just saying we can't hope that he's all psychologically twisted like that."

"Okay," David says. "Then what do we hope?"

"I don't know."

"Okay," David says.

"But?" Tess says.

"But this isn't your responsibility. We have our own problems, and—and I hope this doesn't happen—but I have to say it, or I should, I think? If we do walk into something . . . grisly . . . we have to remember we have our own sons to look after. We have to try to do better at home."

"You think I don't know that?" Tess says.

Tess feels spent, as if she's been crying. But she hasn't. They're speaking calmly. Or if not calmly, it seems to Tess as if logic is driving the conversation more than emotion. And that's good. Sitting next to David feels comfortable. In the same way his arms and big body always felt comfortable. She doesn't need to talk if she doesn't want to. They can sit together without pressure. She realizes how much she'd missed this feeling. It had been more than two years. Since before Jonah.

"So," David says. "This might be nothing, or it might be really hard. Just remember that our boys are okay. We'll do whatever we can here, but then we'll go home to Ethan and Max and start parenting them again. We've gotten really lucky."

"Yes."

"And we'll try harder."

"Angelica said the same thing. And I am trying. But you can't try to be less depressed," Tess says.

"Is that true?" David says. "People say you can't just try not to drink, that you need a program or whatever, and Tazio's been okay for years. He's just trying."

"Tazio should be my role model here?" Tess says, and they both laugh. "You seem a little better," Tess says.

"Thanks for noticing," David says.

"Do you *feel* better?" Tess says.

"Not really," David says. "But I've been doing more. I've been better at imagining the life I want to live. You okay?"

"I think so," Tess says. "Yes."

She wants him to know all her feelings before everything changes, which, she can tell, it's about to. She will feel better before he does. He might be trying, but there's only so much he can do. Even if it is psychosomatic, it's the neuropsych part that's the problem. No one doubts the problem is in his brain. "Psychosomatic" isn't even right. It's more like there's probably a psychology that is affecting his neurology. But, driving down Route 6, she feels on the verge of a change. A quickening of her pulse. An eagerness for the next hour and day. She's felt this before as she's escaped the misery. She forgot all about this feeling. And it might mean nothing, but she embraces it. She wants David to know that it will be okay if she gets a little better and he continues to suffer. Seeing Tazio on television has helped her. And then Teddy's call. She doesn't know why they've helped or if this new momentum, adrenaline, or release is sustainable, and a lot will depend on what happens today, but she's confident for the first time in months. Finding out she can't trust her own memory has been freeing. At first she feared that the mother she remembers might not exist. That she'd lost all connection to the real woman. But maybe that's okay. More than okay—liberating. What is the reality of an abused-then-murdered mother to a young girl? How could Tess have possibly remembered her with any real accuracy? Her mother, Tazio, Jonah. All of it might be wrong. She can start over because, why not? She doesn't know where she's starting.

"You've had it rough," Tess says. But she must have said more, because David is trying not to let her see him cry. She must have said something wrong.

"I'm sorry," she says.

"No—" he says, as she says, "I just want you to know how hard all this—that I know how hard your life is."

He reaches for her with his left hand, which she brings to her lips. She should have waited to go with David that first time she saw her father. Even when David's not himself, he knows how to look after her in a way no one else has since she was a little girl.

"I know these months are my fault," David says. "I know what I'm like to—"

"Wait, fuck, shit, this is the turn," Tess says.

"Seriously?"

"Yes, be quiet!"

"Okay, Tess."

The unpaved driveway is longer than she remembers. There's no purple car on the bed of gray pebbles. Four bikes lean against the vinyl siding alongside lacrosse sticks and a bag of what might be hockey equipment. Trees are bursting with birdsong and pink and white flowers.

Teddy runs out to greet their car.

"You're here!" Teddy says.

Barefoot, in gray cotton shorts and a sleeveless undershirt, he looks barely older than Ethan.

"Teddy?" Tess says in a voice that must hint at her surprise, because Teddy retreats from his initial enthusiasm into false apathy.

Tess rushes to undo whatever pain she's caused, and opens her arms wide. Teddy runs to her and wraps his arms around her waist. He is young. This is the first time they've touched. Teddy doesn't smell like Ethan or Max. There's something peppery—or maybe just older—in his sweat.

"What's going on?" Tess says softly into her brother's ear. "We're here."

"Is he . . . ?" Teddy says, pulling away.

"I'm David," David says. "Nice to meet you."

"You don't look that sick," Teddy says.

"It's something in my brain. So you can't see it."

"Oh," Teddy says.

"So what's going on here?" Tess says.

Any moment, one of Teddy's parents will interrupt them.

"Not much," Teddy says. "How 'bout you?"

"Then why did you call me?"

"Oh! Because Pop found out."

"What?" Tess says.

"Pop found out."

"Found out what?" Tess says.

"That we've been talking. I know you didn't want him to, and I'm really, really sorry. I just didn't know what to say when I accidentally said that you told me how to do a math problem the way that my math teacher just told me to, too. Pop said, 'How'd you know,' to me about you, and I didn't know what to say, so I just told him we were talking because I don't like lying. I'm really, really sorry."

"That's okay," Tess says, holding him into her chest and rubbing his back. "You didn't do anything wrong. It's okay."

"Is everything okay?" David says.

Tess stands, and Teddy hides behind her. She's not much

taller than he is, but he's pressing against her side just like Max does when he feels shy.

"You must be David!" Tess hears from the door, which makes her cringe, which makes Teddy grab on to her and then retreat.

No sign of their mother. Levi joins their father at the door.

"I am," David says. "You're Tess's dad?"

"I am. Andrew."

"David," David says.

There are too many people Tess is worrying about.

"Is there a problem here?" David says.

"I don't think so," Tess's father says. "Is there, Theo?"

"No," Teddy says softly.

"Is there, Theo?" Levi says in a mocking voice—though it's unclear if he's mocking Teddy or their father—from the doorway. Tess wills herself not to dislike Levi. He's just a kid in a stressful situation.

"With all due respect, I wasn't asking you," David says to Tess's father. "I was asking Teddy. Is there a problem, Teddy? Is there another reason you called your sister? Something we can help you with?"

Teddy looks to Levi, who stares back with silent instructions.

"No," Teddy says. "Sorry."

"It's okay," David says.

"Where's your mom?" Tess asks Teddy.

"Out," Tess's father says.

Here is the man Tess remembers. There's an equal chance he'll lie, yell, cry, hit, or apologize. Tess had forgotten her visceral fear of his unpredictability. She finds herself motionless even as she wants to move.

"She left just now," Teddy says. His brother's eyes again command him to be silent, but Teddy can't help himself.

"Why?" David says.

"She'll be back soon," Teddy says.

The trees have grown dense. Each tree has a million branches and each branch has a million flowers. Such bright whites and pinks probably don't last longer than a few weeks each year. They're so beautiful, and there's nothing to look at other than the trees and one another. Levi stands in the doorway. Tess's father, a few steps out from the house toward Tess, forms a triangle with Tess and David around Teddy.

"She's at work," Levi says. His voice is deeper now than it was five months ago.

"At school on Saturday?" David says.

"School?" Tess's father says. He's out on the driveway now.

"Isn't she a teacher?" David asks Tess.

"A nurse," Tess's father says. "A medical assistant. Technician."

"May we come in?" David says.

"I'm not sure that's a great idea," Tess's father says. Tess begins to panic. Breathes deeply. Remembers that her only limits are physical. She prepares her body to enter the house.

"She'll come back," Teddy says. "Soon."

"Come back?" David says.

"What happened?" Tess says.

Tess leaves Teddy, pushes past her father, past Levi, and through the front door, where she sees plates shattered on the kitchen floor, a broom and dustpan out, cracked glass in the cabinet doors, and the stovetop black metal grates strewn across the counter. And somehow, though she'd missed it the first time— and though it startles but doesn't surprise her now—a TRUMP MAKE AMERICA GREAT AGAIN! red-and-white magnet occupies the center of the yellowing refrigerator door.

"David!" Tess yells. David's there with her. They both turn to Tess's father, who followed them in.

"What happened?" David asks Tess's father, and then, to Teddy in a softer voice, "What happened here?"

"Pop found out I was keeping the secret about talking to Tess and he got angry, so Mom left to find a place for us to go," Teddy says.

"You fucking ass-rat," Levi says.

"No one got angry," Tess's father says. In the same room as David, her father looks old and small, but he has more fight in him than David does. He's got the indignance of a man who's lost his life once and is scared to lose it again. Tess is trying to understand, but feels, even to herself, more patronizing than empathetic. But it really is reasonable for her father to want to make his life great again. She wants the same thing. For herself.

"Tess?" David says.

"This doesn't concern you," Tess's father says. "Either of you."

"Go into another room," David tells the boys. "Both of you. Please."

"Fuck you," Levi says.

Teddy is crying, but Tess maintains her composure.

"It's time for you guys to leave," Tess's father says. He is angry but begins pleading: "I'll come into the city soon. Take you two out for dinner. Anywhere you'd like if you'd let me. I'd love to do something like that. I've wanted nothing more for years. I've wanted you to feel free to drop in whenever you wanted. This is great. But not like this. So now get inside, boys. There's nothing to worry about. The boys were roughhousing. We're fine. Go home, Tessie, and I'll call you. I'm sure Teddy can give me your number. Get inside."

But everyone is already inside. Levi closes the door behind him, which has the effect of intensifying the disorder. There are few safe places to step, as shards of glass cover the linoleum. The TV in the nook is on. News about baseball.

"Right now," Tess's father says. "Susan will be home soon,

and this doesn't concern you. The boys were playing rough. Everything's fine."

"Teddy?" David says.

"He hit Mommy," Teddy says.

"You shit-bag fucking ass-rat," Levi yells.

"And she left you two here alone with him after?"

"It was an accident. She told us to watch TV," Teddy says. "He said 'sorry.' "

"What?" David says. "What was an accident?"

"It's time for you to go," Tess's father says. His fists are balled up, but he is rubbing his forehead with his wrists. "Please go. Everything was fine until you two showed up. I was calm. I took my meds. That was what I was telling you last time. Seroquel makes me better. I made a mistake but now I'm better."

"Better?" Tess says between deep breaths. "Teddy, come here," Tess says, and Teddy comes. "Levi, you, too. We'll take you two into the city for the night."

Levi, on the other side of the room, is alternating between crying and making demands. "I'm not going with you," Levi says, "and neither is Teddy. Right, Pop?"

Tess's father moves toward Tess, who hugs Teddy.

Teddy holds on to Tess's arm with his left hand.

Tess's father steps toward Tess and grabs Teddy's right arm. He jerks Teddy away from Tess, but Tess holds Teddy, too, so Tess and her father are pulling the boy in opposite directions. Teddy shrieks in panic or pain.

"Let's just talk for a minute," Tess's father says, still pulling.

David lunges—punches her father first in his jaw and then twice, three times at his cheek and eye. David shifts from preventing her father from doing harm to inflicting harm—punishing her father—himself.

Her father's mouth is open, but she can't hear what he's saying. He falls to the floor.

"Pop!" Teddy is screaming. He watches David with fear and wonder.

David is standing over her father, chest heaving, David's blue polo shirt covered in blood. Tess has never loved him more.

Levi runs at David to defend his father, but he's still just a boy. Standing over Tess's father, David spins Levi around and holds him by his own crossed arms, pressing Levi's back into David's chest. Levi kicks backward at David's shins, while David struggles to keep both Levi and himself unharmed.

"Stop! Stop this!" Susan screams.

Tess doesn't know how long she's been standing at the door.

"Mommy," Teddy cries, and runs into his mother's hug. David releases Levi, who follows his younger brother. Tess and David watch as Levi and Teddy hold their mother and each other. Their father sits against the oven covering his bloody face with his arms.

The boys with their mother, Tess with David, the old man alone on the ground.

"Come with us?" David says to Susan. "We have a pullout couch. Our boys would love it. We'd love it."

"My colleague, she's like an aunt to them. We're going to her house. I just set it all up. Andrew was calm. I was only gone for five minutes."

"You sure?" David says.

"I think you two should go," Susan says, but she doesn't tend to her husband.

"We'll at least stay until you get your things ready," David says. He stands at the sink washing his hands. Tess's father, only a foot away from David's legs, sits in silence.

"Okay. Thank you. Thank you," Susan says.

"Really—the boys can spend some time with their sister," David says. "It'll be an adventure."

Tess expects Teddy to say he wants to come home with her, but neither boy has said anything since seeing their mother.

Susan steadies herself and takes in the room one more time. She sees the overturned furniture and broken glass. She sees her husband slumped and misshapen on the floor.

"You're sure," Susan says. "It's okay?"

"Better than okay," David says. "It's great. Come on and get your things together. You'll take your car and follow us home."

21

Susan is at the stove cooking eggs, bacon, and pancakes, pouring juice, making coffee, and doing what she's done every morning since arriving: pretty much being the best mom in the world. David is sitting at the table preparing plates, paper towels, silverware, and plastic cups. It's only been a week, and though Teddy and Levi are sleeping in the living room with their mother—Susan on the couch and the boys on air mattresses on the floor—there's only one bathroom and one TV, so everyone has had to play nice. Max is overstimulated, Ethan and Teddy thrilled, and Levi quietly sulking. They are really just killing time during the days until school starts, at which point Susan will take Teddy and Levi home. It's awkward, but not unpleasant. Teddy has been playing with Ethan and Max, who have no real sense of what's going on except that people are parenting them again. Tess doesn't let herself think too much about what she'd done: the neglect bordering on abuse, the selfishness that she could or couldn't have controlled. She doesn't let herself dwell or indulge in self-recrimination. It's too much. She's too lucky that nothing terrible happened.

Angelica calls to say she's finally heard from Tazio, and that working in the White House has been his plan all along. Get in there and bring the place down.

"Bring the place down?" Tess says.

"You know, like, sabotage things."

"What are you talking about?" Tess says. "When did you speak to him?"

"Just now," Angelica says. "Yesterday."

"So what is he doing?"

"Working for the American people," Angelica says, laughing.

"For real?"

"Like I said. To bring the whole thing down," Angelica says.

Tess laughs, hears Tazio's arrogance in Angelica's words—
"Bring the whole thing down!"—and still doesn't know what to believe. Everyone looks over to her at the kitchen counter.

"Only Satin knew," Angelica says. "They planned the whole thing together. Tazio says this was Satin's way of apologizing for how she acted after the Edwards campaign. But yeah, Tazio's been showing up to work every day to fuck with Kelly, Pence, and Kushner since Bannon left. Now he's running this branch of government or whatever it is."

"Why couldn't we know?" Tess says.

"Call him!" Angelica says, but when Tess does, Tazio doesn't pick up.

"That was Angelica?" David says. "What'd she say?"

"That Tazio told her he's trying to sabotage things," Tess says.

"Mn," David says, reaching over Levi to guide Max's spoon away from his mouth and into the yogurt side of his combination Greek yogurt and strawberry jam. The large compartment in the plastic container is filled with yogurt, and the smaller one with jam, so unless Max's hand is guided, he eats all the jam and then rejects the unsweetened yogurt left behind.

David is right to focus on the kids. Tess doesn't want to let Tazio—even news like this—get in the way of their breakfast.

"No just sauce, yogit wit sauce?" Max asks.

"Together. Eat them together," David says.

"Yogit wit sauce!" Max says. "Dis good?"

"Yay!" David says.

"Yay!" Max, Ethan, and Teddy say.

Levi sighs, the hood of his sweatshirt covering his forehead and cheeks.

David has agreed to be with the boys for breakfast. It's difficult for him. Every few minutes, he holds the table and grimaces, but he knows that the rest of the morning will be for recovery, and he is proud to be participating again.

"I want to try," David said at a gas station on the ride back from her father's house. "If you try, I'll try," which made Tess hug him with something like girlish abandon, which made David kiss her neck with something like sexual desire, which made her squeeze his hand in a way she hadn't done for a very long time.

"Even when you were healthy, I never thought you could have done that. I didn't know you had it in you."

"I was trying to protect Teddy. You're not angry?"

Tess kissed him again.

"I want to do as much as I can," David said. "Every day. I know I'm broken down, but I might not be better for a long, long time. I might not ever be better. I have to start living where I can. My life is valuable and full of love. Like right now, I'm dizzy and my sight isn't great, but that's okay."

If anyone else had done it, she'd have been horrified by the chauvinistic faux-chivalric insanity of a husband fighting his wife's father. But David isn't masculine like that. He'd become physically and emotionally neutered on top of his already kind and self-abnegating disposition, so it was a joy to see him take control. Especially over her father. She's sure he felt her joy. He didn't want it to end, so he was talking about the future. Let him speak in Monica's dumb aphorisms. He really was, and is, trying.

But still, watching David try his hardest at breakfast and remembering the pride she felt for him a week before, Tess understands that she is not like Angelica. Seeing her father battered on the floor may have been momentarily cathartic, but it wasn't enough for real healing. Maybe this is because her father didn't seem apologetic, while Gerard did, or maybe it's because seeing a man in his late sixties get bloodied up doesn't have anything to do with that same man murdering your mother in his thirties. Or seeing your father kill your mother is something you can't ever get over. Maybe it is worse than rape, especially if you loved your rapist. Or maybe rape is worse when you love your rapist. Or maybe, and most likely, pain and terror can't be quantified, compared, or erased, and Angelica is a different person from Tess, who reacts differently to different atrocities.

"Why didn't he tell Angelica as soon as he had the idea?" David asks, wiping Max's mouth and forking more bacon onto Teddy's plate.

"That's what I asked her," Tess says. "I guess he didn't want to talk about it until it was official, like he'd jinx it or something? He got so excited about Edwards and Hillary and talked about the future in a way he was embarrassed by after, so he didn't want to get too excited with us, and he didn't want to lie to us, so he just kept quiet?"

"Sure," David says. "I guess that makes sense."

Susan and the kids let them talk. Teddy is asking Levi to explain the concept of hunting to Ethan and Max, who don't believe that such a thing could be real.

Tess watches the four boys eat their breakfasts. Max dunks his spoon in the jam and then the yogurt and then jam and then yogurt over and over before each bite so the spoon has some of both. He is covered in yogurt. Ethan watches Teddy eat bacon, and Ethan starts eating bacon in the same way, folding the strips in half and eating each one as a single mouthful. Before this week, Tess doesn't think Ethan has ever tried bacon. Levi takes large bites of waffle and eggs, hardly chewing before he swallows. *So many boys*, Tess thinks as she eats the excess eggs out of the frying pan.

The thought comes to her while staring vacantly into the cooling, empty pan—and it's admittedly an outlandish thought, but all the same: What if Tazio is planning on killing Trump?

Tazio was depressed, didn't like his life, couldn't bring himself to marry Angelica but didn't want to reject her, especially after she told him what Gerard had done to her. He failed at art, at politics, at sobriety (presumably), and at love, so he's found a way to make his life matter. Was it Tazio who said he wanted to be like a kamikaze pilot, sacrificing his life for a worthy cause? Angelica admitted to sitting around after work smoking pot and fantasizing about killing Trump. Tazio could kill Trump to absolve himself of the shame he felt for not being able to kill Gerard. It never made sense that Tazio hadn't confronted Gerard. Maybe Gerard had been a kind of friend, while Trump has no friends and is one thousand Gerards all rolled up into one. He couldn't tell Angelica, when he knew that any one of them might stop him or even turn him in. But, in his mind, what greater gift could he give Angelica or the country? America had chosen its worst person to be its leader, so Tazio wanted to save the country from itself. He would be a hero to more than half the country and much more than half the world. He could save the United States from atomic warfare, economic collapse, Chinese hegemony, racism, sexism, and the xenophobia that hits Tazio, as a Mexican American, particularly hard. He'd be a John Wilkes Booth who'd killed a victorious Jefferson Davis. If David could beat up her father, then Tazio could kill Trump. He could accomplish the greatness he'd always thought himself destined for.

But the more she watches her sons and half brothers eat and drink; the more she sees her husband trying so hard, standing, fetching long-forgotten gummy vitamins from the back of a drawer and offering them to all four boys, three of whom accept with glee; the more she considers the moment Tazio would actually have to bring the gun, bomb, or poison into an actual meeting while wearing an actual suit and tie—it all feels a bit too much like performance art.

Which is actually something Tazio *would* be interested in and capable of.

What better conceptual piece than to act as someone running a task force for a president you despise while actually running the task force? If it was violence Tazio wanted, he didn't need to spend all this time becoming a member of Trump's inner circle. He could as easily have attended a meeting as a member of the press or as a lobbyist or window cleaner or something. Was it easier or harder to get a weapon in as a member of White House staff? Tess didn't know, but if the goal was to kill Trump, this seems like a circuitous way of doing it.

So instead, Tazio creates the greatest political artwork of all time. One that actually matters. What would even come close? *The Problem We All Live With*? *Guernica*? Shepard Fairey's Obama poster? *The Third of May 1808*? Pavlensky sewing his mouth closed? Some Ai Weiwei stunt? Pussy Riot? Banksy? This would be the greatest work of political or conceptual performance art in the history of art as society has come to understand it.

Also, admittedly she wants this second idea to be correct because it would mean Tazio would become famous as opposed to going to jail for the rest of his life or being killed by the Secret Service, and it would also most likely mean that this whole thing wasn't about or for her.

Because that's the third possibility—what she has thought from the beginning.

She had hugged Tazio and told him that she couldn't survive this without him. He was spending all that time at their place, purportedly for David, but maybe it was for her. They've never adequately addressed what happened in North Carolina. David could obviously never know. So rather than deal with their mutual attraction, dependency, or love, and risk hurting himself, Tess, David, and Angelica—and rather than continuing to live what felt to him like a torturous lie—Tazio ran away. He found an excuse—his desire to accomplish—and left the rest of them behind. And then, once gone, why not try to get into power? He always said how awful Trump's surrogates were. Who better than a former Democrat to tell everyone how lucky Americans are to have this president? Tazio probably went down to DC without much thought, and then Satin had the idea to plant Tazio in the administration and sabotage whatever he had access to. It's not like Trump would tolerate a postop trans woman. But this was just incidental to Tazio's actual reason to leave. He loved Tess and Tess loved him, and they couldn't be together. Life couldn't continue as it was. Is this what Tess thinks, or is this fantasy? She has lost track. This—Tazio—is just another example of something unspeakable from which she must let herself move on.

She tells ideas one and two—assassination attempt and performance art—to David later that morning, while the kids are with Susan at the park and the two of them lie in bed. David agrees that number two is more likely. Though he adds the most obvious possibility and one that never occurred to Tess, and the fact of that disturbs her: that Tazio believes much of what he is saying, saw an avenue toward personal acclaim, took it, and then was too embarrassed to talk to anyone about his change of professional trajectory and political heart.

The seven of them sit together at dinner, David's second and final responsibility of the day. This week he has agreed to be present for breakfast and dinner. Next week he will add another responsibility. Lunch or bath time. Or even just a half hour each day contemplating what he might be able to attempt professionally. He is suffering, but he doesn't show it off as he used to. Monica told him that Tess's plan to slowly add activities and responsibilities to David's day was a great one. As much as she hated that he needed Monica's approval, Tess felt tremendous gratitude when Monica gave it. Monica also told David that, along with this transition into more activity, he must stop forcing everyone to know every moment of his suffering. Constantly confronting everyone with his pain didn't make him feel better, and it disturbed other people. Acknowledge your suffering, she said, but don't rub it in everyone's face.

David came home from this session—a few days after Susan and the kids moved in—noticeably calmer. David told Tess that Monica advised him to get through the day trying to enjoy as many minutes of it as possible. Don't define himself by his pain. Assume that the whole day will be filled with suffering, and take joy in the moments that have less suffering. Celebrate, if it comes, even a second of no suffering. Let a few minutes of a child's happiness make him happy while he waits for the meds or bodywork or vestibular rehabilitation or whatever else to kick in. Don't wait to live until he feels 100 percent better. He may never feel that good again. See suffering as a spectrum. He might get to 20 percent and then 30 and 40 percent. Or he might get to 20 percent and stop there. But he has to stop hibernating and start living life to whatever degree possible at every possible moment.

"Why was she saving this advice until now?" Tess asks.

"Maybe I'm only now ready to hear it. Also—"

"What?"

"I have a surprise for you."

"Yeah?" It's been a year or two since he's said anything so teasing or optimistic.

"Check this out!" he says.

David reaches for his laptop and scrolls quickly through images.

"It's taken me a couple weeks, but I think I've finally gotten it," he says.

"What is it?" Tess says.

"Here!"

David enlarges a tiny image, computer designed, of what looks like a cot or hospital bed with a smiling patient and the words HEALING ZONE forming an oval on the top and bottom.

"What is this?" Tess says.

"It's a logo! Do you like it? Surprise! I'm going to try working again! Monica and I were talking about how I had to stop hibernating, like I said. And I believe in this. Iced tea was one thing, but helping people get access to what Monica has to offer? She can see more patients, and I can work on her brand. She said she'd pay me fifty dollars an hour. Eventually I could own a percentage of the business. Isn't this great?"

Disappointment flowers into revulsion.

Tess swallows.

"I'm happy you want to work," she says.

He hugs her and smiles.

"I really like it," she says. "I'm thrilled to hear you were able to focus enough to design it."

"I know!" David says. "Thanks!"

"So you know this guy Tazio?" Susan says at dinner. "Like really know him?"

They eat what Tess assumes is the same baked ziti dish that was in the oven the first time Tess showed up at their house. Ethan and Max keep laughing. One giggles and the other laughs. They hand each other their forks and spoons.

"We're sharing our utensils!" Ethan tells Tess. They hadn't eaten dinner at the same table as their parents in their working memory, and now it's been a week of constant attention.

"Sing depatio?" Max says.

"What?" David says.

"Sing depatio!" Max says.

"Ethan, what's Max saying?" David asks.

"He wants you to play 'Despacito.' They listen to it at school."

David plays "Despacito" on his laptop and Max dances in his chair, looking at his parents for their clapping and commendation.

"He's been David's best friend since high school and became my closest friend in college. Tazio introduced us."

"And he worked for Hillary but now he likes Trump?" Susan says.

"Seems that way," Tess says, unsure if Susan likes Trump. She lives in rural Pennsylvania, and there was a giant Trump magnet on the fridge. But she doesn't seem like the type to stop her husband from doing whatever he wants.

"Then no offense to your friend or anything like that," Susan says, "but he's got something wrong with him. Your father thought Trump was hysterical. A joke, and only a bit better than Hillary, but something different, at least. I never heard him laugh like he did during those Republican debates. I try not to pay attention to that stuff. But what I did see I didn't like."

"Tazio is sick like Daddy?" Ethan says.

"Tazo dance depatio wit me!" Max says.

With so many kids in the house, everyone speaks quickly.

"Make America great again," Levi says, which doesn't make sense, even sarcastically.

"Levi," Susan says.

"What?" Levi says.

"Stop it," Susan says.

"So what if they have a friend who works for Trump?" Levi says. "Half the country voted for him. Dad even reregistered to vote for him. I would have, too. Grab 'em by the pussy!"

"That's it!" Susan says. "I told you that if you said that one more time—"

"I'd be grounded. Right?" Levi mocks her. "Was that it?"

Susan is furious, but she must not want to lose her temper, and there's nothing she can do.

"Well, instead you took all my friends away."

"What did you just say?" Tess says. "Did you just say 'Grab them by the pussy' in my house?" She suddenly wants these people gone.

"He's the president," Levi says. "Isn't he?"

"Turn that down!" Susan says.

"Sorry," David says, stopping the music from his laptop.

"Depatio!" Max wails.

David turns it back on, but more quietly.

"Is Tazio sick like Daddy?" Ethan says.

"We don't know," Tess says, trying to calm herself down. "Tazio isn't sick. No one is sick. We don't know if he likes Donald Trump or not."

"Pick me up," Max asks David.

"I can't, I'm eating," David says.

Symptoms intensify when the boys need him.

"I'll pick you up. Come sit on my lap," Tess says.

"No! Daddy pick me up Daddy!"

"Tess, please," David says.

"Come here, Maxman," Tess says. "You can eat one of my pastas."

"No like pasta Daddy pick me up Daddy!" Max says.

"Jesus fucking Christ," Levi says.

"Levi!" Susan says.

"Oh, fuckadoodle," Ethan says.

The three adults laugh in spite of themselves.

"Ethan!" Tess says.

"Oh, doodle?" Ethan says.

"Sit on Daddy's lap Daddy!" Max yells. "Despacito" is over and replaced by a Dylan song Tess doesn't recognize. "Sit on Daddy sit on Daddy's lap!"

"Please!" David says.

"Wanna play with your trucks?" Levi asks Max and Ethan.

"Pay tucks!" Max says, wiping his eyes and running to the rug.

"That's yours this is mine the bigger one!" Ethan says.

"Can I play with you guys?" Teddy says when he finishes his meal.

"Of course," Levi says. "Come on."

David is still eating his gluten-free pasta with olive oil, salt, and pepper. He is wearing sweatpants and an Eli Manning jersey, but he seems to have patted his hair down with some water. Susan sighs and goes to the freezer, where she retrieves a bottle of vodka that Tess hadn't seen before.

Tess finishes her water, Susan does the same, David picks at his pasta, Susan pours shots into both Tess's and her own water glasses, the women take the shots, Levi looks at them disgusted, Tess sits back and smiles, and Susan pours a double shot into her own wineglass, which is already half filled with eight-dollar Merlot. Susan is only a few years older than Tess.

David excuses himself and goes to bed. The kids sit on the couch and watch *Lego Batman*, which scares Max, who snuggles into Ethan's side. Ethan keeps his arm around Max.

"Does he hit you?" Tess finally asks when the sink is drained and both of them are drying the silverware. She speaks quietly enough that the kids can't hear.

"He was just throwing stuff before you came. He didn't get violent. I've actually been doing better at finding a time to get him to take extra meds. If he's in a bad mood, he doesn't like me to ask. I have to make it nonchalant."

"Forgive me. I know it's none of my business, really. But I always wanted to ask my mother. Why have you stayed with him? Why would you be with him in the first place?"

Susan and Tess lean side by side on the kitchen counter. They're watching their boys watch the movie.

"Your father is a brilliant man," Susan says. "He has a way of making me feel smarter, too. We've been together a very long time. I like having his words in my head. The way he says my name and the boys' names. 'You're the best thing ever to happen to me,' he said a few years ago, and that resonates I don't know how many times a day since."

"Oh," Tess says. The best thing.

"I'm sorry," Susan says. "That wasn't right of me to say that. He was just flattering me, I'm sure. He could have said the same thing about you. Or your mother."

"Everyone says how smart he is," Tess says. "I don't see it."

"I love him. He's good with the boys," Susan says. "Which is part of what makes this so hard. But we'll work it out. He's the love of my life."

Tess has screamed, "Stop! I get it!"

Max is crying.

All four kids are looking at her.

"Mommy?" Ethan says.

Teddy leans toward Levi.

"I just got a little cut," Tess says. "I'm okay. I'm good."

"Mommy's okay," Ethan says.

"Mommy cut hand need Band-Aid?" Max says.

"Good idea, sweetie," Tess says. "I'm going to get a Band-Aid."

The boys return to their movie as Tess puts a Band-Aid on an imaginary cut.

Susan gives her a look that says *what happened here?*

"You can't go back to him," Tess says.

Tess is much drunker than she realized. She's had the shot of vodka and four or five glasses of wine. She hasn't drunk more than half a glass for months. Tess can't remember why this woman is in her house. She remembers, but it still doesn't make sense. She decided to marry Tess's father, so she becomes Tess's responsibility? Tess is the one who should be taken care of. Susan deserves to pay a price for giving happiness to this man who caused Tess so much pain.

"What?" Susan says. She is slim with large brown eyes. She takes care of herself. She has what is presumably a decent job at a doctor's office. She's a catch.

"You're not going back to him," Tess says. "You can't. It's not safe. He could kill you."

"No. He's their father," Susan says.

"He's my father," Tess says.

"I know that," Susan says. "What do you mean?"

"He'll hurt you," Tess says. With or without a knife, he'll hurt her. "We'll work out a way to keep you safe if you have nowhere else to go. He shouldn't have you back. I mean, it's not safe to keep on giving him chances."

"He's my husband. Their father. We've been talking. He's sorry, and his doctor says we can up the Seroquel. We conferenced with him a couple days ago. I'll take care of your father."

"Please. He doesn't deserve you."

"I know you've been hurt," Susan says. She's also drunk. "But I've had quite enough of this. This doesn't really have anything to do with you."

"Your son," Tess says, "wants me to protect him."

"He's ten years old," Susan says. The boys are watching them now, but neither Susan nor Tess can stop. "He just met you. He thinks you're cool. And he just saw his father nearly beaten to death. Both boys. That can't be the last image they have of their father. It'll be what defines the rest of their lives. We have to try to get back to normalcy at home. I'm not going to let what your husband did to them, in front of them, be what defines their lives. It'll just be a bad memory if we go back home. I won't let it mess up their lives like he messed up yours."

Tess's brain is flooded with hatred. "Is this for Teddy, really?" she says. "Not just yourself? You're not risking the boys because you don't want to be alone?"

"You're a middle-aged woman trying to make a ten-year-old like you. Well, you succeeded! Congrats. Listen, enough of this. You take care of your family, and I'll take care of mine."

"They're my family. You three are. I'm trying to help. Let's talk about this tomorrow."

"I am not going to discuss my marriage with you again."

"Fine," Tess says. "Sorry I brought it up."

Susan has already turned around to start inflating her sons' beds for the night.

Tess awakens to the smell of something buttery cooking in the kitchen. She motions for David to stay in bed. Susan must be baking again. Tess creeps into the boys' room. They are still sleeping, Ethan in his bed, Max in his crib. One crib side has been replaced by a half side that lets him get in and out without help. David must have swapped out the side without telling Tess. Sleeping, her children are babies, breathing in through their noses and out through their warm, wet mouths. Their soft child bellies rise and fall. She sits at the foot of Ethan's bed. He doesn't move. She brushes his dark brown hair away from his eyes. He hugs a big stuffed pig to his chest.

Max's stuffed snake has been discarded to a corner of his crib. She sees Max falling through the air, David holding him. His hair, she sees now for the first time, is David's. Messy curls and waves. Will he lose it, too? David's hairline is receding, but he doesn't look bad. It's not like he seems distinguished or any of the other things people say about attractive older men. He just looks like David with less hair. She sneaks back to their bedroom and climbs into bed beside him. He's sleeping, looking like their children.

She won't keep secrets from him anymore.

When Tess wakes up again, Susan and her sons are packing.

"They're leaving," David says to her as soon as he sees her eyes open. He calls to Susan, "You really don't have to go."

"We need to get back." Susan's voice is thick and muted, like she's lifting something.

"Are you sure?" David says. He looks at Tess and shrugs. Tess joins the packing in the TV room.

"Hey, Susan? Please stay," Tess says, rubbing her jaw where she's been grinding. "We'd love for you all to stay. You're no trouble."

"It's time," Susan says.

Still, Tess's relief is stunted by anger. Anger at whom?

"Really?" she says. "The boys will be so disappointed."

"It's just time," Susan says. "Thank you all, you were wonderful."

"Thanks for being with us," Tess says, like a podcast host.

"Anyway," Susan says. "The boys miss their friends. We talked it over."

"And their father?" Tess says, stepping out into the main room. Here it is, the anger.

Susan doesn't answer right away. She is organizing things in the kitchen. Over by the spare room, Ethan and Max gently orbit Levi. As Tess watches, Levi reaches into his bag and—with more ceremony than she would have thought him capable of—removes two T-shirts and hands one to each of her sons. Ethan and Max immediately put the T-shirts on, and they are much too big. All three boys laugh. Max calls his T-shirt a "big dwess!" but Ethan just stretches the cloth of his in front of him, reverently studying the letters looping there in gold script: Hail to Pitt.

"Andy's staying with a friend. For now." Susan says this with a light inflection, as if relating any offhand fact.

"Okay," Tess says, matching Susan's tone. "I just hope you know our door is always open. I mean it. If there's ever anything we can do . . ."

Susan turns from the paper grocery bag she's just finished layering with another paper grocery bag. Her face looks purplish and exhausted.

"Actually . . . ," she says, and Tess fears now they'll end up staying after all. "If you could talk to him."

"Talk to who?" Tess says.

"Andy," Susan says. "Your father."

"About you coming home?"

Susan shakes her head and starts placing lumpy Ziplocs of sandwiches and trail mix down into the paper grocery bag. She holds the bags gingerly. Tess knows what Susan wants her to talk to her father about. But she thinks Susan should have to say it aloud.

"No, not about us coming home," Susan says, looking directly at her. Tess flinches at the cold rage in the woman's eyes. "Honey," Susan says, "you know you hollow him right out." She turns back to her Ziplocs. "Isn't it enough he's got work and meds and his PO and the affliction, and now the poor man's old enough to be retired, and he's still got to take care of all of us?"

"I'm so sorry," Tess lies.

"Truth is, that's the real reason he drinks." Susan gives an angry sigh. Tess's father said he was sober.

"What's the real reason?" Tess is six years old again, watching her father take her mother by the throat. "What's the reason?" Tess says.

Susan stares up at her, disbelieving.

"Honey, you."

By the front door, Ethan and Max are still fluttering around Levi, greedy for their last few moments with him in their home. Susan has gone to pick up the car, and while the boys wait, Levi is demonstrating different kinds of jump-kicks.

David is back in bed. When he can't sleep during the night, he is barely ambulatory in the morning. Tess stands dumbly in the middle of the kitchen, which Susan has left cleaner than it has ever been before. Teddy comes out into the main room and, seeing Tess, runs to her, throwing his arms around her and soundly head-butting her left breast. He swings his sad brown eyes up at her. He'll message her as soon as he gets home, he promises. He'll tell her everything he's doing. Everything everybody's doing. Tess nods, patting his head and shifting it over to a better spot. Teddy rubs at his eyes with the back of his wrist.

"Listen," Tess says, "from now on we can't be texting like we were before. You know I'm your sister and I love you." She feels the boy's slight body slackening in disappointment. "I'll always love you, but I'm a lot older than you." Somehow she's said this in a way that doesn't make sense. "But I want you to know you can call me anytime, and I'll come for you. Understand?"

Teddy nods with fury and thuds his forehead back into Tess's breast.

"You understand?" she says again.

"Yes, I understand," Teddy says. "I do." Tess can feel his hot breath through the fabric of her T-shirt.

There's a soft knock at the front door. Susan walks in and announces it is time to say goodbye. The boys and Susan hug and say goodbye in every obvious permutation. This takes forever. Finally, it's Tess's turn. Susan hugs her fiercely and says goodbye and God-blesses her. She tells Tess she has to promise to thank David again for all of them. Tess promises. Then they are gone.

Tess decides it's not yet time to process anything. That will come later. There is still a half-full bottle of wine in the refrigerator. But when she opens the door to retrieve it, she finds the whole refrigerator has been crammed with rectangular Tupperware cases, shoved in side by side and stacked on top of one another. Each one has a paper label taped to the lid. Meatballs, breaded chicken cutlets, broccoli and peas, baked ziti.

Put there, she recognizes with a twinge, for her. For her and David and the boys. An act of charity. How long must it have taken Susan to make all of it? When did she start? When did she make the choice? Tess shuts the refrigerator and is surprised to find she isn't angry. Everyone needs help. Susan needs help. Teddy, Levi. The three of them will especially need help now that they've gone back to her father. But what can Tess do? What is she supposed to do? Force them to stay? Forgive the abusive murderer—manslaughterer—with hope that he'll find peace and become a better man?

They can all go to hell. Her father for killing her mother. Everyone else for allowing Tess to think he'd done it on purpose. Susan for going back to him and then again for laying Tess's father's mental instability at her feet.

Yet, despite all of this, Tess is grateful for the food. Everyone needs help. Tess simply doesn't want to be the kind of mother who needs help like this, not a surprise refrigerator full of food for her family. She doesn't want to need it, and not needing it is something she can work on. She knows she can. It's something she can make happen. Maybe not for Susan, but hopefully for Teddy, and definitely for David, Ethan, and Max.

22

They are there ironically or symbolically. David suggested the place. They are celebrating. He took the kids to school every day that first half week of get-to-know-the-teacher time. He even picked them up every afternoon. It was difficult and he had to spend the days and nights recuperating, but he did it.

On Friday afternoon, David said Tess should audition for theater work again. She asked if he was sure. He said he was, that he could put the boys down. Or, more precisely, he said, "If I'm going to be incapacitated, I might as well be as useful as possible. Please. For me. Don't sacrifice your life for mine. My mom can help if need be."

David's mom offered to look after the kids Saturday evening so David and Tess could celebrate, but when Saturday came David didn't want to celebrate. He wanted to sleep. David has been in an odd, dreamy mood in general lately, but Tess forced him out. She wanted to celebrate. There was plenty of time for sleep, but they needed to start finding joy together again. Even if it caused him pain the next day, they had to relearn how to be a married couple. And she needs to unburden herself. Be without secrets. Start again from an honest—even if sick—place.

So they sit in their corner booth in an otherwise empty Abel and Cain. The house rules, which had previously been only posted in the bathrooms, are now in small picture frames on every table.

NO NAME DROPPING, NO STAR FUCKING.

NO HOOTING, HOLLERING, OR OTHER BEHAVIOR UNBECOMING
OF APPROPRIATE COMPORTMENT.

NO FIGHTING, NO PLAY FIGHTING, NO TALKING ABOUT FIGHTING.

GENTLEMEN WILL REMOVE THEIR HATS.

GENTLEMEN WILL NOT INTRODUCE THEMSELVES TO LADIES.
LADIES, FEEL FREE TO START A CONVERSATION OR ASK
THE BARTENDER TO INTRODUCE YOU. IF A MAN YOU DON'T
KNOW SPEAKS TO YOU, PLEASE LIFT YOUR CHIN SLIGHTLY
AND IGNORE HIM.

DO NOT BRING ANYONE TO ABEL AND CAIN UNLESS YOU
WOULD LEAVE THAT PERSON ALONE IN YOUR HOME. YOU
ARE RESPONSIBLE FOR THE BEHAVIOR OF YOUR GUESTS.

EXIT THE BAR SWIFTLY AND SILENTLY.
PEOPLE ARE TRYING TO SLEEP IN THE APARTMENTS ABOVE.

Gerard had written these rules in the early days when he felt that Abel and Cain was missing something. He credited them for turning the place around.

People these days tend to start filling up the place around eleven, but there's always room for walk-ins. That's what the waiter says. He asks if this is their first time at Abel and Cain, and they laugh, so he laughs, too. His name is Mark, but he is wearing a Gerard costume. Tess gasped when he met them at the door. Mark's hair is slicked back, and he wears the suspenders, cuff links, sleeve garters, shined shoes: the whole uniform. He is blond, red faced, and pudgy, but he's doing his best. He has a nice way about him.

"Do you know what you'd like?" Mark says. "Or would you prefer to name a favorite spirit and have us prepare something for you?"

"Just a soda water, please," David says.

"He'll have a mint daiquiri," Tess says.

It will be his first drink in six months. Maybe it will fuck him up, Monica said, but nobody could know until he tried it. Monica told them they had to go out and celebrate the successful week. David had helped every morning at breakfast, and he worked for Monica three out of the last seven days. Monica commanded him to have a drink or two—low on gluten, if possible—so David suggested they return here: to the scene of the crime and the origin of their relationship. Monica said that every incremental step should be celebrated.

"And I'll have a Cherry Coke," Tess says.

David laughs and shakes his head. Mark responds that, unfortunately, by way of soft drinks all they offer are soda water and tonic, but he'd be happy to make her a nonalcoholic cocktail if she'd like. "Perhaps something with ginger?" he says, and she says, "No, sorry, it was just a dumb joke. I'll have a scotch, neat, please. Whatever you're pouring these days."

"Very good," Mark says.

They sit silently for a moment, as Chance the Rapper or maybe Kendrick Lamar makes it difficult to have a conversation. David takes Tess's hand. They listen to whoever it is and look around.

"Everything is so shiny," David says.

"It looks like they doused the place in polyurethane," Tess says.

"Somehow, even the ceiling is shiny," David says.

"It looks embalmed," Tess says.

David laughs.

"I'm happy we're doing this," he says. "It's hard, but you're right that it's worth it. Like the work with Monica. Some of it is back-end stuff, getting approval from iTunes, but I actually spoke to a patient today. I've been waiting to tell you! The idea—my idea—was me offering free sessions so people had a sense of what Monica can offer. I had him repeat some of the positive phrases, think about not forcing his condition on everyone. It felt really good. Helping him. It made me feel good. The guy gets debilitating migraines, and I told him about my condition. It made us both feel good. Now he's going to do a Skype session next week with Monica. She'll give me a percentage of every session with him moving forward. He lives in Arizona!"

"Good," Tess says. "That's great. Really great." She doesn't ask how he can be sure Monica is the best person to help someone in Arizona who has bad migraines.

"I'm excited for the first time in a long time," David says.

"And I'm happy, too," Tess says. "But we have to discuss something first. While we're both still sober. When you're feeling okay."

"How scared should I be?"

"I don't know," Tess says.

"You're using the same voice as when you told me about Jonah," David says. "Who'd you sleep with now?"

He's joking. It's just a joke. He thinks she's going to tell him something troubling about Levi or Teddy, probably, or, at the worst, bring up their finances.

"Tazio," Tess says.

"I know. He's supposed to be back in town soon," David says. "I spoke to him, too. It'll be good to finally see him."

"I slept with Tazio," Tess says.

David's hands clench the table.

Time slows down enough that Tess is able to remember Tazio complaining about how Gerard insisted that the tables be shellacked. Not polyurethaned, varnished, or lacquered, but shellacked. Gerard liked the smell and the historical panache, but, unlike polyurethane, shellac leaves white marks from water glasses and needs to be constantly replaced. But now the original shellac seems to have been polyurethaned over, like the rest of the place. Suspended in time. David's nails are digging into the double layer, deepening cracks and creating claw marks in the table's coating.

"Tess," David says. "Talk quickly."

"Sorry!" Tess says, and reaches for his other hand, which he squeezes hard like Ethan does before a shot at the doctor's office. "It was only once. Years ago. We weren't even together yet, you and I."

Right when he should be most upset, all the tension dissolves from his arms and shoulders. David relaxes. He smiles. He looks back for Mark and the drinks.

"Why would you tell me about this now?" David says. But he says it with confidence, almost cockiness. Tess doesn't recognize this tone. And then she does. Anger. She can't remember ever having seen him angry. Only sad.

"Because I can't take the secret," she says. "I want to start fresh. It's selfish of me to tell you, I know that, but I think you and Tazio can get through it, and I don't want him knowing something you don't. He doesn't matter to me. We've already been living without Tazio for all this time he's been in DC. You matter to me. I need you to know that."

"We *were* together," David says with a strange, frightening brashness.

"What?" Tess says.

"You said we weren't together yet," David says. "But we were."

"What do you mean?" Tess says.

"It happened when he was in North Carolina," David says. "You and I were already together."

"I didn't say . . . He already told you? When? You—"

"He told me years ago," David says gleefully. "You think you and Tazio have this thing—this secret life—together that I wasn't a part of. But I've known for years. You think you've been part of some secret friendship, but he's told me everything."

"Why didn't you say anything?"

"Why didn't *I* say anything?" David says.

Mark returns with their drinks, holding David's iced coupe at the bottom of the stem.

A few other drinkers—what did Angelica call them, *clientele?*—have arrived. Neither Tess nor David wears a watch, and their phones have been put away. They've been there just a short time, but in the room with no windows and a thick black curtain concealing the metal door, it could be ten or midnight or four in the morning. Tess feels claustrophobic and confused. She sees Angelica acquiescing after fighting off Gerard.

"I was wondering if you'd tell me," David says. "If you'd ever tell me. And now does feel like the right time. New beginnings and all that. But why did you say we weren't together? We were."

She's scared of him, of what he's saying.

"I've been waiting for you to tell me," he says. "Why do you think Tazio left? I didn't like how close you guys were becoming, always hugging, your looking at him like our savior while hiding your history from me. And still now, when you come clean, you lie."

"What do you mean, why he left?"

"When we went down to DC," David says. "It was because I told him to. I asked him to leave. I didn't feel like I could trust you around him, and I told him that. He understood. He said he'd been offered all these jobs across the country after the election, so he'd be fine taking one."

"What about Angelica? Angelica told me Tazio went down there because of Gerard. Because she told Tazio about what happened."

"That is what Tazio told her."

"Then you knew about what Gerard did?" Tess says.

"Only a few days before you knew."

"But you acted surprised when I told you," Tess says.

"I did," David says.

"He was going to marry her," Tess says.

"Tazio was never going to marry Angelica. He was here for me. Taking care of me. Once I told him I didn't want him around, he was free. He was free to run away like he wanted to."

"Then why'd he propose?" It's too much to be true, but it's true.

"Because he liked her and she wanted him to propose. He's selfish. He's always been selfish. He slept with his best friend's girlfriend. You think he was going to settle down with a dentist?"

"He's an asshole," Tess says. "You both are."

Without clinking glasses, David sips his drink. Color like fire fills his cheeks. Tess is trying to unravel all the implications. David has trusted Tazio but not her? David was more important to Tazio than Angelica was?

"I'm an asshole?" David says. "You were my girlfriend. My first girlfriend. We'd already said 'I love you.' We were spending every night together. And then you slept with my best friend. I forgive you. I forgave you both a long time ago. Tazio was an alcoholic at the time, and like you say, he's always been an asshole, and you were young, so much younger than you are now. We have children and a life together. You've dedicated the last year to taking care of me. But you have to make changes. I'm not going to love you blindly and unconditionally. I'm not Susan to your father.

"We were together when you slept with Tazio. And then when we had kids you slept with Jonah," David continues. "How could I trust you around Tazio again? It would have been insane. I knew Tazio wouldn't do it again, but I didn't like the idea of your living with him at our house all the time, with you in love with him, fantasizing about him while I was miserable and useless. I could feel I was losing you. You read it in my journal. You were acting so grateful to him. You were acting as though you loved him. I had to tell Tazio to get away. I saw the hugs and whispers, and I know how you develop crushes on people and sometimes can't control yourself."

Nausea creeps up Tess's throat. *Tazio just listened to him?*

"I saved his life," David says, as if reading her mind. "I got him healthy and have kept him sober. Except for his one trip to Asia, we haven't gone more than a couple days in twenty years without talking. I'm his best friend, his sponsor, the closest thing—including his mother—that he has to family. We love each other. And anyway, Tazio was looking for an excuse to keep trying to change the world. You know him. There are so few people who have access to real power, and Tazio keeps coming up just a little bit short. He could have been an important figure in an Edwards administration, not to even start about Hillary. He can't give it up."

Tess is trying to process all of this as quickly as possible. "So how long have you known about this plan to sabotage Trump?"

"It was my idea! But not sabotage, to influence. There's no secret here. He's really doing the job Trump assigned him to do. Yeah, he wants the celebrity, he wants the world to see him as extraordinary, but he really is trying to find work for Mexicans and South and Central Americans.

"On the way down to DC, Tazio told me that Satin had been back in touch to apologize for how it all ended in Carolina years ago, and she had this office set up and left-wing financing, and some general odd idea about lobbyists pretending to lobby for one side but actually giving Trump bad info or something like that, and I just asked Tazio why he didn't, as himself, get a job with Trump? How hard could it be? He's mostly honest with Trump. He says what he needs to, to keep the job, just like he said what he needed to on TV to get the job. There's nothing clandestine about anything he's doing, really. He quietly presents reasons for Trump to go back to the left-leaning beliefs he had for fifty years and subsume the racist shit under real infrastructure policy and opioid relief. Or to let Tazio be the token Latino to take some of the heat off the president. You think Kushner or Ivanka or Pence or Mattis or anyone shares beliefs with Trump? You think Trump *has* beliefs? He's happy to have a Mexican working for him. Makes him look better. They're all just doing their best to maintain power and do what they can.

For Kushner and Ivanka it might be about personal gain, for Pence and all those generals, who knows, but Tazio is, along with satisfying his ego, sincerely trying to do good."

"Not sabotage?"

"Sabotage? What does that even mean? No. He's just trying to get people work. He had all these proposals from his time with Edwards and then Hillary. He's just trying to do a good job. He didn't think Angelica would believe him if he told her the truth."

"How do you know?"

"I told you, we haven't gone more than a few days without talking for a decade."

"I'm with you all day!" He's been lying to her for a month, saying Tazio wasn't returning his calls, either.

"Usually I call on the way to appointments with Monica so she can help bring my symptoms down after I talk on the phone. It's been hard. Sometimes we text. I've never had a secret from you before. Only knowing about Tazio. But I didn't know how to tell you just part of the story. I figured I'd come clean with you when you came clean with me. When you told me about Jonah, I thought you were going to tell me about Tazio. You slept with my best friend, then you slept with a coworker, then you sold your engagement ring, and before that you nearly fought a rapist—all without telling me! I'm your husband. We're married. None of this is normal."

Tess doesn't know what he wants her to say.

"I'm sorry," she says.

David says, "I've tried my hardest to protect myself and the kids from you. I didn't know what you were capable of: lying to us, leaving us, crumbling because Tazio doesn't love you back? So yeah, I told Tazio he couldn't visit anymore, which meant he was free to leave the city."

She fights through the fatigue and tries to compartmentalize. She's lost Tazio, but not David. She doesn't know if Angelica
can still be her friend but sees no immediate reason why not. But
David and the kids: they're what matter. She hasn't lost David and
the kids. David said he needed to protect the kids from her? She
doesn't want to let David see her cry.

"How long have you known?" Tess says. "About Tazio?"

"Tazio told me when we were together for all those days keeping him sober. What was that, 2007? We told each other everything. About his mother cheating on his father, what he thinks
drives him to drink, and about why I didn't fully trust you, even
back then, which was when he told me about the night you two
slept together. He said I shouldn't trust you, even if both of you
knew it was a mistake. He was drunk and angry at the world,
and you—he didn't know what your excuse was—but he said you
never made another move with him after that."

"*I* never made another move?"

"Look," David says, "I don't care who made what move
twelve years ago in North Carolina years before we were
married, before he was sober and we had kids and my brain
stopped working. I don't care."

"How can you say it doesn't matter that you don't trust me?
That you've been protecting our children from me, their mother?"

"I don't trust you. I mean, I trust you around the kids and
with me. I trust that you love us as much as we love you. But I've
tried to protect our family against the . . . imperfections in your
personality. You're not reliable. And the kids, especially with me
like this, need a reliable mother."

"Jesus Christ, you're being patronizing."

"Come on," he snaps back. "You've been wonderful to me
this past year. But you cheated on me twice. That I know of.

Once with my best friend and once after we had kids. I could be a lot more than patronizing."

"I've taken care of you all this time."

"Except when you didn't, yes. You did." David is free, furious but free. She has wanted him to stand up for himself, even with her. But this? "Thank you for that," he says. "I think you want to be with me."

"I do," Tess says. And she can't stop herself. "Have you slept with Monica?"

"I've never cheated on you. Even when you hurt me. I never even—"

"Oh, you never even—"

"Yeah, I never even."

"Okay," Tess says. "Sorry I asked."

"You should be," he says.

It is all unraveling. Right now. All the years. The kids. She is going to lose him. He's furious, and he's got a right to be. She'll apologize. She just has to figure out how. Tess wipes her eyes.

"Cheers," David says sarcastically or sincerely, and he takes another sip. She downs half her scotch. Mark arrives with another round.

"On me," Mark says. He's probably overheard enough to know they need it.

David drinks without hesitating or thanking the bartender. Tess wants to tell him to slow down.

"You know, I just feel drunk," David says. "Not dizzy, really. Just drunk. Look at this place. It's depressing as shit."

"Are you okay?" Tess says

"Well, my wife cheats on me, I can't work, I can't see or think, I do my best every day and it's not enough. No, I'm not feeling great. I need the bathroom," David says.

Tess starts to panic. She's struggling to breathe. She's brought all this on herself, and she wants to start over. The past doesn't need to be the past: she wants to explain it to him.

David stands from their corner booth and sways dramatically to the left. He rights himself for a moment against the tin wall, but then unnecessarily corrects and stumbles forward. He stands up straight but then shifts again, which again jars him forward. He reaches for something that's not there and staggers, this time toward the bar, which his arms reach out for too late. His head hits the bar, and he crumples to the floor.

Tess holds David's head in her lap, cradling it as she'd last done with Max's infant body. Then she's in an ambulance with him, and then the rush through the hospital's fluorescent lights and locked doors. She shakes off a sense of déjà vu and only then understands that she's reliving the aftermath of his fall two years ago. He has passed out and she's listing his medications—Lexapro and Serzone—to the EMT, trying to explain his last couple of years. She's in the waiting room as he's in surgery, but she's not certain what for. He lost blood when he fell. Maybe it's an infusion. But it's not surgery. They're just stabilizing him and wanted to get him situated before letting family in.

His heart is beating and he hasn't woken up, but he's not in a coma. He's not bleeding anymore. Doctors haven't told her what's going on. Maybe they don't know. It's two in the morning, and she calls his mother, who is presumably asleep on Tess and David's couch, but it goes straight to voicemail, so Tess is alone.

David is awake now but he can't see well and hardly speaks. He manages to say that he can see blotches from his left eye and nothing from his right. Doctors don't know why, and Tess tries to explain to them that doctors don't know anything and they get offended instead of understanding what she means. David's mother arrives at the hospital, having called Angelica, who's now with the kids. Watching his mother tend to his body, Tess feels—but fights—the usual childhood ache. Transport workers take David in for a CT scan of the brain, but they don't find anything, so they schedule him for an MRI, but that takes a while to set up, so a nurse practitioner sets his wrist, which was broken in the fall. The MRI shows nothing unusual, too, and though David's mother was too polite to ask why he'd been drinking, Tess explained that Monica told them to celebrate. They were celebrating.

Tess cries when she sees him back from the MRI. The IV tugs on the tape near the port on his inner arm, and his other arm is bandaged. But he's awake and talking.

"I'm sorry," Tess says.

David closes his eyes.

He sleeps for hours. The urine test—taken by a catheter—comes back normal, and blood tests are good if maybe a little bit low in hemoglobin, and his heart rate is fine, and so is his blood pressure now, which had been high earlier, but that's normal in falls.

"He's totally fine, he'll be fine," the doctor says.

Tess and David's mother each offer to send the other home to sleep, with promises to call as soon as there's anything to say, but both decline. David is in perfect health, according to every test. He just blinks and sleeps a lot. The kids don't visit. Tess decides it's not good for them to see him like this. She can't sleep, but when she does, she dreams of telling the kids that their father is dead. She wakes up ecstatic he's alive. Angelica is staying with the boys. Tess doesn't want to leave David's side. His body there, quiet, makes her feel so lucky she hadn't said anything worse at Abel and Cain. She doesn't want his body to be without her.

Halfway through the second night, David says, "Tess?" and she is there, waiting at his side.

23

The black marble walls are still there, but without the tumbling water. The ceilings don't seem as high. The floor is the same. It has always been beautiful, but now the marble has been buffed, shined. Little boutiques line each structural wall, as well as around where the bar used to be. And each black marble wall serves as a backdrop to two stalls, both facing out. Music, not so different from what was playing last time Tess was there a year ago, makes it hard to have a conversation with the salespeople. Tess heard the club had become this place and has been looking for an opportunity to see it.

She doesn't teach on Wednesdays, and the boys are in school. David is working. On Wednesdays he Skypes with new patients. Mondays and Fridays he performs his duties as the COO of the Brooklyn Healing Zone, LLC. He schedules Monica's radio interviews and her speeches at holistic festivals around the country, produces her podcast, designs and orders T-shirts and virtual reality headset decals, supervises the building of the Healing Zone app that serves as a combination videoconferencing/meditation/medication-and-treatment reminder platform. He can't work for more than three four-hour sittings per week, but those days when he does work are his favorites. His schedule is manageable, and he owns 20 percent of a company that is starting to make money. Tess thinks Monica is a charlatan. Tess also thinks Monica wants to fuck David. Tess doesn't know what David wants. But Tess trusts David. They're starting to trust each other now.

She wanders past stalls of limited-edition sneakers, handmade buckles and belts, painted chocolates, minor sketches from Austrian masters, fifty-dollar lip gloss, scented soaps, and Motorino pizza. Over the course of less than ten minutes, she thinks she sees two of Max's teachers, a former castmate, Angelica, Susan, Tazio, and Gerard. She's used to this now. She imagines Tazio and Gerard everywhere she goes.

Tess still doesn't understand how that brief interaction with Gerard was enough for Angelica. But it was. She's undeniably freer now. Tess has dinner with Angelica once a week, and sometimes on Saturdays Angelica takes the boys out for brunch. Angelica is a smart, successful, never-married woman looking to have a family. She's dating two men at the moment. Neither is anything like Tazio. One is a patient she'd always suspected liked her. He is Thai, a few years younger than she is, from what she told Tess. At the end of an appointment, she said something along the lines of, "I'm newly single, and I was wondering if you'd like to go on a date?" He said he'd love to. He is beautiful to look at, and he owns a small chain of sushi places across the country. Fast, casual, high-grade sushi. He's going to take her to Japan.

The other man has already proposed marriage. He is a Jewish lawyer from Queens whose wife died seven years ago, just a year after they were married. She drowned during a friend's bachelorette weekend in Miami Beach. He is sad, but he adores Angelica. She met his parents at a heartbreaking dinner where his father took Angelica aside and said, "All we want is Benny to be happy. And he's so happy around you. We haven't seen him so happy. Thank you. Thank you for being such a good person." Angelica has told Tess that she will probably marry Ben. He doesn't ask too much of her, but he loves her, and she loves being around him.

The sex is great—better than with her Thai restaurateur, better than it had been with Tazio—and though there's something cultural or familiar or sexy or who knows what about the Thai guy, she's been spending four or five nights of the week at Ben's place in Tribeca. She told him she's frozen eggs just in case, which made him cry with happiness. They go to movies a lot. She'll take the trip to Japan with the Thai guy just to make sure that she's not making a mistake, but she feels like both of these men could make her happy. Angelica had lunch with Tazio recently, and Tazio said he didn't want to hear about these guys. She said she understood. Tazio told her that he probably isn't cut out for relationships. That he's too selfish, too unpredictable. Angelica said that he probably just hadn't met the right person.

Tess is the right person. Tess could have made Tazio happy. At least for a while. A week or month. They love each other. She knows it. And she knows he knows it. But it doesn't matter. Love is just lust combined with comfort. Love is just compatible pheromones. Love is whatever she wants it to be. Even if she could make Tazio happy, she'd be miserable. With Tazio jealous of whomever she was talking to, while he was off tending to his own personal acclaim. The idea of making Tazio happy still appeals to her. But she no longer believes he'd be able to do the same for her. Tazio isn't someone to rely on. You can't build a life with Tazio. It's all just moments with him. Everything is too much, too heightened, the way it used to be onstage.

Now Tess teaches. A former castmate had to leave her job at a Manhattan private school and posted the opening on Facebook. Tess immediately responded. For David. If she's going to be honest, it was for David and herself. Now they can relax. She can be at home during the evenings. She can make steady money. She can live a life out of the spotlight. A life that doesn't need affirmation. That doesn't feel as much like a reaction to her father or her own ego. Her ego has been dismantled. David knew about her life with Tazio. And, Tess has since learned, so did Angelica. It was before Angelica was with Tazio, so she didn't care. Everyone knew and nobody cared. About any of her secrets or original sins. Except, maybe, for Tess's father. He cares. She sent him a friend request on Facebook, mostly just so she could see pictures of Levi and Teddy. She misses them.

Tess also misses Broadway, but now she can really take care of David, and they get good health care through the school. David isn't doing great, but there's less pressure for him to. There's little practical downside to his work with Monica, but there's potential big upside if he can strategize and market her into a real brand. And that's what he's trained to do. Tess blames Monica for the fall in the bar that set him back a few months, but he's close to where he was before, and his attitude has stayed strong. Dr. Saltman is tinkering with the meds and remains optimistic. They try to go out once or twice a month, just Tess and David, to talk and listen to what each other is thinking and feeling. And her salary plus his work with Monica is enough for the moment if they stay frugal.

Things are different now. She's wary around David. Cautious. And hurt by what he said.

He was protecting the kids from her. She wasn't a reliable mother.

But she's trying to parse what was said out of anger and where he was probably right. They don't talk about it, but they fold their bodies into each other's when they go to bed. She resents him, but for some reason she doesn't understand, resentment isn't much of a force when trying to stand up against history, momentum, need, comfort, and sure, maybe, pheromones and sometimes lust. She needs David, but she wants him, too. She wants to make him happy, and she knows he can do the same for her.

Today she waits in line for a slice of the cremini white pizza about which the man ahead of her said, "It's like biting into an angel." The woman laughed. They're on a date. Maybe a first date. It's not a good joke. The concept of a first date is impossibly foreign to Tess. Tess has never really been on a first date.

Tazio will be fired for something disparaging he said about the administration, reporters say, but other reporters say that Trump doesn't actually fire people, and Tazio has been doing a good job. Tess hasn't heard from him, and he's usually too busy to talk to David, but they still text every day. God knows about what. Trump won't fire him, Tazio texted David. Trump embarrasses people until they leave, but if they don't get embarrassed, they stay. Tess bets that Tazio rides out the administration. Apparently the generals like him. What a dumb fucking world.

She thinks briefly about going to every stall and buying herself suitcases, necklaces, and boots; presents for her husband and sons. She can't buy one of them a present without buying all of them something, and she doesn't need a new suitcase, so she indulges in a second slice of pizza.

When she gets to the front of the line, she orders a slice of the cremini and a slice of the soppressata. This is the only place where Motorino sells by the slice. She finds a bench, alone, where there are two seats open next to each other. One for her, and one for the pizza. David told her not to take the teaching job, to hold on and maybe television work would come, or she'd get the lead role that she'd always dreamed of. She thanked him but ignored his advice. She has liked the students so far. A lot. High school kids. She can hang out with them and provide an outlet and impress them and improve their lives in tiny ways, but she isn't responsible for them. She's directing her first play soon, and the buzz is that tons of kids are planning to audition.

The cremini slice is good, but nothing special. The soppressata is magical. Each bite tastes like dreaming or falling in love. That's not true. Dreams and love can be terrible, and they can last forever, and they're more powerful than she is. Pizza is just pizza. But still, Tess closes her eyes to better taste each bite. Tess wants to yell out in pleasure, but she doesn't want the attention, and she's recovering from a sore throat the boys have been passing back and forth. She looks at the walls that once pretended to be waterfalls, at all the people around her anxiously buying and laughing, and she sees herself clearly. She is a woman in a mall that used to be a nightclub. Things change. Or at least circumstances do. Seasons, bodies, influence, family, friends. She herself used to be a scared little girl. And now what is she? A thirty-eight-year-old woman whose life is good, whose life is fine, at least, and one day will be better.

24

Tazio's mother always puts on a big Labor Day barbecue: half a party for her friends and family, the other half a networking event for real estate agents, sellers, developers, and local politicians. As Tazio walks down the driveway toward the center of the large lawn, kids Ethan's and Max's age run across the grass laughing and playing a game that combines dodgeball and tag. Tazio smells the food—some particular combination of *pollo al horno* and cheeseburgers—and he's lost for a moment, running with his cousins at his mom's old place in Islip. He recoils from the memory. People see him and start to whisper. Forty-five minutes is the longest he can stay. His flight leaves from LaGuardia in less than three hours.

Over the past few weeks, Tazio has been constantly cycling through his life story, itemizing and cataloging significant events. He is proud of nothing except for what he's done for David and, perhaps, this jobs initiative. Each memory has an image associated with it, and along with a few spoken words, they appear in quick succession. Drinking makes the repetition worse, like a cloying song stuck on repeat in his head. *Papa left, Papa died, met David, got into Cooper, met Tess, 9/11, worked for Edwards, slept with Tess, Bush reelected, first solo show, failed liver, recovery with David, David married Tess, Obama elected, reconnected with Angelica, hired at Art for Kids, Obama reelected, Ethan born, Max born, Tess and*

Jonah Carr, David on Tazio's couch, worked for Hillary, David in-
jured, Trump elected, proposed to Angelica, moved to DC, took a
job with Trump to help Latinos.

Tazio has been meeting with city council members about public-private partnerships. Without publicizing it, he has exchanged tax cuts for minority hiring. He goes on television to talk ambiguously about Latino outreach. He is snickered at on public transportation. He has lunch with Satin, and sex with strangers. He has started drinking again, but he doesn't tell anyone about it. Not even David. He drinks alone, in his hotel room or DC apartment, before falling asleep. It's harmless—if not to his liver then at least to Tess, David, Angelica, Satin, and his mother. Angelica says that she's been dating. Good for her. David says that Tess doesn't want to talk to Tazio because Tess is angry that Tazio told David that Tazio and Tess had slept together without telling Tess that he had told David. The explanation is confusing and, frankly, silly. Tess. They missed out on what could have been a true friendship or love affair. Something of value. The problem is that they never named it. They never figured out what they were together.

His mother smiles, or she affects a smile, or the smile is genuine but for reasons Tazio can't guess. His mother's emotions have always been ambiguous. No matter what happens, he will be on that plane, heading for LA. He no longer blames his father for leaving. If he could, he'd blame his father for dying before he could go and find him again. But not for leaving. The man wanted to live without shame.

Tazio's mother greets him, same as always: perfect posture, brown hair, lipstick smile, tailored pants, white blouse. "Come here," she says. She hugs him. They haven't seen each other for a couple of years. Not since he invited her into the city to meet Angelica.

Papa left, Papa died, met David, Cooper Union. "Ven acá, away from all these gawking people," his mother says in Spanish. He follows her into the house, then through hallways into her office. On her desk, there's a photo of him when he was little, riding a bike with training wheels. His expression is concentrated and grave.

"You've come in person to tell me you're engaged!" she says.

Tazio laughs. "I'm sorry to disappoint," he responds in Spanish. "I know you liked Angelica. I did, too. But we weren't a right fit."

Papa left, Papa died, Tazio met David, got into Cooper, met Tess, 9/11, worked for Edwards. "I'm sorry to hear that," his mother says.

The way she says it, Tazio can't tell if she's sorry for him because he lost someone important, or if she's disappointed in him for having done so.

"I don't think I'm cut out for marriage," Tazio says.

"That makes two of us," his mother says, and laughs.

. . . Slept with Tess, Bush reelected, first solo show, hospital, recovery, David, Tess, Angelica elected, Art for Obama . . .

"I've come to ask you something," he says. Finding the right words here is more difficult than when he proposed to Angelica. He can't just come out and say *Are you proud of me now? Now do you approve?* "It's exciting," Tazio says, smiling. "My new job."

Her smile remains inscrutable.

"Or at the very least," he adds, "it's funny? We'll sit down with everyone, have a bite to eat, and I'll tell you all about it?"

He knows what's coming before she says it.

"I'm sorry, *cariño*, but it isn't funny," she says. "No. I know you're trying, but this isn't the right way."

Tazio should be numb by now, but this hurts. From his bowels up through his throat. But it's okay. Nothing real is lost. Tazio hasn't spoken to his mother in years, and this is his specialty: disappointing women who love him.

"When you were a child, you used to beg to go to the mall to play those games where you put in coins and won tickets," she says, walking him out of her house, and then, as though it's natural, back to his rental car. He's only been there for ten minutes. "In the beginning, when you were seven or so, you played the basketball game, the game where you hit some animals as they poked out their heads, and some other ones. You ate foot-long hot dogs and drank Sprite. You didn't want to go with friends anywhere. You liked playing those games.

"And then you found a machine among the games where all you did was drop your quarter in and see if your quarter was enough to pile on top of the other quarters to make an avalanche. After you saw that machine, you stopped playing the games. You just put quarter after quarter into the slot, and sometimes you would win, and other times you wouldn't. It didn't make sense to me or your father. It wasn't a game. There was no fun. You hogged that machine, spent five dollars in ten minutes, and you traded in your tickets for some toy worth less than five dollars. If you want to help, help. Become a lawyer—it only takes three years—and represent people in need. Or sell your paintings and then spend weekends at a soup kitchen. You two always needed to make such grand gestures. But why?"

Acknowledgments

Thank you to the family and friends who cared for Owen, Sam, Alex, and me while we struggled with my health over these past few years.

Thanks to Trena Keating, the best literary agent in the United States; to Sarah Cantin, for her generosity and editorial genius; and to Rakesh Satyal, who vastly improved and then fiercely guided this novel to publication.

I'm fortunate to have friends, collaborators, and early readers who are better writers than I am. To John Paul Carillo, Andrew Palmer, Matthew Buckley Smith, and Rafael Yglesias—my work is as much yours as my own.

Thanks to the doctors—Joseph M. Furman, MD, PhD, of UPMC; Jeffrey P. Staab, MD, of the Mayo Clinic; Nomita Sonty, PhD, of Columbia; Richard K. Mark, MD, of Concorde Medical Group; Patrick J. McGrath, MD, of Columbia; and Frank Rosen, PsyD—who diagnosed and treated my condition.

Thank you to Rebecca Katz and Simon Vance for background on life in politics, and to Rebecca Naomi Jones for insight into life onstage.

My writing owes a substantial debt to that of Gwendolyn

Brooks, John Cheever, Dave Eggers, Kazuo Ishiguro, Alice McDermott, Philip Roth, and Dai Sijie.

I'm grateful for the warmth and intelligence of my students, colleagues, and fellow parents at Grace Church School; my family at Lake Owego; my neighbors in Bed-Stuy; and my teachers at Grace, Dalton, Columbia, and Hopkins.

Thank you, Eli, for always making sure everything is as it should be.

And thanks of course, always, and mostly to Alex, the beating heart of my life. And to Owen and Sam: my life, itself. I love you three the world.

About the Author

Brian Platzer is the author of the novels *The Body Politic* and *Bed-Stuy Is Burning*, as well as the forthcoming parenting book, *The Homework Handbook*. He has an MFA from the Johns Hopkins Writing Seminars, and a BA from Columbia University. Brian's writing has appeared often in the *New Yorker*'s Shouts and Murmurs and McSweeney's Internet Tendency, as well as in the *New York Times*, the *New Republic*, Lit Hub, Salon, and elsewhere. He suffers from chronic dizziness and lives with his wife and two sons in Bed-Stuy, Brooklyn.